"LOOK AT ME, ALLISON."

"Why are you so determined to deny the obvious?" His voice was quiet.

She jerked away from his hand and stood up, then realized instantly it was a mistake, because she now stood so close to him that she was almost touching his broad chest. He blocked escape with his massive body. Unless she wanted to dive off the boat and swim for shore, she couldn't move.

He bent his head slowly toward hers, and she didn't turn away. As his mouth claimed hers, a sweet fire rose within her, burning away every reality but one: her desire for him. His arms enclosed her firmly and her own hands lifted to curl around his neck, her fingers stroking the powerful muscles of his upper back and the thick hair at the base of his neck. She had no will of her own, only an aching hunger . . .

Island Summer Love

Amy Belding Brown

ST. MARTIN'S PAPERBACKS

For Duane

Chapter One

"Allison Curtis, you aren't seriously considering going to California *now*!" squealed Martha, in a voice so shrill that even Allison, who was used to her friend's histrionics, had to wince.

"My aunt invited me," Allison said. "Just to give me a breather before the wedding."

"Breather!" Martha uncurled from the antique Queen Anne chair and stood up. "When there's so much left to do? And everybody in the world has showers planned? You can't run away at a time like this!"

"I'm not running away." Allison bent her head and let her long, auburn hair swing forward over her face. "Anyway, it's all arranged. And even Cabot said it would be a good idea. I'm twenty-four years old, and it's time I met my father's sister."

Martha crossed her arms over her chest. "It's beyond me why you'd want to go now, Allison. You're just about the luckiest girl in Massachusetts, and you're certainly marrying the handsomest man! One of the wealthiest, too. Everybody knows that Cabot Wilder is *the* most eligible bachelor of the decade!"

Allison sighed. "I'm not breaking the engagement,

Martha. I'm just going to visit a relative for a month."

"Halfway around the world. While the man you love stays home alone slaving over trust funds and stock reports. How can you stand to be apart at a time like this? I thought you two were crazy in love!"

"We are. And Cabot will manage just fine." Allison fingered the silver-backed hairbrush on Martha's marble vanity. "He always does."

"You've had a fight, haven't you?"

Allison shook her head and smiled. "We never fight. Cabot is too good-natured. You know that."

"I don't get it. It's not like you to leave when everything's so exciting. If it isn't Cabot, then what is it?"

"I don't know. Just premarital jitters, I guess. I need some sun and a sandy beach. A few weeks on my own. I'll be fine when I get back."

Martha raised her slim arms above her head and arched her back in a slow body stretch. "I know what you mean about getting away. Boston's unbearable in June and July. I'm dying to go to Maine. But my parents are leaving for Kenya in two weeks and they don't want me up at our cottage on Harper's Island alone." She let her arms drop and grinned at her friend. "After last summer's escapade in France, they claim they don't trust me unless I'm chaperoned."

Allison laughed. "I can understand why. Chasing Raoul all over Europe when you were supposed to be studying at the Sorbonne! You're lucky they didn't lock you away in a castle tower somewhere."

"I know." Martha sagged back into the chair, curling a long leg under her body. "It looks like I'm stuck. Either I go to Kenya with my parents"—she rolled her eyes in a melodramatic grimace—"or I roast in Boston. I've asked everyone I could think of to come to Maine with me, but it seems that everybody's got a cruise scheduled. I didn't even consider asking you because of the wedding, but if you're thinking about going to California anyway . . ." She leaned forward, her eyes shining. "Come to Maine with me, Allison! Your aunt can wait until next summer."

Allison smiled doubtfully. Much as she liked Martha, she was daunted by the thought of spending an extended period of time in her upper-crust world of money and elegance. Ever since they had met at Mount Holyoke College and Martha had become her friend, Allison had felt like a poor country girl. At times it was all she could do to remember that being middle class didn't exactly place her in the ranks of the underprivileged. She came from a good home in the Boston suburbs; her parents worked hard to provide the necessities and even a few luxuries for her and her brother; growing up, she had never felt impoverished. Yet it had been a shock to go to college and find herself among girls like Martha. Temperamentally, too, she felt at odds with her friend. Martha's high spirits and proverbial recklessness were foreign to Allison's own quieter nature. She had always been known as the bookish type, studious and thoughtful. In fact, she thought of herself as boring.

It had been a major surprise to everyone when Allison became engaged to Cabot. The rich, handsome grandson of one of New England's industrial giants, Cabot had a reputation for dating glamorous, exciting women. When he finally chose Allison as his future wife, it shocked all but his closest associates. They alone knew that the characteristics Cabot was seeking in a wife had nothing to do with excitement and flair. He wanted a woman who was quiet and self-possessed, attractive without drawing attention to herself, someone who would be able to live in his shadow. A precise description of Allison.

Cabot had done everything in his power to sweep her off her feet, and Allison had fallen rapidly in love with him. His good looks and dark, enchanting eyes had charmed her completely. When, on Christmas Eve, in the company of his mother and three cousins, he had presented her with an enormous diamond ring, she had been stunned with excitement.

The next morning she'd announced her engagement to her parents. They'd been thrilled. Her mother immediately started to make plans for the wedding, until Allison reluctantly informed her that the Wilder family would be making all the arrangements.

"They have all kinds of traditions they have to follow, Mom. It would be too confusing for us to try to figure it all out. I thought it would be easiest just to let Cabot's mother take care of everything."

How could she begin to explain to her parents the way that people in Cabot's world operated? Allison wondered. Just thinking about Sarah Wilder, Cabot's brilliant and sophisticated mother, intimidated Allison. The first time Allison had met her, by special invitation to Sarah's Beacon Hill home, she had been spellbound by Sarah's character and fire. The elegant older woman had looked at her with a penetrating, gray-eyed stare that made gooseflesh form on Allison's arms. Allison had spent the evening struggling to remember all the social graces Martha had taught her, praying that she wouldn't commit some outrageous faux pas in the older woman's presence.

As always, Cabot had been pleasant and relaxed, and his composed expression gave Allison no clue as to how she was doing. It wasn't until the next evening, when Cabot informed her that his mother had decided they could continue to see each other, that she realized she'd passed a crucial inspection.

Since the wedding plans had all been left up to Sarah, and Cabot had important financial reports to attend to, Allison was left alone to while away the weeks until September. When her aunt had written from California, inviting her for a month-long visit, Allison had jumped at the opportunity.

"Allison, you're a million miles away!" Martha's voice brought Allison back to the present; she looked uncertainly into the laughing face of her friend. "You haven't heard a word I said, have you?"

Allison blushed. "I'm sorry. I was daydreaming."

"About Cabot?" Martha leaned forward, always eager to hear about Cabot. Privately, Allison wondered if Martha still carried a torch for him. She knew they had dated for a while, a year or so before she introduced him to Allison, and it wouldn't have surprised her if Martha was still a little bit infatuated. It was hard not to be, with a man like Cabot.

Allison grinned and held up her hand. "I confess. But I did hear what you said about going to Maine."

"Well?"

"I don't see how I can. I already promised my aunt."

"She'll understand! After all, this is your last summer of being a single girl! Everyone deserves one last fling. And visiting an aunt doesn't exactly qualify as a fling, does it?"

"I suppose not." Allison shrugged. It didn't really make much difference to her whether she went to Maine or California. Though she wasn't about to admit it to Martha, her real reason for wanting to visit her aunt was to take her mind off the overwhelming responsibilities she was about to face as Mrs. Cabot Wilder. "It's not as if it's the last chance I'll ever have to go to California. Cabot flies out there all the time."

"Of course he does! Oh, Allison . . ." Martha bounced up from her chair and flung her arms around Allison. "It'll be wonderful having you there!"

"Okay," Allison said, unable to suppress a grin. "You talked me into it. As long as your folks don't mind."

"Mind? They'll be thrilled! They think you're the most sensible person in the world. A good influence on me, Mama's always saying."

It was hard for Allison to believe she could ever have any influence at all on Martha, but she was flattered by her friend's enthusiasm. "When are you going to leave?" She hoped Martha wouldn't have a million reasons to delay her departure. "I have to be back by mid-July for my gown fitting."

Martha opened her arms expansively. "We'll leave Saturday. That way we'll have almost a whole month and a half." She cocked her head. "That isn't too long, is it?"

"I guess not."

"The cottage is already open for the season; the caretakers always have it ready by the first of June. So we can go any time. As far as I'm concerned, the sooner we go the better! I'm dying to get out from under Mama's eagle eye."

Allison nodded. "The city heat is really getting to me."

Martha rose and floated toward the door. "I'll go talk to Mama right now. You won't be sorry, Allison. It'll be a wonderful summer, I promise you."

* * *

Allison had expected that Cabot would try to talk her out of spending the summer in Maine, but she was surprised at the intensity of his remonstrances. It wasn't like Cabot to be intense about anything. As she sat with him in the elegant den of his mother's home the evening before her departure, she felt a sharp pang of regret.

"I love you so much, Allison," he whispered, his finely chiseled face grave with yearning. "I wish you didn't have to leave. Are you sure you can't back out?"

"Martha's counting on me to go with her," Allison said, savoring the warm admiration in his eyes. "I'd feel terrible, letting her down at the last minute."

"I understand." He stroked her cheek. "I just wish I could go with you. It would be wonderful to have all that time to ourselves." He ran a hand through his dark brown hair and tightened his arm around her waist. "But there's so much going on right now —that merger I told you about is very precarious at the moment, and I don't dare be away from the phone for more than a minute."

Allison nodded. "We wouldn't be seeing much of each other anyway until that's completed. Besides, this is my last chance to be a single girl." She wrinkled her nose as she reached up to touch his cheek. "One last fling."

Cabot sighed and shook his head. "I'll be glad when we're married, darling, so we can have our flings together." He kissed her again. Allison pressed herself against him and let her fingers play across the back of his neck. She wondered if he would finally make love to her tonight. It had always surprised her that Cabot was satisfied with their relationship. He embraced her often, but never pressed her for further intimacies.

At first she had considered herself lucky that she was engaged to a man who wasn't always trying to get her into bed. But recently, in her private fantasies, she'd begun to imagine a muscular, blond stranger carrying her away to his private lair and ravishing her. She told herself she'd been reading too many romance novels, but it was exciting imagining being caressed by this make-believe lover. She knew her fantasy would evaporate once she and Cabot were married. Cabot had kept his passionate side well hidden, but his reputation as a ladies man certainly suggested that he could be ardent when he chose.

"I really want to go with Martha this time, Cabot. Once we're married, we'll have all the time in the world to be alone together."

Cabot smiled. "At least promise to call. If I can't kiss you, I want to hear the sound of your voice."

"Of course. I'll call every day." She smiled up at him with the meek look she knew he loved. "And the summer will be over before you know it."

He kissed her lightly. "I can hardly wait for our wedding day."

Allison bent her head away from his gaze. Her hair fell across her face, hiding her sudden pallor.

Cabot brushed her hair off her cheek. "One more thing, darling. You *will* cut your hair before the wedding, won't you?"

Allison looked up at him. She knew it was unfashionable to wear her hair down to her waist, but she loved it that way, loved the sensuous ripple as it fell the length of her back, the way it lifted like a curtain in the wind. She forced a small smile. "I'll cut it, Cabot. I promise. As soon as the summer's over."

* * *

The trip to Maine took four hours by car, and Martha insisted on driving all the way. Allison sat back in the comfortable bucket seat of her friend's red Porsche, watching the miles of dark green pines fly past, while Martha chattered happily about her plans for the summer ahead.

"We'll have the place all to ourselves. Harper's Island is right out in the middle of Penobscot Bay. You won't believe the air up there—it's like crystal. So clean and quiet you'd hardly believe you were on the same planet as Boston. There's a constant sea breeze, and the weather's almost always wonderful! You're going to love it, Allison. Our cottage is really a house, you know: six bedrooms with private baths. There's a pool and a tennis court. And just last year Mama had a new hot tub installed. So it's not as if we'll be roughing it. There's a native couple who take care of the place year 'round, Abel and Isabel Cutler. They're real darlings! They're like grandparents to me."

"I thought you said we'd have the place all to ourselves." Allison wondered how Martha would actually feel about having two grandparent types looking over her shoulder all month.

"Oh, they're no trouble." Martha waved her hand, dismissing Allison's fears. "They live in the village and keep pretty much to themselves. Every once in a while Isabel cooks up a pot of lobster stew or makes a batch of sinfully delicious brownies. When I was growing up, I spent a lot of summers in the kitchen, listening to Isabel's stories about the island, so I think she feels she helped raise me."

Allison yawned and leaned back against the soft headrest. "Do you mind if I take a little nap? I'm afraid I was up late last night."

Martha grinned. "Heavy date with Cabot, huh?

Lucky you! Sure, go ahead. I'll try to keep my mouth shut, at least until we get to the ferry. You won't want to miss the ride over."

Allison dozed off slowly, rocked by the tranquilizing hum of the wheels on the road. She wasn't aware of anything until she felt Martha's long finger jab her shoulder.

"We're here, sleepyhead. Wake up!"

Allison opened her eyes. The car was parked at a large wharf-like structure, and beyond it was the most brilliantly blue water Allison had ever seen. Approaching the wharf, advancing slowly through the swells, was a large, gray ferry. She watched it ease into place at the end of the wharf, and a moment later a corrugated metal ramp was lowered. A few cars drove off, then a dour-faced man in a red fishing cap signaled Martha to come on board. Allison held her breath as Martha eased the Porsche down the ramp onto the ferry. A moment later, when the man came over to her side of the car, Martha unrolled her window and leaned out.

"Hello, John," she bubbled. "How was the winter?"

The man grunted noncommittally and handed her a small orange ticket. "Where's your folks this year, Martha?"

"They've decided to trust me finally, now that I'm twenty-five." She dug in her purse and handed the man a five-dollar bill, then gestured to Allison. "This is my best friend, Allison Curtis. She'll be spending the summer with me. Allison, meet John Bailey."

John nodded at Allison and she smiled back. The man seemed pleasant enough, and he clearly knew Martha, but Allison couldn't help noticing his reserved manner. She wondered what he really thought of Martha and her flashy red Porsche.

When the ferry began to move a few moments later, Martha climbed out of the car and gestured for Allison to follow. They stood together at the waist-high metal rail that surrounded the deck, facing the open sea. The breeze was strong and salty, more refreshing than any air conditioner. Allison found herself enjoying the fine salt spray that misted her face.

The ferry ride took almost an hour, and Allison felt as if she had undergone an enchantment by the time Martha drove onto the wharf at Harper's Island. The island was thickly covered with pine forests, except for a little cluster of houses at the western tip, where the ferry docked. As Martha drove down the street of the little village, Allison felt a strange flutter of recognition deep within her. It was almost as if she had been on the island before, as if it were a beloved, familiar place. She shook her head to clear it. It must be the effect of the fresh air and sunshine, she thought; she had never been to Harper's Island, or any island like it, in her life.

"There's just a handful of families that live here year-round," said Martha. "They're mostly fishermen. The rest of the houses on the island are summer places, like ours." She gestured expansively as she drove along the narrow dirt road. "There's the general store. It has everything anybody needs, or so they claim. Actually, it's the island social spot. The post office is in there, too, tucked away in the back corner. So is the only telephone on the island."

"Only telephone? You mean there isn't one at your parents' cottage?"

Martha shook her head. "No. My folks like it that way. When they come to Maine, they want to get away from everything except the sun and the sea."

So she wouldn't be able to call Cabot every day.

Allison swallowed a pang of disappointment and looked out at the dark green building. A gas pump stood out front, and two dilapidated benches were propped on either side of the screen door. A rusted oil barrel stood near the corner of the building. The long window was dirty and grease-spotted. Through it, she could make out a human shape moving in the semidarkness. Two young boys dashed around the corner of the building; their faces were smudged and their overalls were torn at the knees.

"It doesn't look very prosperous," Allison murmured.

"I don't suppose it is. But I don't think it bothers people here. The islanders don't seem to care too much about style or anything."

Don't care, or can't afford it? Allison wondered. She studied the small group of lobster boats in the little harbor. It was a very picturesque setting; it had probably been photographed hundreds of times. But these weren't props on a movie set; they were the tools of real working men and women, who farmed the sea for a living. She wondered what it would be like to actually live in the village year-round. The houses looked shabby and run-down. Poverty must be a way of life for these people, she thought, as natural to them as luxury was to Martha. For a fleeting moment she almost felt ashamed to be sitting in such an expensive car. But then she shook off the sensation and brought herself up straight in her seat.

"Look out!" She jabbed Martha, who was craning her neck to look at something out in the harbor.

Martha swerved the car just in time to narrowly avoid hitting a tall, blond man who was walking down the middle of the road. She screeched to a stop, the car's wheels halting only inches from a deep ditch.

"Oh God! That was Brent Connors! I'm never going to live this down!" Martha threw a desperate glance at Allison, jerked open her door and scrambled out of the car. Allison got out, too, intrigued by the scenario of the nervous Martha Hollingsworth facing an angry villager.

The man had turned to face them and put down the large metal bucket he was carrying. He was standing with his arms folded across his chest, his legs braced apart as if he were about to repel an attacker. Dressed in blue jeans, a white T-shirt, and knee-length, muddy boots, he looked to be about thirty. His rugged face was chiseled into a hard scowl under the thick, tousled blond hair. Allison found herself staring at his firmly muscled arms and legs, then blushing as she realized that he was steadily returning her gaze.

Chapter Two

"**O**H, BRENT, I'm so sorry!" Martha rushed up to the blond man, waving her hands helplessly in the air. "I didn't see you! If Allison hadn't said anything, I might have hit you! Oh God, are you all right?"

Brent cocked his head to one side and looked down at Martha as if he were watching a clucking chicken.

"So you've come back to terrorize the island again," he said in a deep voice. "What happened, did they kick you out of France?"

Allison saw that he was trying not to smile. Martha apologized again, still swinging her arms, as if flapping them in the crystalline air could erase the events of the last few moments. Brent seemed to be enjoying her distress; the hidden smile crept into the corners of his mouth and lifted them toward his cheeks in a wide grin.

He unfolded his arms and reached to place a hand on Martha's shoulder. "Who's your friend, Martha? She doesn't look like the weekend airheads you usually bring up here."

"Brent, don't be nasty!" Martha turned and waved her hand at Allison. "This is Allison Curtis. She's vacationing with me until the middle of July. Allison, come over here and meet Brent."

Allison walked over to Martha, who beamed at her eagerly.

"This is Brent Connors, Allison, the number-one lobsterman on the island. He's also Abel and Isabel's favorite grandson."

Allison looked up at Brent, trying to meet his penetrating gaze with composed poise.

"How do you do?" She extended her hand, intensely aware of his square jaw and wide mouth.

"Allison Curtis." He took her hand, wrapping it firmly in his large palm. "I guess I have you to thank for saving my skin just now."

Allison forced a smile. "There's so much beautiful scenery, it's hard to keep your eyes on the road," she said, quickly withdrawing her hand.

"That's right!" said Martha.

Brent turned to her, a twinkle in his blue eyes. "You weren't watching the scenery. Unless I miss my guess, you were jabbering about your latest escapade."

"I was not!" Martha cringed under his skeptical frown. "Okay, I wasn't paying attention, and I'm really sorry." She fluttered her hands. "Look, I'll treat you to dinner at my place tomorrow night. Will that help?"

"It's a deal. As long as you don't do the cooking." He grinned, and Allison felt a strange, responsive lurch inside her chest.

Martha drew herself up. "I've been taking lessons, Brent. I'm much better than I was two summers ago."

Brent's doubtful glance slid toward Allison. "Can *she* cook?"

"Allison's a great cook!" Martha beamed.

"Fair enough," Brent said. "I'll take my chances. But it better be good."

Allison felt herself bristle; she opened her mouth to speak, but a sharp jab from Martha's elbow silenced her.

"It'll be great," declared Martha. "Just come at six, and I promise you that by the time you're done eating, you'll be in raptures!"

Allison sighed inwardly. Since Martha was obviously determined to impress this man, she would do what she could to help. She sent her most brilliant smile in Brent's direction, and then colored in embarrassment when he winked at her. Before she could recover her dignity, he had picked up his pail, turned his back, and was walking away from them with long strides.

"You like him," Allison said when they were safely back in the car. "Is he another one of your conquests?"

Martha shrugged. "Everyone likes Brent. But he isn't anyone's conquest, unfortunately. He's not the type to let himself get wrapped around one woman's finger. He's too independent."

"Are you saying he's a womanizer?"

Martha grinned. "Maybe 'confirmed bachelor' is a better way to put it."

Despite her disclaimer, it was obvious that Martha had a crush on Brent. She had chosen well for once, thought Allison, remembering the way Brent's rugged masculinity had instantly affected her. She almost envied her friend's freedom. She mentally pulled herself up short. She had no right to think such thoughts. Not only was Brent a complete stranger, but *she* was engaged to be married!

Allison watched Martha closely as they continued on the dirt road that wound along the shoreline. Her friend was uncharacteristically quiet, her face still flushed from the encounter with Brent Connors. She wanted to ask Martha point-blank about her feelings for Brent. But her friend seemed so tense and withdrawn that Allison was afraid her question might provoke another accident.

Martha finally slowed the Porsche and turned left up a narrow, winding road. They climbed through thick stands of pine trees and emerged finally in a broad clearing dominated by a huge cedar-shingled house that overlooked the water. The structure had obviously been designed by a professional architect; it blended perfectly with the surrounding forest and the broad sweep of lawn that overlooked the ocean. A wooden balcony circled the second floor, and the roof was dotted with skylights. The overall impression was one of elegant simplicity.

Martha pulled up in front of a low breezeway that jutted from the side of the building.

"Welcome to the cottage," she said, turning off the engine.

"Cottage?" Allison gaped at the enormous building. "This looks more like a mansion."

"I admit, it's not exactly cozy." Martha got out of the car and opened the trunk with a twist of her key. "But it's very pleasant, once you get used to it." She marched into the breezeway and unlocked an elegantly carved door. "Come on in. I'll give you the grand tour. But don't expect to know your way around right away. It'll take a few days."

Allison followed her friend through the door and

into a wood-paneled foyer that opened directly into a large, sunlit living room.

"This is the family room," Martha said. "We practically live here. I don't honestly know why Mama insisted on having so many other rooms built downstairs. We never use them."

Allison noted the comfortable couches and easy chairs arranged around the room, and the massive stone fireplace opposite the wall of windows overlooking the water.

"It's lovely." She wanted to curl up with a book on the big, blue chintz couch. "I thought it would be more formal, knowing your mother's decorating tastes."

"Oh, Daddy insisted on the informal look." Martha laughed. "He said it was a summer cottage and it ought to look like one." She crossed the room to the windows. "Our boats are moored in a little cove right below us. You just follow that path." She pointed to a trail that disappeared into the trees. "Daddy has a forty-foot yacht which he won't allow anyone to set foot on unless he's aboard. But there's also a twenty-foot sailboat and a sunfish, which I'm allowed to use to my heart's content."

"I have a confession to make." Allison followed her friend to stand in front of the windows. "I've never been sailing before. I've never even been on a boat, except for the ferry we just came on. In fact, I'm kind of afraid of the water. When I was a kid, my cousin Daniel decided the best way to teach me to swim was to throw me in. I almost drowned."

"Well, you can't come to Maine and stay away from the water. I'll reeducate you." Martha grinned and patted Allison's arm reassuringly. "Now come and see the rest of the house."

She led her through a series of quiet, sunny rooms

that enchanted Allison. A sense of peace and serenity pervaded the house. It seemed to be a place where worries and concerns would melt away, where the pleasant rooms seemed to be saying that things would always work out for the best.

"It's beautiful!" Allison marveled, peering into a large, sun-splashed solarium on the second floor. "Where do I sleep?"

"Oh, you can choose your own bedroom," said Martha. "Only the master bedroom is off-limits."

"It really doesn't matter," Allison said, as Martha showed her into one sky-lit bedroom after another. "They're all so lovely—so spacious and relaxing."

Martha shook her head. "You have to decide. It's a family tradition: guests choose first."

"Then I guess I'd like the room in the back of the house—the one that overlooks the town." Allison felt a hunger to watch the working fishermen as they plied their boats back and forth to the island, and the room she mentioned had a clear view of the array of lobster boats in the harbor.

"Are you sure?" Martha looked at her curiously. "That's smaller than the others. And it's not the one with the best view."

"I thought it was. The harbor's so interesting." She wondered suddenly, with a shock of surprise at her own thought, which lobster boat belonged to Brent Connors.

"Then it's yours," Martha said. "I'll take the one in the front of the house. I love seeing the moonlight on the open water."

Martha's tour ended in the kitchen, a charming, country-style room complete with fireplace, antique hutches, and a huge trestle table with benches.

"This is where we'll do the deed." Martha ran her

hand over the wide wooden countertop that circled the room.

"Deed?"

"When Brent comes tomorrow night. Don't tell me you forgot already! We promised him supper."

Allison nodded. She hadn't forgotten the verbal banter on the road, but had assumed the invitation hadn't been taken seriously. Would Brent really show up the next evening?

"I thought we could have steak and mashed potatoes." Martha turned a starry-eyed gaze on Allison. "He likes that kind of meat and potatoes fare." She grinned. "He's very down-to-earth."

"Are you sure he'll come?"

Martha nodded. "He'll come, all right."

"You like him, don't you?"

"He's a great guy. Very sexy. Unfortunately, he's not suitable."

"Suitable?" Allison had trouble thinking that something like suitability mattered to Martha.

"Oh, Allison, you might as well know the truth." Martha flung herself into a rocking chair by the fireplace and gave Allison a desperate glance. "Two summers ago I had a terrible crush on Brent. He even took me out a few times before Mama found out and put an end to it. That's why they sent me to Europe last year."

"If your mother doesn't want you going out with Brent, why in the world is she letting you come up here this summer?"

"I assured her I wasn't the least bit interested in Brent anymore. And if I have anything to do with him, they'll yank me home so fast, I won't know what hit me."

"Then why did you invite him for supper?" Allison sank down on the trestle bench.

"I don't know!" Martha wailed. "It just seemed that I had to do *something*! I mean, I almost ran over him!" Martha looked wistfully at Allison. "I really thought I was over him until I saw him standing there."

Allison shook her head in mock sympathy. "Martha, your heart's on so many strings, how do you keep them all straight? What about Raoul? Every handsome man you meet is Mr. Right."

Martha's mouth curled upward slowly and finally broke into an irrepressible grin. "I am a bit crazy, aren't I? You're right—I love them all."

"Well, one of these days you're going to have to settle on just one."

Martha bounded out of her chair, all her despair having instantly evaporated. "I'm afraid you've already nailed the only one Mama and I could ever agree on. You see, it's not enough just for *me* to decide. I have to choose someone acceptable to my parents."

"Is that why you always get crushes on working-class men?" Allison couldn't suppress a grin of her own. "Are you just trying to drive your mother crazy?"

"Well, I'll stop as soon as you let Cabot go."

"Sorry. He's hooked." Allison playfully flashed her ring at Martha.

Martha pushed out her lower lip in a momentary pout, then her face brightened. "I should take you down to meet Abel and Isabel right away! You haven't been properly introduced to the island until you've met them!"

Moments later Allison found herself following Martha along a well-beaten forest path that wound down the hill toward the village. Martha danced along the path, chattering about a mutual college friend who had recently become pregnant.

"You won't catch *me* having babies until I've had a chance to experience life." Martha giggled. "Children only tie you down."

Allison smiled. One of the things she liked about her friend was her childish irresponsibility. It balanced her own quiet seriousness, and helped her to put things into perspective when she felt discouraged or confused.

When the path opened out on a little meadow, Allison saw a small gray house and a tidy garden beyond it.

"That's Abel's garden," Martha announced. "He grows the best vegetables on the face of the earth. You won't believe how heavenly beans can taste until you eat some of his!" She took Allison's hand and pulled her quickly across the yard to the back door. It opened before she had a chance to knock, and Allison found herself looking into a pair of blue eyes that seemed disquietingly familiar. As she watched Martha throw herself into the arms of the round-faced, elderly woman, she realized with a start that they were Brent Connor's eyes, and then she remembered that this woman was his grandmother. Martha was uttering little squeals of excitement as she embraced the woman; when she finally pulled away and turned to introduce her, Allison felt uncomfortably intrusive, as if she had been eavesdropping on a pair of very dear friends.

But the older woman shook her hand warmly.

"Come on in and join us for supper," she said, and held the screen door wide. "If I know Martha, you haven't even had a chance to unpack your bags."

Allison laughed and followed her friend into the small kitchen, where she was greeted by the delicious aroma of baked apples emanating from the oven.

"Abel's out in the shed, knitting trap heads. Half his lobster traps were lost in that big storm we had last May; he's still trying to catch up." Isabel turned to Martha. "How nice for you to have a friend with you this summer. I hope you give us plenty of chance to get to know her."

"Oh, I intend to, Isabel." Martha winked at Allison. "Especially when you make brownies."

Isabel laughed and led them into a small, unfinished room at the far end of the kitchen. A slender man in his early seventies was sitting on an upturned wooden crate, weaving some narrow rope together in a complicated pattern. Abel greeted them warmly, but didn't move from his crate, nor did his fingers stop their flying motion.

A few minutes later Isabel had put Martha to work mashing potatoes, and Allison to buttering a steaming bowl of fresh peas. When they all sat down at the worn kitchen table, Allison found herself eating with more appetite than she had had in a long time. She enjoyed listening to the teasing banter between Abel and Isabel, and followed with interest Martha's questions about island residents. Isabel answered with a string of anecdotes about each islander, and every once in a while Abel inserted a droll comment that set them all laughing.

It was during dessert, huge slabs of hot apple pie, that Martha finally asked about Brent. Allison found herself intensely aware of the sudden silence in the room.

"Well," said Isabel slowly, throwing a long glance at Abel, "he's been pretty busy this winter. Had some trouble out on the fishing grounds one day last February. Got caught in an awful storm, but lucky for him, the Coast Guard heard his SOS and towed him in. It's not like Brent to get himself in such a predicament. But I suppose all boys have got to learn the hard way sometimes. It took him a while to get his boat back in shape, so he lost some money. He's trying to make up for it this summer. Hope the price of lobster is better than last year."

Abel coughed and wiped his mouth with his napkin. "It never would have happened if it hadn't been for that Lawton woman. He was awful gone on her. Thought she was going to get her claws in him for good and take him right off the island."

Isabel frowned. "Now, you know nothing could get Brent to leave Harper's Island, Abel."

"Well, that woman sure gave it a try. I was some glad to see the back of her last spring when she went back to Portland. I like this one he's seeing now a lot better—what's her name?"

"Emily Potter." Isabel clicked her tongue. "And you know there's no need putting two and two together and coming up with five." She turned to Martha. "Emily is Mildred's granddaughter, here for the summer. A pretty young thing, kind of caught his eye. But I don't believe he's too serious about her."

"He's not likely to be serious about anybody for a while, after what he went through last winter," put in Abel. "But it's good to see him on an even keel again. That Tracy Lawton had him acting like a lovestruck boy."

"You're exaggerating, Abel. Brent's not so foolish as you make him out to be."

Abel nodded, chewing. "Any man's foolish when he's head over heels for a woman like that." He peered down the table at Allison. "You got a boyfriend, Miss Curtis?"

"Allison's engaged," said Martha quickly, "to the handsomest man in the world."

Abel laughed. "If anybody ought to know, it'd be you, Martha. I believe you've looked them all over already."

"Abel!" Isabel's black look made Abel swallow his grin and turn back to the remains of his pie. She turned to Martha. "Don't mind him. He's just giving you a hard time. He knows it'll get your goat, all this talk about Brent."

Martha had colored, but she looked calm as she put down her fork and slid her hands into her lap. "I'm afraid I've set my heart on somebody I met last summer in France."

"Oh?" said Isabel.

"His name's Raoul, and he's wonderful. European men are so sensual."

Abel was studying his plate closely. Allison thought she saw him try to swallow a grin several times, but he kept his head bent as he poked determinedly at a scrap of pie crust.

Isabel cleared her throat. "Well, I'm sure he's very nice. Is he coming to visit you on the island?"

"Oh, no! Mama's declared him off limits." Martha smiled. "For the time being, at least. I'm working on her, of course."

"Of course," muttered Abel.

Martha leaned toward Isabel. "But who is this Tracy Lawton? And why was she on the island in the off-season? I don't believe I've ever heard of her."

Abel grunted and raised his head, but Isabel spoke before he had a chance to comment.

"None of us had ever heard of her, either, dear. She just showed up one day last fall with a trunk full of books and papers. She said she was doing a study of island life for a book she was writing."

"Only she didn't do much studying that I could see," commented Abel. "Just set her sights on Brent and went after him like a hound goes after a rabbit."

"Brent's hardly a rabbit. He's a grown man," said Isabel. "Besides, she was a very attractive woman. You can't blame the boy for wanting to spend time with her."

"Well, I'm glad he finally got shed of her." Abel put down his fork and rocked back in his chair. "It's the first time I ever saw him like that about a woman."

"Well, it won't be the last," Isabel said cheerfully, collecting the empty pie dishes. "One of these days he's going to find the right woman and settle down for good."

"Can't be too soon for my taste," said Abel. "I don't believe there was ever a man who was more meant for marrying than Brent."

Allison smiled. "It's funny you should say that. Martha told me he was a confirmed bachelor."

"Brent?" Abel shook his head. "He's sowed his wild oats already, that boy. He's ripe to settle down, you mark my words."

Martha coughed lightly, folded her napkin and placed it on the table. "Can we help you with the dishes, Isabel?"

"No, of course not! This is your first night on the island! There'll be time enough for chores in the days to come. Especially if you're running that big house all by yourself this summer."

"Thanks for a wonderful dinner," Martha said, hugging the older woman once again before she and Allison left the little gray house.

Isabel smiled. "You're more than welcome, dear." She turned to Allison. "And so are you. I hope you'll come back often." To Allison's surprise, the older woman gave her a brief hug, as well. "Welcome to Harper's Island."

The forest path had darkened as Allison and Martha walked back to the cottage, and Allison was relieved when they arrived at the house. She had heard stories as a child of people getting lost in the woods, and they had always seemed disturbingly real to her.

Fatigue overcame her almost immediately. After unpacking her things and listening to Martha enthuse for a while about sailing, she said good night and went upstairs. She took a long hot bath in the private bathroom off her bedroom and slipped into her white lace nightgown. For a moment she stood at the long bedroom window, looking down at the moonlit village below. Impulsively, she slid open the window and stepped out onto the balcony, then shivered as the surprisingly cold air enveloped her. Yet something about the peaceful scene drew her, and she didn't go back inside immediately.

Below, sleeping serenely in their houses, were the island villagers, hardworking men and women who struggled daily for survival. It was a life that had always alarmed her, one that appeared full of privation and hardship. But now, strangely, she felt drawn to the little town; she found herself wondering if she could be happy living in a community like it, where life seemed so straightforward and uncomplicated, where people like Abel and Isabel Cutler shared their lives with friendly neighbors. Of course, she would never have to find out. In a few weeks she would be one of the wealthiest young women in America.

She sighed and continued gazing down at the village. Somewhere down there was Brent's house. She felt a sudden flush of excitement, and an image of the tall blond man rose in her mind. She realized, with a shiver of recognition, that Brent Connors was an exact likeness of her fantasy lover.

Chapter Three

DESPITE HER FATIGUE, Allison slept fitfully. She dreamed that Cabot was running toward her across a brilliant green meadow, while she waited with outstretched hands. For some strange reason, she was weeping, almost as if she were dreading the imminent touch of his hands. When she woke, at dawn, she had the uneasy feeling that Brent Connors had been somewhere in her dream. She lay motionless in bed, watching the room lighten around her, trying to recall more details of her dream. But the more she tried to remember it, the more it all became a vague blur. Why did she have the distinct impression she had been in Brent's arms? She sighed and closed her eyes, willing herself back to sleep.

It was no use. She was wide awake. Outside her window the birds were singing frantically. It was a beautiful sound, very different from the grind of traffic outside her apartment window in Boston. But it could hardly be called silent. She smiled. Who had ever invented the myth that rural life was quiet?

She got up and went to the window. The sun was rising on the far side of the house, but her part of the balcony was still in shadow. She stepped out into the cool, morning air and squinted down at the harbor. Most of the boats that had been moored there the previous afternoon were gone. Apparently, fishermen went to work early in the day. She sighed. She knew from past experience that Martha liked to sleep well into the morning. It always seemed to Allison that the best part of the day was already gone if you didn't wake up until ten o'clock.

She went into the blue-tiled bathroom adjoining her room. Last night she'd been so sleepy she'd hardly noticed the elegant touches that made it so attractive: a low skylight over the bathtub, a chrome and white vinyl armchair, and an antique étagère holding blue and white plush towels. She saw for the first time how it blended with the bedroom; the same soft hues were carried throughout, as was the feeling of comfortable and subdued elegance. Clearly, Mrs. Hollingsworth had had her say in the decorating scheme on the second floor, no matter how much her husband had insisted on the place's cottage-like appearance downstairs.

The birds were still caroling when Allison went downstairs, dressed in a comfortable pair of blue linen slacks and a matching chamois blouse. She briefly considered taking a walk down to the private beach below the house, but decided to save that for later in the day. Right now she wanted to explore the grounds around the cottage. Martha would wake up soon enough and proceed to assault her with a whole list of activities for the day.

Allison left a note on the trestle table in the kitchen, and then slipped quickly outside. The house was surrounded by wide green lawns, and, on the south side, an informal garden of fruit trees and flowers flanked a winding gravel path. From almost any vantage point, Allison discovered, she could get a glimpse of the sea. It was an idyllic setting, a place for lovers. She tried to imagine Cabot strolling with her through the garden, and something froze inside her.

She closed her eyes and took a deep breath. This was ridiculous. She loved Cabot deeply. His courtesy and good looks had swept her off her feet; his money had been a heady aphrodisiac. Perhaps her love didn't correspond to the flighty passion of heroines in romance novels, but then, that was just fiction. She'd never loved any man before Cabot, despite her numerous dates.

From the beginning, when she first started going out with Cabot, she had known he would make a perfect husband. How could anyone not be dazzled by the world he lived in? Everything was so easy for Cabot; he merely had to pick up the phone and he could have anything he desired. He showered her with gifts; he was always sending her flowers or baskets of gourmet foods; he presented her with expensive pieces of jewelry on each monthly anniversary of their first date. Once, he had arranged a catered dinner aboard his father's private yacht and they had dined under the stars while the ship plied the waters of Boston Harbor. Later that evening they had danced on the open deck to live band music. It was a world that was totally captivating, a dream come true.

It was obvious that the strange feelings she'd been having lately were just prenuptial jitters, the same nagging doubts that every bride experienced as the big day approached. She loved Cabot and he was the perfect fiancé. There was no doubt in her mind.

She shook her head and looked across the lawns at the dark pine forest. Spotting the path she and Martha had taken to visit the Cutlers, she suddenly decided to follow it all the way down into the village. She had a desire to see the harbor up close, to watch the fishermen working on the dock.

She walked quickly across the clearing to the path and headed down through the deeply shadowed trees. She found herself hiking along with an uncharacteristic buoyancy in her step. There was no good reason for the growing excitement in her chest, but she couldn't deny the pleasant prickle of anticipation there. It was as if she knew something delightful was just about to happen.

When she came out of the woods into the Cutlers' backyard, she was surprised to see Isabel just coming out of the back door carrying a basket of wet clothes.

"Hello!" the older woman called cheerfully. "Glad to see not all of Martha's friends are stay-abeds!"

Allison grinned and waved. "Can I help you?" she called, but Isabel shook her head.

"This is my favorite exercise on summer mornings. Nothing's more satisfying than hanging out clean laundry. You go on about your business."

Allison continued across the meadow and came out on the main road. To her right she could see the harbor in the distance, and she headed eagerly in that direction. It wasn't until she was in front of the general store that she knew she was being followed.

Three years of city living had made Allison alert to the signals of danger. She never went anywhere without paying attention to her surroundings, and especially the presence of other people. Now she detected the sound of heavy footsteps which seemed to precisely match her own stride. She knew better than to look back over her shoulder and alert her pursuer to her fear. Automatically she quickened her pace and turned into the driveway of a small, red house. She could ask for help if anyone was at home. Hopefully, whoever was following her would just continue along the road. The daylight itself offered her considerable protection.

She was just a few steps from the porch when a hand fell on her shoulder. Allison let out a sharp cry and would have run except for the sudden, iron grip that hooked her elbow. She spun around, her mouth open to scream in earnest, and looked up into the laughing blue eyes of Brent Connors.

"You're up wicked early for a summer person." He released her elbow and cocked his head. "You planning to cook breakfast for me instead of supper?"

His accent was pleasantly clipped. Allison noted his red flannel shirt and tight blue jeans as her rapidly beating heart gradually slowed to normal.

"Breakfast? Why would I make your breakfast?"

"Looks to me like you planned on paying me a visit. Only sorry I wasn't here first." He nodded past her toward the house.

"Oh!" Allison flushed. "Is this your home?"

"Has been for nearly eight years." His grin widened, and Allison found herself grinning back sheepishly.

"I—It's hard to explain. I thought somebody was following me."

"Well, you were right. I was." His mouth quirked upward. "But that doesn't explain why you came visiting."

Allison looked into his bright blue eyes and flushed. "I was scared. I thought I might be in danger."

"Danger? Here on the island?" His laugh came from deep in his throat; a rich, generous laugh. "You watch too much television. This is Harper's Island, not New York City. Besides, Miss Curtis, when I have dishonorable intentions toward a woman, I don't sneak up on her. I usually just come right out and say what's on my mind."

Allison swallowed. "Well, I'm sorry, Mr. Connors—"

"Brent," he interrupted, grinning so broadly that a long dimple appeared at the corner of his mouth. "Let's skip the formalities. I'm not very fond of etiquette. Come on in and have some breakfast. I'm starved."

He walked past her to the house, clearly expecting her to follow.

"This is ridiculous," she protested. "I can't eat here."

He spun to stare at her. "Why not?"

She looked back at him, the color rising once again in her cheeks. "I was just going for a walk. I only turned into your driveway because I was nervous."

"So?" He shrugged. "Does that mean you're not allowed to eat?"

She was suddenly aware that she wanted to eat breakfast with Brent. And there was no good reason not to. It would give her a chance to learn about the island from a native's perspective. And that was something she had been curious about, from the first moment she had arrived on the island.

"Okay," she said, smiling. "I'll have breakfast with you." She felt a strange pleasure light her from within as Brent grinned back at her.

"Good. How about scrambled eggs?"

Allison could hardly believe she was actually following this stranger into his house, but she went up the steps behind him without hesitating. When he opened the door and held it for her, she stepped past him, accidently brushing his arm with her hand.

She was instantly aware of a current passing between them, a jolt not unlike an electric shock. She started, looked quickly at him, and found him gazing at her intently. She dropped her eyes, letting her long lashes shield her startled glance, but her heart was pounding wildly, and she knew that Brent had felt the same tremor. She put her fingers to her throat in a futile effort to calm herself. Brent stepped over the threshold behind her and closed the door.

They were standing in a small living room, paneled in light pine and decorated with fishing paraphernalia. A woodstove stood in one corner opposite a worn couch, flanked by two sagging easy chairs. The room had a casual, friendly look to it, but it also suggested a life lived on the threshold of poverty. Allison waited for the familiar shudder of revulsion to course through her, but it never came. Instead, something about the room attracted her; it was snug and well-cared for; it emanated a cozy, warm aura, an atmosphere of having been lived in. She knew, just looking at it, that it was a place that was *loved*.

"The kitchen's right through here." Brent opened a door to her left. She felt a mild tremor run up her spine at his nearness; to cover her agitation, she moved quickly through the doorway.

Blue-checked curtains hung at a sun-splashed window overlooking the harbor; the stove and counter were spotlessly clean. In the center of the kitchen sunlight drenched a circular wooden table.

"Have a seat." Brent pulled a ladder-backed chair away from the table. "I'll get you a cup of coffee."

Allison flicked him a curious glance. "I thought you wanted *me* to cook breakfast."

He grinned down at her and tapped the back of the chair. "I don't really expect my guests to fix me breakfast, Allison."

Something about the way he said her name made her breath tighten. She sat down and spread her fingers on the clean table. "You have a nice little house."

Brent's amused snort startled her. "Little is right. It's certainly not much compared to the Hollingsworth place. But I like it this way, strange as that may sound. I wouldn't trade this little shack for the Hollingsworth cottage if you paid me."

"Really?" Allison gave him a puzzled look. "What's wrong with it?"

He laughed. "To begin with, it's not a cottage. *This* is a cottage. Second, Mrs. Hollingsworth may be rich, but she's about the unhappiest person I've ever met. All that money doesn't do her any good when it comes to relating to other people."

"You sound bitter."

"Let's just say her world isn't everything it's cracked up to be." He had his back to her, spooning ground coffee into a percolator. "So tell me something about yourself."

"Me?"

"Sure. Like where you got that big rock on your finger."

Allison looked down at the diamond solitaire on the fourth finger of her left hand. She was so used to wearing it, she no longer thought of how ostentatious her engagement ring was. She remembered her initial reaction to its size, a mixture of shock and embarrassment.

"A friend gave it to me," she said quickly, wondering why she wasn't able to say the word "fiancé."

"Then you're engaged?" He turned to look at her, and she was instantly unnerved by the penetrating look in his blue eyes. She nodded.

Without taking his eyes from her, Brent opened the refrigerator door and took out a carton of eggs.

"When's the wedding?"

"September twentieth."

"So, tell me why you're here on Harper's Island with Martha."

"I wanted to get out of the city for a while. Martha invited me, and I've never been north of Portland before. It sounded like a nice vacation."

"Funny," he said, bending over the frying pan and cracking eggs into it rapidly, "but something about you doesn't strike me as being Martha's type."

Allison stared at him. She had no idea how she was supposed to respond to such a statement. She'd never met anyone so blunt, so forthright.

Brent turned, lifting the frying pan from the stove. He gave her a quick grin. "I offended you, didn't I?"

She shook her head, wishing suddenly that she'd braided her hair. A long strand hung over her right eye and she quickly brushed it away. "I'm just not used to people being quite so direct."

"Martha should have warned you. I'm known for being candid. It gets me in trouble sometimes, but most people appreciate it, once they get used to it."

He spooned the eggs onto two plates and set one of them down in front of her. "But you didn't satisfy my curiosity yet. What's your real story, Allison Curtis?" He slid into the chair across from her and handed her a fork.

"I don't really have a story." She looked down at the enormous pile of scrambled eggs. The aroma was delicious, but she no longer had any appetite.

He laughed. "Everybody has a story. And I'd put money on the fact that yours is fascinating. For instance, how'd you get hooked up with Martha in the first place?"

Allison looked up at him. "I met her at college, and she took me under her wing. If you're saying I don't come from her social class, you're right. But she's not snobbish or anything. She's friendly, fun-loving, great to be around. She was the one who introduced me to Cabot—"

"Cabot?"

"Cabot Wilder. The man I'm engaged to."

"And Cabot doesn't mind you going off for a whole month?"

"I think he understands."

"Well, he's either a blind man or a darn sight more liberal than he ought to be."

She felt herself color as he met her confused gaze. "Cabot's not like other men."

He grinned. "He must not be. If you were my fiancée, I wouldn't let you get farther away than the end of my arm."

She bent her head quickly and scooped a forkful of eggs into her mouth. She was grateful for the protective shield of hair as it slid across her blazing cheeks.

"By the way," said Brent quietly. "I like your hair. Long hair on a beautiful woman is very sexy."

She looked up at him. He was leaning toward her, smiling. He finished the last of his eggs and stood up, carrying his plate to the sink. "Coffee's ready."

Allison could hardly swallow. She didn't speak when he placed a mug of steaming coffee in front of her. She found that she could no longer look at him directly. His frankness and rugged masculinity challenged something deep within her. With great difficulty she managed to gather her wits and ask a question.

"Do you really catch lobsters for a living?"

He raised his mug to his lips and smiled. Once

again she saw the dimple deepen beside the corner of his mouth. "Ay-uh," he said, drawing out the word in an exaggeration of his down-east accent. "It's not really much of a living by most standards. I like it, though." He sipped his coffee and regarded her more seriously. "I'll never be wealthy enough to buy my woman a rock like that." His glance flicked to her hand. "But I'm happier than most men. And free. Got nobody to tell me what to do with my time. No clock to punch, no supervisors to deal with. What about you, Allison? Do you work for a living?"

She brightened. "I teach—that is, I taught—at a private school in Boston."

"Taught? As in past tense?"

She shrugged. "Well, I'm getting married, and I don't think I'll have much time for teaching as Cabot's wife."

"What, he's going to put you to work in his office?"

"No, it's just that there are all kinds of volunteer things I'll be expected to do as his wife."

Brent nodded but didn't say anything. Allison drank her coffee nervously under his penetrating gaze.

"You see, Cabot's family is different. They trace their ancestry back to the *Mayflower*, so certain things are expected of them—charity work and things. . . ." She fumbled for words, conscious only of Brent's hard stare.

"He must be a very important man. And well-off, judging by the size of that diamond."

Allison nodded. "He is. Very."

"Well." Brent cleared his throat and rocked back in his chair. "Seems like you got yourself quite a catch, Miss Allison Curtis. Congratulations."

"I'd better go." Allison stood up quickly. "Martha will be wondering where I am."

He didn't move, but sat gazing at her with a long, knowing stare. Allison felt a shiver flick across her shoulder blades and looked quickly past him out the window. The wind had come up, rippling the surface of the harbor; the colorful lobster boats rocked gently at their moorings.

"Which boat is yours?"

"The blue and white one," he answered proudly. "I'll take you out in her someday."

"No! I couldn't!"

"Why not?"

"I . . ." She shook her head.

"You can and you will," he said in a low voice. "Wait and see." He got to his feet.

For some reason, Allison couldn't take her eyes off the harbor. Her heart started beating wildly as Brent stood up and came around the table to her. She was sure he was going to touch her, and, if he did, she was afraid she would burst into tears. She didn't know why she was feeling this way, her body so filled with a tumult of confused emotions. Why was she so shaken by Brent's presence, and his words? She didn't know him, didn't even like him; he was nothing to her.

She walked quickly into the living room and past the couch to the door. She was about to open it when Brent's powerful arm reached out in front of her, blocking her exit.

"Allison." His lips were very close to her ear. "Sooner or later you're going to have to face the truth. It would be easier for you if it was sooner. Believe me, I know."

"What?" She spun to face him, and found that her

mouth was only inches from his. She took a step backward and bumped into the door.

Brent put his hand on her arm. "Are you okay?"

"I'm fine." She straightened, lifting her chin. "And thank you for the breakfast. It was very good."

"Forget the breakfast. Did you hear what I said?"

"Yes, but I have no idea what you're talking about. And I frankly find it insulting that you would even suggest that I'm not facing some truth. I hardly know you."

"Allison." His hand was still on her arm, and he was smiling calmly. "I happen to know what I'm talking about. Believe me, it doesn't do any good to run away from it. The truth has a tendency to catch up with you and hit you from behind, if you don't face it straight on." He sighed. "I only wish somebody had said this to me six months ago. It could have prevented a lot of pain." He slid his hand away; her skin tingled where his fingers had been.

"I don't know what you mean," she said hoarsely.

"I think you do. Your body betrays your feelings, even if you don't want to recognize them." He leaned closer. "You don't love Cabot."

The explicitness of his statement shocked her. She gaped up at him. He was smiling at her gently.

"Just think about it." He opened the door, and Allison hesitated only a moment before stepping into the sunlit morning.

She stumbled down the steps, aware that Brent was still gazing after her. In the driveway, when she glanced briefly over her shoulder at him, he flashed his grin once more and waved.

"See you tonight, Allison," he called softly as he closed the door.

Chapter Four

ALLISON WALKED QUICKLY back up the wooded path to the Hollingsworth cottage. She felt as if she were suspended on a tightrope over an enormous canyon; one look down and she might fall to her death. The only thing to do was to keep walking, praying that she wouldn't lose her balance.

She knew one thing. Brent Connors had a powerful effect on her; she had never met a man who made her pulse race so wildly, or whose words disturbed her so deeply. What had he meant, that her body had betrayed her feelings, that she didn't love Cabot? Of course she loved Cabot! How could anyone not love him? What woman wouldn't give her right arm to be his fiancée? All right, so maybe she and Cabot didn't have the kind of passionate relationship that was written about in books. That didn't mean she didn't love him. There were other things that mattered in a marriage: comfort, compatibility, future security. And Cabot could provide all those things. She would be an idiot to turn her back on her good fortune. She had heard stories of women who waited all their lives for the man of their dreams to come along, and he never came. As she entered the house, she tried to compose herself; she had no desire to let Martha see how upset she was.

She found her friend in the kitchen, wearing a pink satin bathrobe, spooning strawberry preserves onto a toasted English muffin. Martha grinned at Allison.

"Where have you been? I've been waiting for ages to talk to you! Come and have some breakfast. You must be starved!"

Allison shook her head and slid into the rocking chair by the window. "I'm really not hungry. I guess the exercise must have taken the edge off my appetite."

"Don't tell me you explored the island already!" Martha wailed.

Allison kicked off her shoes. "Just the village. I'm really not used to so much fresh air all at one time."

Martha laughed. "Well, anyway, I'm glad you're back. We have to get our plans straight for tonight."

Allison felt her cheeks grow warm. "I've been thinking about it, Martha. I don't think having Brent for supper is such a good idea."

"What?"

Allison shrugged. "You can still entertain him, of course. I'm just going to beg off. I'm not up to it."

"Is this about Cabot?"

"Well, I doubt that the idea would please him very much," she said quickly, grateful that Martha had supplied her with an excuse for her reluctance. "I mean, he practically had a fit that I was going off to Maine without him, and if he knew the two of us were entertaining a man . . ."

Martha laughed. "Cabot's not some Neanderthal macho type, Allison. You keep thinking he's like all the boys you knew in public high school. It's different in the world Cabot and I grew up in. Social occasions are just part of our everyday lives. They're *duties*." She grinned. "You might as well get used to it. It'll be part of your daily routine soon enough."

Allison gave her a doubtful look. "I can't believe he would take it so calmly."

"Cabot doesn't have a jealous bone in his body. Besides, do you think that he doesn't see other women socially? He's always going off to dinners and parties with a beautiful woman on his arm."

"It's not the same thing."

"Of course it is! Anyway, you have to do it. For me." Martha jumped to her feet. "And we'd better start planning or we'll never be ready by the time Brent comes."

Allison realized that unless she revealed her disquieting morning encounter, she had no valid reason to balk at her friend's plans. And she certainly had no desire to put the disturbing details into words.

"All right," she sighed. "But just remember, this wasn't my idea."

Allison grew increasingly nervous as the day went on. In the afternoon Martha insisted on driving down to the general store for food supplies, and Allison rode along, hoping that the trip would distract her mind from its preoccupation with her morning conversation with Brent. As they pulled up in front of the store, Allison's gaze swung out over the harbor and she noted that Brent's boat was gone from its mooring. She felt herself relax, and realized that she had been unconsciously dreading the possibility of another encounter with him ever since she'd agreed to go to the store.

The general store had a surprising abundance of supplies tucked away in its dark corners. Allison walked slowly up and down the aisles, studying the miscellaneous items, while Martha ordered sirloin steaks from the stocky, affable man behind the meat counter. The store sold everything from finishing nails to gourmet teas. It even held a shelf of pharmaceutical supplies. Allison reminded herself that she was on an island, and that such a store, while appearing quaint to her city-bred eyes, was probably viewed as a great convenience, even a luxury, to the year-round residents. Its hardwood floors were polished to a dark patina by years of muddy boots and shoes. It occurred to her suddenly that Brent's feet were among them; they had probably been familiar with these floors since childhood. She felt a warm rush in the pit of her stomach as she imagined rounding the corner of an aisle and coming face to face with him. What, she wondered, would it be like to live on Harper's Island year-round?

As Allison left the store fifteen minutes later, carrying a heavy bag of groceries, she saw that Brent's boat was coming into the harbor, moving slowly toward the long wharf where the ferry had docked. She felt a thickening in her chest and forced herself to think of Cabot as she climbed into the car beside Martha. She was relieved as they left the village behind and sped back up the hill toward the cottage.

"I'll show you around the rest of the island tomorrow," Martha promised, apologizing for not having given Allison a full tour. "But I really want tonight to be special."

"I'm sure it will be," Allison murmured. There was nothing to be done but grin and bear it. The evening ahead might not be so terrible after all, Allison told herself. Martha's presence would be certain to keep Brent's focus off her; if he was still as interested in Martha as she hoped, he might not pay her any attention at all. At any rate, she planned to make herself as inconspicuous as possible and to retire to her bedroom at the first opportunity.

The dinner preparations went smoothly. By five-thirty the salad was made, the steaks had been basted with a special barbecue sauce that Martha had concocted out of tomatoes and Worcestershire sauce, the stove-top grill had been checked out, and Allison was standing in front of her bathroom mirror, trying to decide what to wear. Although she didn't want to draw attention to herself, it went against her nature to ignore the finer points of good grooming. She finally decided on a lavender chamois dress with three-quarter-length sleeves, a self-belted waist, and a softly tailored neck. It wasn't new, but she knew that it complemented her hair and figure. She decided not to bother with makeup; it was something she used only sparingly anyway, and the fresh sea air had heightened the natural color in her cheeks and lips. She spent a long time working with her hair, first braiding it and winding it around her head, then tying it back with a wide barrette, before she finally brushed it out and left it hanging, unadorned, to her waist. She couldn't forget Brent's comment about long hair being sexy. Perhaps she should pass that piece of information along to Martha, who had often asked her if she should grow out her short, brown curls.

As she descended the stairs in her low-heeled, white sandals, Allison heard the sound of an engine outside. Through the circular landing window she could see a black pickup pulling up in front of the house. A moment later the door opened and Brent stepped out, his blond hair glinting in the late afternoon sun. He wore a blue knit shirt and brown corduroy pants. Obviously he had dressed up for dinner. It was the first time she had seen him in something other than blue jeans.

The doorbell rang, and she waited for Martha to come running. The front door was in the foyer immediately below her. She started back up the stairs; the last thing she wanted was for Brent to catch her observing him as he entered.

"Allison, can you get that?" came Martha's frantic wail from her upstairs bedroom. "I'm not quite dressed!"

The doorbell rang again, more insistently. Allison put her hand on the banister to steady herself.

"Allison?"

"Yes, I'll get it." So much for remaining in the background for the evening. She descended the rest of the stairs and crossed the foyer to open the heavy door.

"Hello, Allison." Brent smiled down at her with the same gentle expression he had left her with that morning. "You look beautiful tonight."

"Good evening, Brent." She forced herself to smile up at him. "Martha will be down in a minute."

He stepped through the doorway, his body only inches from hers.

She took a step backward. "Won't you come in and sit down?" She led him into the living room and sat on the edge of one of the couches. She expected him to sit in the easy chair opposite her, but when he sat next to her, she tensed and inched away.

"Is something wrong?" She heard the smile in his voice.

"No," she said carefully. "Whatever gave you that idea?"

"Maybe it was the look on your face when you answered the door. Like you didn't want to see me. Like you were afraid I'd take up our conversation where we left off this morning." The amusement in his voice was unmistakable.

Suddenly, it was more than she could bear. She whirled to face him. "What you said this morning—about my feelings for Cabot. You're dead wrong. I love him and we're going to have a wonderful marriage. Besides"—her face reddened with the heat of her growing indignation—"you have no right to tell me what I feel about Cabot or anybody else! I don't even know you, and you certainly don't know anything about me!"

"I really hit a nerve, didn't I?" The teasing tone was gone from his voice; there was something wounded in the deep, resonant timbre. "I'm sorry; I honestly didn't mean to upset you. I just wanted you to realize what was happening before it was too late."

"You act like you have some kind of right . . ." Her words drained away under his intense blue gaze.

"No, not right, Allison. Experience."

She had a sudden suspicion. "You're talking about Tracy Lawton, aren't you?" The words were out of her mouth before she could stop them, and she saw immediately that they had hit home.

A shadowed look crossed Brent's face and he leaned back into the couch. "What do you know about Tracy?"

"Nothing. I just heard the name mentioned, that's all."

His eyes darkened. "Whatever you've heard about her, you'd be wise to forget."

"Oh," she fumed, "it's all right for you to evaluate my relationship with my fiancé, but I'm not supposed to mention the woman you love."

He gave her a long, slow look. "I don't love her, Allison. I'm not sure I ever did. That's what I'm trying to tell you; people can fool themselves about their true feelings. It's better to be honest from the beginning."

"Well, I *am* being honest, for your information!" She stood up. "And you have no right to say these things to me!" She heard Martha's feet on the stairs and pressed her hands against her blazing cheeks. "No right at all!"

But there was not a trace of apology in Brent's eyes. Unable to face Martha, she turned and ran for the kitchen. Brent would have to invent some excuse for her strange behavior.

From the safety of the kitchen she could hear Brent's and Martha's voices, a soft interweaving of sound, almost musical in tone. She scurried around the room, checking on the food and table settings, wishing there was some way she could make herself fade into the woodwork for the evening. When the timer rang, signaling that the potatoes were done, she felt more in control, and was able to face Brent and Martha when they appeared in the doorway a few minutes later. Brent sent her a questioning look over Martha's head, but Allison ignored it. Determined to say nothing that wasn't totally polite and aloof, she simply smiled.

"You two go ahead and sit down. I'll be your waitress tonight."

She was a bit surprised when Martha didn't protest, but understood the reason a moment later, when her friend slid into place next to Brent, leaving Allison to take the chair on the opposite side of the table.

The dinner conversation went smoothly, thanks to Martha's constant chatter. She managed to engage Brent's attention on almost every subject under the sun. Allison felt a reluctant admiration for her friend's verbal skills. If she didn't always put people immediately at ease, at least Martha was able to entertain them.

When he had finished eating, Brent leaned back in his chair and crossed his arms over his chest. "That was some meal. I'll have to return the favor, and have you down to my place for supper." He took in both young women in his admiring glance.

"Oh, no," Martha said, laughing. "No more meat and potatoes for me! I'm going to have to diet now for the rest of the summer!"

Brent cocked his head. "Who said anything about meat and potatoes?" He glanced across the table. "You don't mind my cooking, do you, Allison?"

Allison flushed deeply and glanced at Martha, who sent her a dark, questioning look.

"Allison had breakfast with me this morning," Brent explained casually. "She didn't seem to object to my hospitality then. Unless she was just being polite." He sent her a piercing smile. "You're not given to meaningless etiquette, are you, Allison?"

"If you'll excuse me, I've got a splitting headache." Allison rose quickly and hurried from the room before either Brent or Martha could object. She knew that Martha was probably furious, but hopefully some time alone with Brent would take the edge off her anger. She ran up the stairs and down the long hall to her bedroom. Maybe she should leave Maine and go to California after all. It wasn't too late to change her plans. She had made such a mess of things here, Martha would surely welcome her departure.

Allison was surprised to hear the sound of Brent's truck on the gravel driveway only a few minutes later. She wondered briefly if he and Martha had gone somewhere together, but a moment later Martha knocked at her door.

"Come in," Allison called, bracing herself for Martha's wrath. She knew from experience it could be devastating.

"He loved it!" Martha crowed, dancing across the room and embracing Allison. "And he invited us to his place! That's a first! Do you have any idea how reluctant he is to invite people into his house? It's almost as sacred as his boat! I can hardly believe it!"

Allison looked at her in surprise. "Aren't you angry?"

"Angry? Why should I be angry?" Martha's eyes were glazed with bliss. "Would you believe he actually kissed me good-night? Well, just on the cheek, but that must mean he still cares for me. Brent never does anything just for form, you know."

"You mean you're not upset that I had breakfast with him?"

Martha smiled. "Well, if you weren't engaged to Cabot, I might be worried. But I know how devoted you two are. You could never have eyes for another man. And I know Brent would never touch another man's woman. He's very old-fashioned that way. He probably asked you as a favor to me."

Allison managed a wry smile. She felt relieved, and strangely deflated, by Martha's attitude. Apparently she'd been making too much out of the morning's events. Of course, Martha was right. She had no interest in other men, and Brent hadn't expressed any interest in her. The confusion and agitation she had felt had been of her own making. The chemistry was all in her head.

Martha giggled. "I'm pretty sure he still likes me. I wouldn't be surprised if he asks me out on his boat before the week is out."

"Is that supposed to be a privilege?"

"Of course it's a privilege! Lobstermen are practically *married* to their boats, and Brent is no exception! Two summers ago I practically begged him to take me out hauling with him, but he said I was too flighty." Martha pulled herself into an erect finishing-school stance. "But I'm so much more mature now, don't you think?"

Allison smiled, but all she could think about was Brent's confident declaration that he would take her out in his boat sooner or later. Did that have more significance than she'd believed?

"Well, what would you like to do tomorrow?" Martha asked. "Sail, swim, hike?" She threw out her arms expansively. "Or just laze around on the beach?"

Allison took a deep breath. "I think maybe I'd better go home tomorrow, Martha. I don't think it's a good idea for me to be away from Cabot, after all."

"But you can't leave now!" Martha wailed, looking at Allison in horror. "Everything depends on your being here!"

"Everything?" Allison frowned in confusion. It was clear that Martha's budding romance with Brent could only be enhanced by her return to Boston.

"Of course! Don't you understand? If you leave, Mama will be up here like a shot to investigate the situation. If she even *sees* Brent look at me, she'll yank me out of here so fast I won't know what hit me!"

Allison sighed. It wasn't the first time she'd felt irritated by her friend's extreme dependence on her parents. In some ways, Martha behaved more like a sixteen-year-old than a grown woman. Allison knew that it was because of her friend's coming inheritance and social position, yet it seemed strange to her that Martha could put up with her mother controlling her life to such an extent.

"I really don't see how my presence keeps your mother from being suspicious."

"Oh, Mama trusts your good judgment implicitly! If you leave, she'll know something's wrong. Besides, I'm not going to do anything stupid with Brent. Just a little fun and romance."

"Entertainment for the summer?" Allison wondered how Brent would react if he knew what Martha had planned.

Martha smiled sheepishly. "There's nothing wrong with that, is there? You've got to admit, there's nothing better than a sexy man to keep you from being bored."

Allison went to the window. The lights of the village glowed through the darkness. "Well, I don't want to ruin your plans, Martha, but I really think I've made a mistake in coming." She swallowed. "I miss Cabot."

"Oh, Allison, of course you do! I understand completely!" Martha flung herself onto the bed and stretched out at full length. "You won't believe how terrible I felt last summer after I came home from France! I thought I would absolutely *die* without Raoul's arms around me! And I can imagine it's even worse when you're engaged to someone—especially someone like Cabot." There was a pause, and Allison tried to say something, to echo Martha's thought, but no words came to her.

Martha rolled onto her side and then sat up quickly. "I've got the perfect solution! I'll invite Cabot here! He can use the guest house, so everything will be perfectly proper, and we can all have a wonderful summer together!" She bounced on the bed. "Why didn't I think of that before?"

Allison frowned. "I don't think he can get away. There's a big merger coming up, and he has to be in touch with his lawyers. It's much better for me to just go home—"

"Nonsense!" Martha spoke in the stubborn tone that meant she was certain she was doing something for the absolute good of all concerned. "He can bring a cellular phone and work here, if his lawyers can't handle it themselves. They really *ought* to be able to; he pays them enough." She bounced again. "It's the *only* solution, and I just don't know why I didn't think of it sooner. Cabot will love it up here. We can all go sailing and swimming every day if we want to!"

Allison sighed. There was not much point in arguing with Martha once she'd made up her mind. "Maybe you're right. If you can drag him away from Boston."

"Of course I can." Martha stood up, grinning. "I'm going down to the general store right now and call him. And I won't take no for an answer." She disappeared before Allison could murmur a word of thanks.

Allison turned back to the window and looked down at the little village below. So much for a summer on her own. The invitation was as good as sent. And it was a good thing. Her current emotional turmoil only proved how badly she needed Cabot by her side.

Chapter Five

FROM HER BALCONY Allison watched Martha drive the Porsche down the long driveway toward the road. A strangely heavy feeling settled over her as silence enveloped the house. If only she'd been able to laugh off Brent's remarks! The man had an uncanny ability to unnerve her.

She stood on the balcony until the sky was black and a cold wind rose from the water. Martha's errand was taking a surprisingly long time. But then, it was like Martha to talk for hours on the phone. She probably had a number of arrangements to work out with Cabot if he accepted the invitation, and Allison was increasingly sure that he would. Martha was an expert at talking people into things; her own presence on Harper's Island testified to that.

Shivering, Allison returned to her room and lay down on the bed, drawing the thick, down comforter around her for warmth. The headache she had professed to escape Brent's presence was now a reality. She closed her eyes and pressed her fingers against her throbbing temples. She drifted slowly toward sleep, great waves of relaxation sweeping through her like the sea caressing the shore.

The sound of the doorbell roused her. A quick

glance at the clock on the nightstand next to the bed told Allison that it was nine-thirty. More than an hour had passed since Martha left for the store.

The doorbell rang again. Allison put her hand to her pounding forehead. Martha must have forgotten her keys. Irritated, and still in pain, Allison stumbled down the stairs and pulled open the door.

"Brent!" she gasped.

"There's been an accident." Brent's pale face and pained expression were in tune with her own aching head.

Her hand rose to her throat. "It's Martha, isn't it? Something terrible's happened!" She sagged back against the wall.

"Her car hit a tree." He spoke slowly, his words measured, his voice painstakingly calm. "She's alive and conscious, but she's broken several bones. They don't know the extent of her internal injuries yet."

"Oh my God!"

"My grandparents are taking her over to the mainland right now. I thought you'd want to know. She may be in the hospital for a while. It all depends on what they find."

She stared up at him with wide, frightened eyes. "But I have to be with her! She's my friend!"

He nodded. "I figured you'd want a ride over tonight. That's one of the reasons I came. Do you have a jacket or something? It gets pretty cold on the water at night."

"Yes . . ." She continued to stare at him. "I can't believe this happened! She was just going down to the store to make a phone call."

"Do you have a jacket?" he repeated.

She nodded.

"Tell me where it is. I'll get it for you."

Allison shook her head, trying to clear it. "I'll get

it." She turned blindly and started to stumble up the stairs. When Brent followed her, offering her his arm, she let herself lean against him, wondering if she would ever stop trembling.

He stood in the doorway of her bedroom while she rummaged through the closet and finally found her blue windbreaker. She pulled it off the hanger, fumbling awkwardly with it for a moment before Brent helped her into it. With his steadying hand once again on her arm, Allison felt calmer.

He glanced down at her stylish sandals and frowned. "Don't you have any sneakers? Those will just get in your way."

She returned to the closet, where she fished out a pair of worn Nike jogging shoes. She had brought them along on a whim; they were old and comfortable; she hadn't worn them much since she met Cabot. She sat on the edge of the bed and slipped off her sandals, then started to pull on the Nikes with trembling hands. The shoe slipped off her foot and dropped to the floor. Instantly Brent knelt to pick it up and slide it smoothly onto her foot. The touch of his fingers on her skin was like a caress. He slid on the other shoe, tied them both and stood up quickly.

"Let's get going."

He led her out of the house to his pickup and helped her into the cab. She curled up on the seat, her arms wrapped tightly around her. When he climbed in behind the wheel, she started shaking uncontrollably. The thought of Martha lying crushed and broken by the side of the road made her feel sick and dizzy.

Brent's hand touched her cheek. "Take it easy," he said softly. "She's going to be all right."

Surprisingly, Allison felt herself relax. She gave

him a weak smile. "I'm sorry. I guess I'm just nervous."

"Of course you are." He removed his hand, started the engine and backed the truck around to head down the hill.

"How did it happen?" Her voice was hollow in the darkness.

She felt more than saw him shrug as he bent over the steering wheel and guided the truck expertly down the hill. "I don't know. She must have been taking that corner too fast, not paying attention. I've warned her before to slow down."

Allison remembered the disapproval she'd seen on his face when she first met him, when Martha had barely missed running him down. Martha had made light of it at the time, as if he were simply teasing her. Apparently he'd been serious. She was beginning to realize that Brent, unlike most people she knew, rarely said anything he didn't mean.

They didn't speak again until Brent pulled to a stop in the little parking lot next to the village wharf. Allison sensed that all thought and feeling had been drained out of her. She was grateful for Brent's steadying hand as he helped her from the truck.

He reached past her and groped under the passenger seat. When he straightened and closed the truck door, he was holding a flashlight. "My boat's moored out in the harbor. We'll have to take the painter out to it."

"Painter?"

"It's a small boat—like a skiff." He led her down the sloping parking lot to the wharf. Her shoes made soft padding sounds on the wooden boards. At the end of the wharf a narrow ramp led down to a long float where the skiffs were tied. Brent pointed his flashlight beam down the ramp. "It's a bit steep and slippery, so hold onto the rail," he cautioned as he started to descend the ramp.

Allison followed warily, holding the rails on both sides with her sweating hands, anxious to stay as close as possible to Brent and the flashlight. At the bottom of the ramp Brent took her hand as she stepped onto the float. She felt it rock beneath her and clutched his hand more tightly.

"What's the matter? Haven't you ever been on a boat before?"

She shook her head.

"I thought all of Martha's friends were boat lovers. You really *aren't* like the others, are you?"

Did she detect amusement in his tone or was it just her imagination? "I had a bad experience as a kid," she murmured.

"I'm glad you told me." He squeezed her hand gently. "But there's nothing to be afraid of. All you have to do is step into the painter." He aimed his flashlight at the flimsy boat tied to an iron hitch on the side of the float. The gap between the float and the boat was dark, abysmal. Water slapped the sides of the float. Allison felt dizzy; her skin was clammy. She had a wild desire to run back up the ramp and to keep running until she reached the safety of the Hollingsworth cottage. She looked at Brent.

"Go ahead," he said. "There's nothing to it."

She took a deep breath and stepped into the boat. It rocked wildly beneath her, and she clawed frantically at the air.

"Sit down!" Brent was suddenly beside her, pushing her down on a low plank that ran between the sides of the boat. "Just take a couple of deep breaths and sit still. You're doing fine."

She did as she was told, clenching her hands together in her lap, her eyes riveted on Brent as he dropped the small outboard motor attached to the boat's stern into the water. He started the engine and they began moving almost at once, gliding noisily out over the black water, trailing a dull white wake. Allison couldn't remember when she'd ever felt so frightened. The whole evening had become a nightmare. She started shivering again, violently this time.

"Cold?"

She shook her head. "I think it's just nerves."

When the painter was only a few yards from Brent's lobster boat, he cut the engine and moved into the bow. He crouched expertly on the gunwales and reached out over the water. Allison felt the painter bump against the side of the larger boat. Almost instantly he had tied the skiff to the mooring and climbed into the lobster boat. Leaning toward her over the gunwales, he spoke calmly but firmly.

"Hold my hand, Allison. Take your time."

She stood up slowly, moving carefully along the boat until she could touch Brent's hand. She no longer felt quite as terrified, despite the nearness of the dark, lapping water. Brent circled her wrists in two iron hands and pulled her smoothly upward while her legs scrambled to get a footing on the slippery side of the lobster boat. A moment later she was standing next to him.

"Welcome aboard the *Blue Lady*. I'm afraid my timing's terrible, but I'm going to have to kiss you." He smiled apologetically.

"What?"

"It's an old tradition on this island. When a lady comes on board a boat for the first time, she has to kiss the captain."

"You're kidding."

He shook his head. "It's to ensure good luck."

"You're making this up." She backed away from him.

"Absolutely not. One thing you can count on, Allison, I don't tell lies." He stepped close to her. "You don't want to jinx the trip, do you? The way things are going tonight, we need all the luck we can get. Believe me, if it wasn't an unbreakable tradition, I wouldn't ask." He cocked his head and his smile widened slowly. "On the other hand, maybe I would."

He put his arm around her and bent his head. As his lips brushed hers, Allison felt an intense wave of pleasure pass through her body. Her hands reached involuntarily for the back of his neck, but he had already stepped away. Allison felt jolted, acutely aware that she wanted him to kiss her again, a deep, lingering kiss.

"Thanks," he said softly. "Now we'd better get this old tub moving."

He went forward into a sheltered area covering the wheel, and started the boat's engine. It made a powerful, throbbing sound deep inside the boat. Allison ran her fingers slowly over her lips. She'd never known a man could kiss that way. Cabot's kisses had always been hard and dry. She felt weak and dazed; she didn't know how much of her feelings had been generated by worry and how much by Brent's kiss.

"Come on inside the cuddy," Brent called, glancing over his shoulder at her as the boat started to move across the broad arc of the harbor. "You'll freeze out there."

She went to him, into the dimly lit pilothouse, and sat on the wooden crate he indicated. She gazed up at him and at the black sky and water that framed his body. She tried to think of Martha and the hospital where they were headed, but all she could do was remember Brent's lips against hers. His physical presence seemed to be the only reality in the world.

Two hours later Allison was sitting in the hospital waiting room between Abel and Isabel Cutler, while Brent telephoned Martha's parents. Isabel had filled her in on all the details of Martha's condition: the broken leg and rib, the mild concussion, even the bruises and scrapes. Luckily there had been no serious internal injuries. Allison listened anxiously at first, but Isabel's matter-of-fact tone eventually reassured her that Martha was going to be all right.

"It's really a miracle," Isabel said. "She could have been killed instantly. It happened right in front of our house, you know. At that awful curve. I sometimes think they shouldn't allow cars on the island. A lot of places don't."

"They didn't have them on Harper's before the summer people came," put in Abel.

Isabel laughed. "They didn't have cars, period, before the summer people came."

"She's really going to be all right, then?" Allison asked again. She felt numb with relief.

"Of course, dear." Isabel reached over and patted her hand. "She'll be laid up for a bit, though. She'll need somebody to be with her."

"I expect they'll send her back home to Boston," Allison said, suddenly realizing that her stated desire to return home was about to become a reality.

"I doubt that," Abel said. "More likely they'll hire somebody to wait on her hand and foot and leave her up here where she won't bother them."

"Abel!" Isabel's sharp voice silenced her husband, but Allison had caught a hint of the truth behind his words in her own dealings with Martha's parents.

Their relationship with their daughter was one dominated by attempts to control her behavior.

A young, dark-haired doctor approached them, striding quickly across the gray-tiled floor. Allison and Isabel looked up expectantly; Abel got to his feet.

"Dr. Silverman. How is she?"

"Sit down, Mr. Cutler." The doctor smiled down at them pleasantly. "Martha's doing fine. You can see her now, if you like. She's out of recovery; her bones have been set, and she's resting comfortably. She may be a little woozy still, but that will pass in a few hours."

Allison swallowed. "How long will she be staying in the hospital?"

"About a week, I'd say. Maybe less. Of course, she'll need some care at home for a while, but I understand that won't be a problem."

"Certainly won't," said Abel.

"Are you her grandfather?"

Abel shook his head. "No relation. Just friends. Her folks live in Boston."

The doctor nodded. "Well, be sure to have them see me when they get here."

Brent appeared at his elbow. "They won't be coming."

The doctor turned to him. "Excuse me?"

"I've just spoken with the Hollingsworths on the phone. They don't think it's serious enough to warrant disrupting their busy schedules." Allison could read the disgust on his face.

The doctor shrugged. "Well, in that case, I'll keep in touch." He nodded briefly and walked away.

Brent raked a hand through his hair and shook his head. "Those people have all the money in the world, but they don't have time to come to the hospital to see their own daughter!"

"They've always been like that," Isabel said, rising and putting her hand gently on his arm. "She's used to it, Brent."

"How can anybody get used to *that*?"

"They live in a different world. Now, come on and put on your best smile. The doctor said we can see her now."

"They only allow two visitors at a time. You two go ahead. I need a few minutes to calm down. Allison can keep me company." He flicked a glance in her direction.

"Yes," Allison said quickly. "Go ahead. And please don't hurry on my account."

"Thank you, dear." Isabel smiled and gathered up her coat, nodded to Abel, and the two of them headed down the hall.

Brent sank into the chair next to Allison. "People like that make me sick," he muttered. "And they wonder why we natives resent summer people!"

Allison turned to him. His bitterness was almost palpable. She felt the waves of anger flowing from him into the room.

"Everybody isn't like that," she said. "I'm sure there are good, decent people who vacation on the island."

"Are there?" He looked at her and smiled grimly. "I suppose you're right. But Mr. and Mrs. Hollingsworth have always made my blood boil. They come here and act like royalty, but they don't have an ounce of humanity in their souls. They've come up here for years and never had the slightest connection with the people who live on the island year-round, except to hire them for menial jobs. I never understood why my grandparents put up with it.

The Hollingsworths never treated them like human beings. I had the misfortune to make their acquaintance two summers ago, and I wish to God I'd never laid eyes on them!"

"Was that the summer you had an affair with Martha?" Allison had blurted the question before she could stop herself. Brent's dark scowl told her that she should have held her tongue.

"I never had an affair with Martha."

"I'm sorry. I meant to say romance," Allison corrected herself quickly. "Martha told me about it, how her parents found out and made you stop seeing each other. . . ." Her voice trailed away.

"One thing you should know, Allison. I've never let *anyone* tell me what to do. Not since I was sixteen years old. That includes the Hollingsworths. One of the reasons I'm a lobsterman is because it's one of the last ways to make a living in America where you can still be your own man."

"I'm sorry," she said, unnerved by the vehemence in his tone. Obviously, his anger was generated by more than simple disgust at Martha's parents. It must have something to do with his relationship with Tracy Lawton. Had she been wealthy? Had she tried to make him change his life? Hadn't Abel said something about her attempting to get Brent to leave Harper's Island? She felt a strange spark of curiosity run through her. "I guess you've had some bad experiences."

"Yes, as a matter of fact." He took a long, slow breath and his face softened. "Maybe I'm overreacting, but I'm afraid I have yet to meet somebody with a lot of money who didn't have his or her values pretty thoroughly mixed up."

She looked away from his penetrating gaze. "I really want to thank you for letting me know about

Martha. And for bringing me here," she said, anxious to change the subject. "If you hadn't come to the house, I'd be going crazy with worry by now."

"No problem." To her surprise, he grinned. "I told you I'd take you out in my boat. I just didn't expect it would be a moonlight cruise."

She smiled back at him. "It wasn't as bad as I expected, once I was aboard the *Blue Lady*."

"No," he agreed softly, "that wasn't bad at all."

Startled, Allison realized that he was referring to their kiss, and her heartbeat quickened as she felt the telltale heat of a blush rise in her cheeks. Quickly she looked away, and felt a distinct sense of relief at the sight of Isabel and Abel coming through a door at the far end of the hall.

"I guess it's our turn," she said brightly, standing up and starting toward them. She knew that Brent's eyes were still on her as he followed her down the hall. Never before had she been so keenly aware that you could actually *feel* someone's eyes. It was as if she were being caressed by a very soft, gentle hand.

Chapter
Six

MARTHA WAS SITTING UP in bed when Allison entered her hospital room, but she looked pale and shaken. There was a long scratch down her right cheek, and her jaw was dark and swollen.

Allison embraced her carefully. "How are you feeling?"

"Sore." Martha smiled grimly. "I feel like a real jerk."

"You ought to," said Brent from the foot of the bed, where he was examining her chart. "You were driving much too fast."

"We're just glad you're all right." Allison patted Martha's arm, hoping to moderate the impact of Brent's blunt comment. But Martha didn't seem to hear her. She was smiling at Brent as if he had just complimented her.

"You certainly scared the hell out of everybody." Brent replaced the chart on its hook and came around the bed to stand beside Allison. "When Abel found you, he thought you were dead. What in the world were you doing, chasing around in the middle of the night?"

Martha's eyes widened suddenly and she turned to Allison. "Oh, I meant to tell you! Cabot says he'll come. I was so excited! I guess that's why I took the corner so fast. I wasn't thinking about my driving. I was just happy for you and eager to tell you. I knew you'd be thrilled!"

"Cabot? Allison's fiancé?" Brent leaned forward, frowning.

Martha nodded. "He'll be free in about two weeks. We made all the arrangements over the phone. He'll bring his files and stay in the guest house, where he can spread out to his heart's content. Turn it into a real bachelor pad, if he wants." She wrinkled her nose. "I'm just sorry I had to go and get myself busted up like this. But I won't let it spoil things for the two of you."

"Martha, I have to go back to Boston. It isn't right for me to stay in your parents' place while you're not there. And you'll be going home yourself as soon as you get out of here. Don't worry." She shook her head as Martha's face lengthened. "I'll call Cabot and explain everything. He'll understand."

"But you can't!" Martha wailed. "Besides, I don't want to go home! I'll heal just as quickly in Maine as I will in Boston. Quicker, even."

Allison looked doubtfully at the thick bandages around Martha's ribs and the bulging cast on her leg. "You're going to need help, Martha. At least for a while. You won't be able to manage alone."

"That's right! So you have to stay! Doesn't she, Brent?"

"I certainly don't see how you can go home at a time like this, Allison," Brent agreed. "When I spoke with Martha's mother, she was assuming you'd stay."

Allison glanced at him; the look in his eyes reminded her again of his kiss. Something knotted in her throat.

"See, you're outvoted. And what Mama says, goes. You know that!" Martha reached for her hand. "Please, Allison! You can't desert me at a time like this! Can she, Brent?"

"Of course not." There was gentle amusement in his voice. "Not when you've just been seriously injured."

Allison sighed. "Oh, all right. But I think we should call Cabot. He might not feel comfortable about coming with you laid up like this."

Martha laughed. "By the time he gets here, I'll be back on my feet. I promise! Even the doctor said I'd be able to get around on crutches in a couple of weeks. So you're not allowed to call him, Allison. Except for a love chat."

Brent shifted his feet. "We'd better go. You both look beat. And I could use a little sleep myself before I go out hauling tomorrow." He glanced at his watch. "Make that today."

His hand brushed Allison's back in unspoken command that she say good-bye. She felt the heat of his fingers through her dress, sending ripples of electricity over her skin.

She smiled at Martha. "Brent's right. You get some rest. I'll come and see you again as soon as I can. I'll find out when the ferry runs are—"

"Don't worry, Martha," Brent interrupted her. "I'll see that she gets here often. She won't have to wait for the ferry, either. Now say good night." He reached down and touched her arm.

Martha smiled. "Is that all I get, a pat on the arm?"

"That's right." Brent grinned back at her. "You've been a bad girl."

"Come on, Brent, just one little kiss!"

He shook his head. "I don't give my kisses away lightly, Martha. You know that."

Allison knew from the laughter in his voice that Brent was joking, but as she bent to hug her friend good-bye, she couldn't escape the memory of his mouth on hers just a few hours earlier. When she straightened and headed to the door, she was still blushing.

The beauty of the return trip was blurred with fatigue for Allison, but as she watched the smooth indigo sky lighten with dawn, she felt a deep peace settle over her. The *Blue Lady* rode the water easily, her powerful engine throbbing quietly beneath them. Brent seemed absorbed in his own thoughts; after a while Allison fell into a half sleep, her head rocking gently against the pilothouse wall, a faint smile on her lips.

It wasn't until Brent cut the engine and spoke her name that she realized that they had returned to Harper's Island. The sun was just rising over the green hill beyond the village. She had never seen a more beautiful dawn.

At Brent's prompt, Allison climbed gingerly into the painter, holding her breath as if that might prevent the dangerous rocking she dreaded. When Brent clambered in beside her and set the boat swaying, she instinctively clutched his arm.

He grinned at her. "Still don't have your sea legs yet, do you?"

"I'm afraid not." She shook her head.

"Well, with all the trips you'll be making back and forth to the mainland on the *Blue Lady* in the next few days, I'd be surprised if you're not as salty as the rest of us by the time Martha gets out of the hospital."

"I really don't want to put you out," she said. "I'm

sure it would be much easier for you if I took the ferry."

He narrowed his eyes. "I'll decide what's easiest for me." He slid into the stern and quickly started the outboard. A moment later they bumped gently into the wharf pilings and Brent helped her quickly onto the dock.

"I'll drive you home." He stood beside her, his mouth very close to her ear. Her pulse quickened once again at the deep timbre of his voice, and she berated herself for her reaction. It must be a function of her fatigue, she thought. There was no reason why a man's *voice* should make her heart race. Certainly, if she were going to react to anyone's voice, it would be Cabot's.

"There's no need," she said quickly. "It's light enough. I can walk."

But he hadn't heard, or had chosen to ignore her words. He walked ahead of her, his powerfully muscled legs carrying him rapidly up the ramp to the truck. She followed wearily, wondering where he found his energy after being awake all night. He was holding the door open for her when she reached the truck, and she let him hand her up without objecting, secretly grateful that she didn't have to walk up the long hill to the cottage.

"I'm afraid I wasn't very good company on the ride back," she apologized as he climbed up beside her. "I was almost asleep."

He started the truck. "You were exhausted. You needed the rest. I've told you before, I don't hold etiquette in very high regard. Actually, it's kind of refreshing to be with a woman who doesn't chatter all the time."

She wondered if she was supposed to laugh. "At

least you can get some sleep yourself now," she offered lamely.

He shook his head. "Not for a while. Sun's up and I'm hauling today."

"You mean you're going right back out in the boat again? Now?"

He nodded, grinning. "It won't be the first time I've been up all night."

She looked away. She assumed he was referring to his relationship with Tracy Lawton. They had undoubtedly been lovers. Perhaps they had spent days at a time together on his boat. Not that it mattered to her, she told herself angrily.

He turned into the long Hollingsworth driveway. "I'm glad you told Martha you'd stick around for a while," he said quietly. "She really needs you right now."

She looked at him. "I don't think Martha needs *me*. It's obvious that a lot of people here love her."

"You're wrong. She *does* need you. She desperately needs a friend who isn't one of her family's hirelings, someone who cares about her as a human being."

She swallowed. "You have to understand about the Hollingsworths. They don't live in the same world as other people. The rich have different customs, different traditions."

"Their children still have feelings."

"But they're used to it. Cabot told me once—"

"Cabot?" He glanced at her, frowning. "Is your fiancé's family like the Hollingsworths?"

"Well, not exactly. The Wilder money is much older. . . ." Her voice died as his frown deepened.

"So tell me about this world you're going to marry into, Allison. Are your children going to go for months at a time without seeing their parents? Are they going to be brought up by nannies and tutors?"

"No!" Allison said hotly. "I'm going to raise my children by myself!" She realized, with a little shock of alarm, that she had never discussed the raising of children with Cabot. She had just assumed that she would spend her time caring for them once they were born. But the thought gnawed at her. Was there some truth hidden in Brent's words? Would being married to Cabot Wilder force her to forgo an intimate relationship with her own children? She shivered as they pulled up in front of the massive Hollingsworth cottage.

"Thanks for everything." She turned stiffly to Brent and tried to smile.

He was watching her closely. "You're more than welcome."

She found the door handle and pulled it. To her chagrin, she couldn't make it move.

"Sometimes it sticks," Brent said. He leaned across her and hit the handle with the heel of his hand. "Try it now." He didn't move away from her, apparently waiting to see if she could open it by herself. His chest was just inches from hers. Allison pulled at the handle with moist hands and finally felt the door click open.

"There!" she said with forced brightness. "Thanks."

"Any time." Brent straightened. "Actually, I'm not sure you are welcome, though. It was an awful temptation to sit there and watch you struggle. You make a beautiful prisoner."

Her eyes widened as she felt his glance roaming slowly over her slender body. Nervously, she gave the door a hard push and it swung wide.

"Sorry." He grinned. But she could tell he wasn't sorry at all.

She smoothed her skirt down over her legs. For some reason she felt unable to move.

"As a matter of fact," he continued, shifting toward her slightly, "if you weren't engaged, I believe I'd kiss you again right now."

"Another island custom?" she said tightly.

"Not this time, I'm afraid. Just a darned good idea." He lifted his hand toward her face.

Her tiny gasp was less surprise at his action than shock at her overpowering physical awareness that she wanted him to kiss her.

He stroked her cheek and cupped the nape of her neck, the subtle pressure of his fingers bringing her face close to his. His mouth grazed hers with an exquisite tenderness; the pressure of his lips drove a wedge of desire deep into her body. Her arms rose involuntarily, her hands trembling in the air beside his shoulders. Then, suddenly, she understood what she was doing.

She wrenched violently away from him. He gave her a bewildered frown as his hand dropped onto the seat between them.

She slid quickly toward the open cab door, aware that her lips were still burning with his kiss. Her breath was coming in tiny, pinched gasps. As she jumped to the ground, his eyes met hers in a glance that thoroughly unnerved her. Nervously, she smoothed her skirt and tucked a loose lock of hair behind her left ear. It was all she could do to speak.

"Thanks again," she said.

"No problem."

Standing on the ground, only her head and shoulders were above the seat of the cab. She could no longer see his face clearly. It was both a relief and a visceral loss. She reached to close the truck door.

"Wait a minute." Brent turned off the engine and slid across the seat to the passenger side so that he was sitting directly above her. He reached down to hand her something, a small, bright object that glittered in his big palm. It was a gold barrette, gently bowed and etched with a delicate pattern of climbing roses.

"It's lovely!" She reached to touch it, then drew back. "But it's not mine, Brent."

"It is now. I saw it in the hospital gift shop and I knew it was made for you."

She looked up at him. "You shouldn't have bought it. It must have cost a lot of money."

"Take it," he said in a low voice. "Wear it—right there." He grazed her hair above her right ear. His hand was gentle, caressing. She shook her head. "I can't accept it." She felt his frown.

"It's yours. It was made for your hair. If you won't take it now, then I'll save it for later." He curled his fingers over it and moved back into the driver's seat. Allison watched him start the ignition. He glanced at her, but it took her several seconds to realize he was waiting for her to shut the door.

"I appreciate the thought, Brent." She was strangely reluctant to close the door and be left alone with the big house. "It was very kind of you."

"Kind has nothing to do with it, Allison. Like I said, it was made for your hair. When you change your mind about accepting it, let me know."

"I don't see how I ever could." She fumbled for the right words to express her inner turmoil. "It just wouldn't be right . . . under the circumstances."

"Meaning Cabot?"
She nodded.

"I'm looking forward to meeting him. He must be one hell of a guy to keep you so loyal when you have so many doubts."

She swallowed. "Doubts?"

"About your feelings for him. The fact that you don't love him."

"I *do* love him!" she flared, suddenly furious. "I'm engaged to marry him, aren't I? And besides, it's none of your business *what* my feelings are for Cabot! You have no right to interfere—to come on like some authority on the subject!"

She started to slam the truck door, but he reached across and held it open with his powerful arm.

"You go ahead and play these games if you want, Allison. The only person you're hurting is yourself."

"I'm not hurting anybody! Least of all me!" She was choking on her anger; she saw him shift off the seat and out of the truck through a blur of hot tears.

"Take it easy." He took her shoulders and turned her so that her back was against the truck fender and he was blocking her path to the house. "You're in no condition to be left alone right now, are you?"

She started to move away from him, but his hands tightened like a vise on her upper arms, and she knew she had no strength to match his. Abruptly, he lifted her, scooping one arm under her legs and the other behind her back.

"Put me down!" she screamed.

But he paid no attention. He marched around the cottage to a back entrance and pushed it open with his shoulder. "Glad Gran keeps this door unlocked," he muttered.

"What are you doing? Where are you taking me?" Allison was suddenly frightened.

"I'm putting you to bed." He moved rapidly

through the labyrinthine house to the stairs. "You're exhausted."

"Stop it! Let me go!" But she had no energy to fight him. She stopped struggling and let him carry her up the stairs and deposit her on her bed. She knew he was right. Waves of fatigue were coursing through her, weakening her resistance.

He sat beside her, straddling her with his arms.

She blinked up at him. "I really do love Cabot," she murmured.

He stared at her, his eyes a dark, piercing blue. "I know you think you do," he said softly. He sighed and stood up, raking his hand through his blond hair. "Have it your way. For now, anyway. Get some sleep. I'll see you later."

He closed the bedroom door as he left, and Allison heard his footsteps on the stairs a moment later. She turned on her side and stared out the window. The sky was a deep, rich blue; sunlight poured through the sheer curtains. She heard the pickup start, and thought about Brent going back out on the *Blue Lady*. She thought of his mouth on hers, and a tremor went through her body. How long would he have to work hauling lobster traps out of the ocean today? She knew he was exhausted, too.

An image came unbidden to her mind, of him beside her on the bed, asleep. She shook it away angrily, but it persisted. She saw his firmly muscled body beside her, the handsome profile, relaxed in sleep. No matter what she did, she couldn't blot out the image. What in the world was she going to do when Cabot came?

She sighed and rolled away from the window. Instantly her eyes widened and she sat up. There, on the night table right beside her bed, was the gold barrette. Brent must have placed it there before he left. She touched it gingerly, as if to be certain it was real, and then picked it up. It was as if Brent knew that she still had a little girl's love for decorative barrettes. It touched her deeply; the gift was, oddly, more poignant than any of the expensive jewels Cabot had given her. Was it because she knew Brent's money was so much harder to come by? Or was there some other, deeper reason?

She examined the barrette carefully. It was clearly not a child's barrette. The etching was exquisite, a delicate scroll of climbing roses riding the barrette's broad curve. It was precisely the kind of thing she would have admired in a shop window but would never have had the nerve to buy. And it was certainly not fashionable enough for Cabot to even consider purchasing it for her. She relaxed back onto the bed and held it up to the light. The gold glinted and winked, shining with quiet beauty. She felt weary, but strangely at peace. Still holding the barrette, she closed her eyes and slept.

Chapter
Seven

ALLISON SLEPT DEEPLY AND PEACEFULLY for the rest of the morning, and when she woke at noon, the gold barrette was still in her hand. She sat up, blinking in the bright room, trying to recall the events of the night before. Her only clear memory was Brent's kiss.

She changed into jeans and a flowered blouse, brushed her hair and put the barrette in it without thinking before she went down to the kitchen. She felt weird, being alone in the big house without Martha. Rummaging nervously through the cupboards and refrigerator, she found sandwich materials, and was just biting into a salami and cheese sandwich when the doorbell rang.

She found Isabel standing in the breezeway, smiling brightly.

"Good morning!" Isabel handed her a jar of creamy liquid. "Thought you might like some fish chowder for lunch."

"Thank you!" Allison beamed back at the older woman. "Please come in. I was just getting a bite to eat. Will you join me?"

Isabel shook her head. "I've already eaten. But I'll join you for a cup of tea."

"Great!" Allison led her into the kitchen. "I feel sort of strange playing hostess here. You probably know this house better than I do."

Isabel laughed merrily. "It is pretty familiar."

A short time later Isabel was seated at the big trestle table, sipping a cup of hot tea, while Allison sat across from her, savoring delicious spoonfuls of fish chowder.

"I'm so glad you're going to be staying for a while," Isabel said. "Abel and I want you to come and stay with us until Martha gets back. This is an awful big house to live in all by yourself." She took another sip of tea. "Young people, especially, need company."

"Oh, I couldn't!"

Isabel laughed. "Brent warned me you'd be stubborn. But you have to remember, this isn't the city. We still know how to be neighborly up here."

Allison found herself grinning back at Isabel, infected by her contagious warmth. "Thanks, but I'd feel like I was imposing."

"Nonsense! I insist!" Isabel reached across the table and patted Allison's hand. "It's all settled. In fact, I've already made up the guest bed with fresh sheets, so you mustn't make me feel like I've wasted my time."

Allison hesitated. She was drawn to Isabel's warmth and generosity, and she had to admit she didn't like the idea of spending nights alone in the Hollingsworth cottage.

"I won't take no for an answer," Isabel warned, eyeing Allison sternly over the rim of her cup.

"All right," Allison grinned, "if you're sure I'm not imposing. I'll bring my things down after supper."

"Heavens no! You're having supper with us! I've already got it stewing on the back of the stove. Abel will be up with his truck for your things in a couple of hours. In the meantime, I want to show you around the island."

Allison felt slightly dazed by Isabel's radiant smile. She smiled back uncertainly.

A half hour later she was sitting beside Isabel in an old Ford sedan, gazing out the window at the breathtaking island vistas.

"One hundred years ago the village was much bigger," explained Isabel. "There was a thriving fishing fleet here. The island was pretty self-sufficient. A lot of these trees have grown up since. There were at least a dozen saltwater farms on the island." She waved her hand at the tree-covered hills. "It's all changed now. Not one farm left. When I was growing up, it was already going downhill." She shook her head sadly. A wisp of white hair feathered her ear.

"What's that?" asked Allison, sitting forward and pointing to a square building with a cupola that stood on a hill. It was shaded by tall maples and surrounded by a field of uncut grass that rippled in the breeze.

Isabel smiled. "It's the old schoolhouse. Or was. It's been closed since the last teacher left the island almost twenty years ago. Abel and I both went there to school. And Elizabeth, too."

"Elizabeth?"

"Brent's mother. She went to high school on the mainland, of course. There's never been a high school here. And then she went on to college in Orono, where she met Phil. They live in Portland."

Allison glanced at Isabel. It had never occurred to her to wonder about Brent's parents. She had just assumed they lived on Harper's Island, too.

Isabel caught her glance and smiled. "Brent's something of a throwback, I guess. He used to spend summers up here as a boy, and he followed Abel everywhere. He always said he wanted to be a lobsterman when he grew up, but we never took it too seriously. It's a typical boy's dream." She laughed. "But even back then he always meant exactly what he said. We shouldn't have been surprised, I guess, when he quit that law firm in Augusta and bought the old Jenks place. He was headed for a partnership, and his parents were fit to be tied, but there's no stopping Brent once his mind's made up."

"Brent's a *lawyer*?"

"Oh, yes. He was good at it, too. Has a mind like a whip, that boy. But he's always had his heart set on lobstering. He's a born fisherman. Seems to know exactly where to lay his traps."

"I would think it would be a lonely kind of life."

"Well, in a way, I suppose it is. But it seems to suit Brent quite well. And it's just wonderful for us to have him here. You have no idea how much help he's been to us." She tilted her head toward Allison. "I don't mind telling you, I was scared, though, when he took up with Tracy Lawton last winter. She was always trying to talk him into going to Boston or New York and buying a condominium. 'Where the action was,' she said." Isabel screwed her face into a grimace. "I'd never say it to Brent, of course, but the day she left, I felt like throwing a party."

Allison looked down at her hands where they were twisted in her lap; the big diamond glinted up at her. "I've heard you mention her before," she said slowly. "What was she like?"

"Tracy?" Isabel frowned thoughtfully. "Well, she was beautiful, that was certain. Long dark hair, and the darkest eyes I ever saw. And she was real smart, you could tell that from the way she talked. But . . ." She shook her head. "I could never quite understand what Brent saw in her. She was way too sophisticated. Kind of a snob, too, if you want my private opinion."

"It's hard to imagine Brent falling in love with a snob."

Isabel nodded. "You're right. And when he realized who she really was, he broke off the relationship. But I think for a while she reminded him of everything he'd given up. You know, all that money and power, the excitement of city life. Even though that isn't really his style."

Allison laughed lightly. "Most people dream all their lives about being rich."

"I know, dear. But if you don't know it already, you'll soon learn that Brent isn't like most people. He's very much his own man." She shook her head slowly. "Sometimes I could wish he was a little more like everybody else. Maybe then he'd be married and settled down with a wife and children. I'm beginning to wonder if I'm ever going to live to see my own great-grandchildren. It would do my heart good to watch them growing up on Harper's Island."

Allison felt a strange thickening in her throat. She swallowed. "Are there many children on the island?"

"Quite a few, actually. Enough to get into trouble when there's nothing to do in the summer. Of course, the older ones usually help out with the lobstering. It's the little ones that are at loose ends. And their mothers are usually too busy making ends meet to spend time entertaining them." She sighed. "It really is a pity. Some of them are half wild by the time they go to school."

Allison looked out at the pine-covered hills and the water beyond. They rounded a bend in the road and Isabel stopped the car at the top of a rocky bluff.

"Come on," she said, getting out of the car, "I have something to show you."

She led Allison to a promontory at the edge of the bluff. The ocean was spread out before them for miles, while far below, blue and green waves crashed against the high rocks. Sunlight glinted off the water, sending reflections scattering in a hundred directions. The wind blew Allison's long hair away from her body and caressed her face.

"It's beautiful!" she whispered.

Isabel smiled. "This is the opposite end of the island from the village. It's called Lookout Point. The story goes that fishermen's wives used to watch for their returning husbands from here. I've always loved being surrounded by the sea. When things get hard, I come out here and just soak it all up. It makes all the hard times worth it."

"I can see why. I think I've just fallen in love with Harper's Island."

Isabel pointed to a spot at the base of the cliff. "There's a big thunder hole down there. It's hard to get to, so I won't try to take you. My old legs can't navigate the rocks anymore, I'm afraid. But maybe I'll get Brent to show it to you sometime. It's well worth it."

"What's a thunder hole?"

Isabel smiled. "It's a sort of cave that the sea's carved out of rock. At high tide the water rushes in and makes a booming sound. Kind of like thunder." She glanced at her watch. "We'd better run. Abel will be wondering where you are, and I have a few more things to do at the house before supper."

Allison climbed reluctantly back into the car, promising herself that she would return to Lookout Point with her camera as soon as possible.

Isabel continued to point out island landmarks as

they continued along the road that circled the island: the huge boulder known as King's Rock, a favorite play spot for the children; the ruins of a nineteenth-century mansion that had been built by an eccentric millionaire from Rhode Island; the many summer cottages. At last they turned the corner and came back into the village. Allison was overwhelmed by the richness of the island's history. It was hard to believe that such a little piece of land out in the ocean held such a wealth of folklore. As they drove past the town wharf and the harbor, she noted that the *Blue Lady* was at her mooring, bold and bright in the late afternoon sun.

Isabel stepped on the brake and the car swerved to the side of the road. Startled, Allison turned and caught a glimpse of three young children running into the woods. Their strawberry-blond hair was matted, and their dirty clothes were ragged. Isabel shook her head and sighed as she returned the car to the road.

"Those Flory children! I swear every one of them has nine lives! It's a miracle none of them have been killed."

Allison felt her heart go out to the children. "Were those the children you meant when you said some of the little ones were at loose ends?"

Isabel nodded. "They really need someone to take an interest in them. But their mother's got two younger ones, and their father's out all day lobstering, and then he works a night shift on the mainland."

"Maybe a play group could be started," Allison mused. "Something to entertain the children during the day. Not school, just activities they'd like: arts and crafts, music, dance. Maybe they could even put on a play!"

Isabel sighed. "It's a wonderful idea, but I'm afraid no one has the time. Everybody's too busy putting food on the table. For most of these families, life is a hand-to-mouth struggle all the time."

"Well, I could do it!" Allison blurted. "At least for the next four weeks. To get it started."

Isabel glanced at her quickly. "If you could, it would be the best thing that's happened to the island children in more than forty years. But I'll be honest with you. I'd hate to see something start and then fall apart because you left before the summer was out. It would break those kid's hearts, and they can't stand much more pain in their lives."

Allison nodded thoughtfully.

"Don't get me wrong," Isabel continued. "I'm sure the whole town would get behind your effort. But four weeks isn't very long. And Brent said something about your going back to Boston—"

"I'll be staying here," Allison said firmly. She wondered what else Brent had told his grandmother. Was her whole life now public information? "I have to go back for a gown fitting in mid-July, but there's no reason I can't come back the next day. The wedding's not until September, and someone else is making all the arrangements." She turned to Isabel. "I know Martha wants me to stay as long as I can, so why not the whole summer?"

"It sounds good to me," Isabel said. "But I don't want you to jump into anything without thinking it through." She pulled into the Hollingsworth driveway. "You think about that idea a little longer, and then let me know. I can get things rolling in a matter of hours. It won't be an easy task, mind. Some of those children are almost wild. But it would be the best thing in the world for them." She rounded the curve at the top of the hill. "There's Abel now, with the truck." She pointed to a small, battered red pickup. Abel sat at the wheel, smoking a pipe. Isabel pulled the Ford up beside the truck and turned to Allison. "Don't let him hurry you," she said. "Supper's not until six, so there's plenty of time. Just gather up anything you might like to have for the next week or so."

"Thanks so much—for everything." Allison felt almost buoyant as she slid out of the car. The idea of starting a children's program excited her, and gave her an energy she hadn't felt in a long time. It was the first time she'd ever had the chance to design her own program to meet the needs of a particular group of children, she reflected. The curriculum she taught in Boston was well researched and intellectually sophisticated, but it wasn't something she had created herself.

She smiled at Abel as he climbed out of his truck. "I won't take long," she said. "Why don't you come in and make yourself at home?"

"That'll be easy," Abel said, grinning back at her. "Seeing as how I practically live here."

Allison laughed and ran inside.

When Abel brought her back to his house, Allison moved her things quickly upstairs to the guest room that Isabel had fixed up for her, then went to the kitchen to offer her help.

"There's not much left to do, dear." Isabel glanced at the clock. "We'll eat in half an hour. Why don't you just relax?"

"But I feel so useless!" Allison protested, and Isabel smiled knowingly.

"All right, then you can set the table. The plates are in that cupboard."

Allison took down three of the large blue ironstone plates and carried them to the round wooden table that was already covered by a blue-and-white-checked cloth.

"We'll need four plates, dear," said Isabel.

"Four?"

"Yes. Brent's coming for supper. He often does when he's spent the day hauling. Besides, beef stew's his favorite meal."

Allison felt a vague uneasiness as she returned to the cupboard for another plate. The prospect of sitting at the same table with Brent troubled her. How was she going to react to him after last night?

But she had no time to wonder, because at that moment the sound of a door slamming in the back shed off the kitchen announced Brent's arrival. Allison concentrated on setting the table while Isabel welcomed her grandson with a hearty embrace.

"When will you learn to come in by the side door, like a regular person?" she chided him fondly.

He grinned. "I'm afraid I'll never fit into the category of 'regular person,' Gran. I've been coming in this way ever since I started digging clams as a kid."

She nodded. "Well, at least you know enough now to take your boots off before you walk across my kitchen floor. I remember wiping a lot of clam-flats mud off this floor in my time!"

"That wasn't all *my* mud, and you know it!" He wagged his finger at her playfully. "Abel tracked in his share of dirt, as I recall." He turned to Allison. "Has my grandmother got you all settled in already? Smells like she's going to feed you right, at least."

Allison smiled. "I'm fine. Isabel gave me the grand tour of the island this afternoon, and I fell in love with it."

Brent's face assumed a more serious look. "Now you know why I live here," he said softly. He pivoted back to his grandmother. "Is there anything I can do to help?"

"Not a thing. But tell me, how was the haul today?"

Brent grunted. "Disappointing. They just don't seem to be running well this summer. It should pick up in a couple of weeks, though. Too many shedders right now."

"You look pretty tired. Did you get any sleep at all?"

He shrugged. "A few winks after I cleaned up. I tell you, it was tempting to just call it a night, but I wouldn't miss your beef stew for the world."

Again he looked at Allison, and this time his glance rested on her hair. She felt a cold shiver run the length of her spine. She'd forgotten she was still wearing the barrette. Her hand instinctively reached up to touch it, and Brent's slow smile told her that he was aware of the reason for her discomfort.

"I'll bet you gave Allison my old room," Brent said to Isabel. "It probably still has my baseball glove in the closet."

"It's a guest room now." Isabel poked a long wooden spoon into the kettle on the stove. "And your baseball glove is long gone, I'm afraid. Now don't tease her, Brent. She's almost as tired as you are."

He came toward Allison, grinning, and she involuntarily blushed. Her heart was pounding wildly against her ribs. Brent's knit shirt could not hide the strong muscles underneath as he reached out and took her hand. He squeezed it gently, and then dropped it to move past her into the living room and join Abel.

Allison stood, frozen, wondering what his gesture had meant. Was it a silent reminder of the events of the night before? Approval of her acceptance of the barrette? And what did that acceptance mean to him? Was she being disloyal to Cabot in wearing it?

She swallowed and looked quickly at Isabel, but the older woman was opening the oven door, apparently oblivious to her confusion.

"Would you tell the men-folk that it's time for supper, dear?" Isabel asked over her shoulder. "If we don't eat now, those two will get so wrapped up in boat talk we won't be able to have a decent conversation at the table."

Chapter Eight

THE MEAL WAS both simple and delicious. Large bowls of hearty beef stew were complemented by hot, flaky buttermilk biscuits, slathered in fresh butter. Allison ate eagerly, surprised by her own hunger. Apparently, what they said about fresh air was true; it stimulated the appetite. She sat opposite Brent at the table, and as she lifted the spoonfuls of wine-flavored stew to her lips, she was aware of every glance.

The conversation was light and entertaining. Isabel and Abel exchanged stories about eccentric islanders, and Brent recalled some of his memories of boyhood summers spent on the island. Then, after a silence during which everyone simply savored their food, Isabel spoke.

"I must tell you—Allison has the most wonderful idea for a summer recreation program for children here on the island." She threw an apologetic glance at Allison. "I'm sorry to spill the beans before you've made a final decision, but I just can't keep it to myself a minute longer! It's such a marvelous plan!"

Brent emptied his bowl of its last spoonful of stew and sat back in his chair. "Sounds interesting. Why don't you let us all in on the secret, Allison?"

She flushed as she met his curious glance. "It's not really ingenious or anything. I just thought that a sort of play group during the summer might help to keep the children out of trouble. You know—games, arts, crafts, that kind of thing."

Brent nodded. "And who's supposed to run this program?"

"I thought I would. I've had teaching experience, and it wouldn't be too difficult if I had a central place to work out of. Maybe even the old schoolhouse itself. A lot of the arts and crafts could be done with natural materials—pinecones, shells, seeds—things the kids could find around the island. And I'm sure somebody must have an old baseball bat and a softball."

Abel nodded thoughtfully. "It just might work. You know, if someone's willing to get it off the ground, kind of coordinate things, I'll bet everybody'd pitch in. It could be good for the whole community."

"I told you!" Isabel beamed at Allison. "If you can sell Abel on the idea, you can sell anybody."

But Brent was shaking his head. "The local people wouldn't be too likely to trust a summer resident. Anyway, what's to keep you here? I thought you were only up here for a month."

"The *children* will keep me here," she said staunchly. "I've decided to stay through the summer."

Brent frowned. "If Cabot calls you home to Boston three weeks after the program starts, you'd leave in a minute."

"I would not!" Allison flared. "When I make a commitment, I stick to it! And I'd make sure Cabot understands what my priorities are!"

Brent looked at her skeptically.

"People will trust the program if we stand behind

it, Brent," said Isabel firmly. "I think it's important to make this a community project right from the start."

"You make it sound as if Allison's already made up her mind to do it," replied Brent. "I had the impression she was still deciding."

"I *have* decided," said Allison. "And with all of your help, we can start the ball rolling tomorrow."

Isabel beamed. "Wonderful! Then it's settled." She stood up. "Wait until you see the dessert I have for you."

Within minutes she had set a plate of shortcake heaped with ripe, juicy strawberries in front of each person.

"The season's first wild strawberries," she announced proudly. "Now eat and enjoy."

Allison had never tasted such sweet strawberries. They were small, but incredibly juicy, with a delicate, honeyed taste. Was it because they were wild, or did their taste have something to do with Brent's presence at the table? She shook her mind away from the thought and turned to compliment Isabel on her cooking.

When they finished eating, Brent rose. "Gran, you and Abel go relax in the living room. Allison and I will do the dishes tonight."

Isabel smiled. "Why, thank you, dear. That would be lovely. Maybe I can get Abel to take a stroll with me. It's a beautiful evening."

Abel grunted, but a few minutes later he was shrugging on his jacket.

"We won't be long," Isabel said as she followed Abel out the door.

"Take your time," Brent called. The door banged shut. He turned to Allison, flashing his quick grin. "Hope you don't object to K.P. duty tonight."

"Not at all," she said quickly. "I'll wash."

"Suits me." He sagged briefly against the wall, and Allison was reminded of the fact that he'd been awake for most of the past forty-eight hours.

"In fact," she suggested, "why don't you go home and get some sleep? There aren't many dishes, and you look pretty tired."

"No thanks. I may look crazy, but I'm no fool. I've never yet turned down the opportunity to be alone with a pretty woman."

She smiled. "Thanks for the compliment, but you must be tired if you've forgotten that I'm not available."

His expression turned serious. "I haven't forgotten, Allison. I was hoping that maybe you'd thought over what we talked about."

She felt weak and dizzy; she turned away from him and ran water quickly into the porcelain sink.

"All right, I get the message: wrong subject. Anyway, right now I'm too beat to try anything out of line." He laughed. "Let's get these done so we can both get some sleep."

"Good idea." Allison was grateful that his tone had lightened again. She was becoming less and less able to defend her emotions against the onslaught of his bluntness.

She squeezed liquid detergent into the sink, unfolded Isabel's blue dishcloth and watched the foam of bubbles rise toward her hands. She slid the silverware under the lather, lowered the glasses one by one into the warm water. For a while it was silent in the kitchen, as Allison carefully washed each article and rinsed it under hot, running water before setting it in the yellow dish drainer. Brent dried things and put them away with a calm, serene air that seemed pleasantly comforting and domestic. As her hands plunged in and out of the soapy water, it occurred to

Allison that this must be one of the most profound pleasures of marriage, this simple, quiet intimacy between a man and a woman, sharing the household chores in the evening.

And then she thought of Cabot. As his wife, she would never experience such a scene. They would have servants to prepare the meals and wash the dishes. After dinner there would be social functions to attend: concerts and gallery openings, cocktail parties and charity balls. The quiet simplicity of honest work would be something only in her past.

She began to feel uneasy as Brent moved back and forth behind her from the sink to the cupboards; she wondered if he could read her thoughts, if he knew the turmoil inside her heart. She had to say something to break the silence.

"I didn't know you were a lawyer."

She saw him hesitate, his hand poised above a wet plate in the dish drainer. He glanced at her. "I'm not. I'm a fisherman."

"Isabel told me you used to work with a law firm in Augusta."

"That was a long time ago."

"Didn't you like the law? What made you change and move to Harper's Island?"

He smiled. "I got smart. I woke up one day and realized that I'd spent the past twenty years doing things to impress other people. I decided it was about time to impress myself." He picked up a plate, dried it slowly. "I consider myself lucky. Some people never have the courage to follow their hearts." He gave her a sharp glance.

She scrubbed nervously at the crust of stew on a bowl. She cleared her throat. "Will you be hauling tomorrow?"

He laughed. "No way. I intend to sleep all morning,

and then some. I figured I'd take you over to the hospital in the afternoon. We can have dinner at the Blue Lobster after we see Martha. It's a great little place right on the water. They serve some of the best stuffed lobster in the state of Maine. We'll make an evening of it."

She was startled that he had included her in his extensive plans. She wondered if she was supposed to be flattered. More likely, he had just assumed she would like the idea. And in fact she did. A part of her wanted to accept on the spot, the way a girl with a crush jumps at the chance to be near the object of her affections. But she couldn't. She'd already accepted the barrette. Going out to eat with Brent would be a step in a very dangerous direction.

"I can't. I mean, I *would* like to see Martha, but I really don't think—"

"—you should go out to dinner with me," Brent finished. He put the last plate away in the cupboard and came to stand behind her. She felt the back of her neck prickle in response to his closeness. "There's nothing to be afraid of," he said quietly. "It's just a simple dinner at a restaurant."

She didn't turn. She bent her head over the spoons she was washing and scraped hard at an imaginary stain.

"It's just that I don't know what Cabot would think," she said weakly.

"Do you genuinely care what Cabot thinks? Isn't it what you're feeling inside right now that really bothers you?" His voice was very low.

He touched her then, before she could think of a reply, his fingers moving lightly at her waist, turning her gently around to face him. Her hands dripped soapsuds onto the floor, and she lifted them away from her sides in a helpless gesture.

"I thought you said you were too tired to do anything out of line," she murmured, wishing she had the willpower to tell him to stop.

"I was wrong," he said softly.

He bent his head and his mouth claimed hers, tenderly at first and then with increasing passion. She didn't even try to resist. Her own lips responded hungrily to his kiss, and her arms went around his neck, her wet fingers seeking the strong muscles there. She melted dizzily against him as his hands played up and down her spine. She had never dreamed that a kiss could evoke such overwhelming desire; all she wanted was to surrender herself, body and soul, to Brent Connors.

When he finally released her, Allison felt dazed and drained. She looked up into his eyes and met his direct gaze. Then it slowly dawned on her what she had done. Horrified, she backed away.

"You see?" she said faintly. "You see why I can't go to dinner with you?"

He smiled and shook his head. "I see why you have to break your engagement. I wasn't the only one who wanted that kiss."

"I never . . . I didn't . . ." She couldn't think of anything to say.

He sighed. "All right, you go on playing your imaginary games, pretending you're in love with your fiancé. But don't expect me to play them, too. And I'm not going to promise that what just happened won't happen again. You're far too beautiful for me to ignore."

"What about Martha?" she blurted. "Don't you feel some loyalty to her?"

"Martha?" He frowned. "What kind of loyalty should I feel toward Martha?"

"Now *you're* the one who's playing games!" She

moved to the far side of the room, hoping for some safety in distance.

"I don't play games, Allison. And I honestly don't know what you're talking about. How in the world does Martha enter into this?"

"Don't you know how she feels about you?"

The trace of a smile crossed his face. "Martha is infatuated with any working-class man under the age of forty. As long as her parents wouldn't approve, she's convinced she's in love."

"She's not like that!" She felt her cheeks growing warm under his gaze. "She told me about the romance you had with her two summers ago. You can't pretend it didn't mean anything!"

His smile disappeared. "I'm not pretending, Allison. That so-called romance was ninety percent in her head." He stepped toward her. "But I don't see how my relationship with Martha has any bearing on your problems with Cabot."

"I don't have problems with Cabot! And if you want to talk about problems, what about Tracy Lawton? You shouldn't go around kissing other women, getting them all stirred up, when you're still in love with somebody who dumped you last spring!"

His face darkened. "You clearly don't know anything about my feelings for Tracy." He took another step. "Don't project your guilt onto me. *I'm* not engaged. We were talking about you and Cabot."

She flushed hotly. "What makes you so certain we're not meant for each other? You don't even know Cabot! And what gives you the right to judge me?"

"I'm not judging you," he said softly. "And I don't have to know Cabot to see how you feel about him. Every cell of your body tells me."

She turned away. She refused to argue with him

any longer. He obviously knew very little about her, and nothing at all about Cabot. The fact that Brent was able to unleash so much passion in her was merely an indication of how badly she missed Cabot.

"I won't take you to dinner tomorrow," he said quietly. "You can pack a lunch when we go to see Martha."

"I'm not going with you." She moved back to the sink and immersed her hands in the dishwater.

"Martha will be disappointed." He reached out to touch her cheek. The heat of his fingers against her face startled her and she stiffened.

"I'm planning to take the ferry."

He shrugged. "Have it your way, then. I'm too tired to point out the drawbacks right now. Maybe you'll change your mind by tomorrow afternoon."

"I can assure you I won't!" In her frustration, she splashed water onto herself, then gave a sharp cry of outrage.

He grinned and leaned close to her. "You sound like my four-year-old niece. Only she's not half so pretty when she's angry."

With a groan of fury she lifted her dripping hands to push him away. Instantly, he caught her wrists and stretched her arms to the sides. She struggled to break his grip, but his hands were like iron shackles.

"Let me go!" she cried. She was trembling now with a white anger she'd never felt before.

He released her hands immediately, but didn't drop his penetrating gaze. His eyes held her for a long time, and for an instant she thought she detected something sad there, a kind of poignant tenderness she'd never noticed before.

He swallowed and took a step back. "I'd better leave before this gets out of hand," he said huskily.

Without another word he turned and left the house.

Allison had finished the dishes and had finally stopped trembling when Isabel and Abel returned from their walk.

"We saw Brent on our way back to the house," Isabel said. "He says he may sleep all day tomorrow."

Abel chuckled. "It'll be a first, if he does. That boy never did seem to need much sleep." He glanced at Allison. "You look pretty tired yourself, young lady. Don't feel you have to stay up on our account."

"That's right," Isabel put in quickly. "We usually turn in pretty early ourselves, especially when Abel's hauling."

Abel nodded. "Up at four tomorrow, I reckon. Looks like it'll be good weather."

Allison was glad to retire to the little bedroom on the second floor. As she undressed and slipped into her nightgown, a wave of fatigue washed over her. She went to the window and opened it. A gentle breeze lifted her hair and caressed her face. She leaned out, gazing down at the little village. The houses along the street were somehow friendly and comforting, despite their sagging lines and faded clapboards. How different the look was from the widely-spaced homes in the suburban development where she'd grown up. There, each house had been isolated on its own neatly manicured lawn, but here the houses seemed to lean toward each other like old friends. She found herself staring at the little red house near the end of the street. Brent's house. The only light came from the kitchen window. It seemed to beckon her warmly.

She sighed, wondering what kind of community

she would be living in a year from now. She probably wouldn't be able to even see another house from her window. Cabot already had plans to build a beautiful, ten-room house on twenty acres of land he'd purchased in Concord. Even though the site was well off the road, it was surrounded by trees and protective shrubbery. Privacy, he had often told her, was the hallmark of good taste.

Well, it was obvious that you didn't have much privacy on an island. She went to the bed and slid wearily under the covers, pulling the blanket up to her chin against the cool night air. She closed her eyes and felt herself fall quickly toward sleep. Her last thought was of Brent, bending toward her, his lips parted in a slow smile.

Allison woke slowly, roused by the caroling of birds. For a moment she forgot where she was; she lay with her eyes closed, drifting out of a pleasant dream of lying in someone's arms. When she opened her eyes, she saw sunlight streaming in through the window, and clear, cool air gently blowing the white curtains, and she remembered that she was in the Cutlers' house. Brent's grandparents. She knew suddenly whose arms had been around her in her dream.

She sat up quickly. She must find a way to make it clear to Brent, in no uncertain terms, that she was off-limits. And the only way she could make that plain was to convince him that she really loved Cabot.

She looked down at the diamond ring on her left hand. In its large, oval setting, it seemed to glare at her accusingly, like some cruelly faceted eye. She had a strange urge to remove it and slip it into the bottom of the bureau drawer. She wished Cabot had given her something smaller, more inconspicuous.

She flipped off the bedcovers and swung her feet to the smooth wood floor. She didn't want to think about Cabot this morning. It was a glorious day; the air was cool and crisp; the sky was exploding with sunlight. She felt alive and energetic. It was a perfect day to begin her play group project.

She showered in the little green bathroom at the end of the hall, and dressed hurriedly in khaki pants and a soft, pink blouse. She tied her hair back at the nape of her neck with a matching ribbon, reluctantly discarding the gold barrette on the bureau top. She was determined not to give Brent any confusing signals. She was engaged to Cabot, and although he might not be the world's greatest lover, that could be an advantage. At least he didn't arouse an unbearable emotional turmoil within her every time he entered a room.

She found Isabel in the kitchen, busily kneading bread dough. A quick glance at the clock told her she'd slept later than she realized; it was almost ten.

"I guess I'm too late for breakfast," she said wistfully.

"Not at all, dear. There's granola in the cupboard, or if you prefer something hot, I'll cook up some oatmeal." Isabel turned to her and smiled.

"Granola will be fine." Allison helped herself to a bowl and spoon, and was soon sitting at the table pouring creamy milk over the grainy homemade cereal.

Isabel placed a bowl of fresh strawberries in front of her. "Help yourself. There's more where they came from. And take all you want; they don't last forever."

"Thanks." Allison took one of the red berries and

bit into it, savoring the sweet, juicy taste. "I was hoping you might introduce me to some of the parents on the island today, so I can sound them out about the possibility of a play group."

"I'd love to," Isabel said. "But you don't need to worry about getting their support. You already have it." She smiled at Allison. "I mentioned it to a few people this morning when I was at the store, and let me tell you, everyone's very excited. Pete Hayes even said he'd get a crew together to clean out the old schoolhouse this weekend. So all you have to do is be there to greet the kids Monday morning."

Allison blinked at her. "You mean things are already started? Before I even talk to anyone?"

"You talked to me, dear. And Abel. In a community this small, it doesn't take long for things to catch fire."

"I really appreciate it, Isabel. Not just that, but everything you've done. I had a wonderful night's sleep."

"I'm glad, dear." Isabel plopped the bread dough into a large wooden bowl and covered it with a towel. "I've made arrangements for you to see the school this morning, and then this afternoon, when Brent takes you over to the mainland, you can stock up on some supplies. Pete Hayes—he owns the store, you know—said to charge it all. We're already planning a fund-raising dance for later in the summer. Hope to catch some of the tourists that way."

"That's fantastic!" Allison felt a heady rush of enthusiasm, and then suddenly remembered that she wasn't going to the mainland with Brent. "But I'll need to know the ferry schedule."

"Whatever for, dear?" Isabel slid into the seat across the table and gave her a puzzled look. "Didn't Brent offer you a ride? I'll have to speak to that boy."

"No, he offered. But I don't feel it's quite right for me to go with him."

Isabel frowned. "The *Blue Lady* is the fastest boat on the island. It'll certainly get you there and back in half the time it'll take on the ferry. Is there something I'm missing? Did Brent say something that offended you? I know he can be awfully blunt at times."

Allison shook her head and bent over her bowl of strawberry-laden granola. "I told him yesterday that I'd take the ferry."

Isabel chuckled. "Well, I doubt he thought you were serious. The ferry only runs twice on weekdays —at nine and three—so if you went this afternoon, you wouldn't be able to get back until tomorrow. He was probably too tired to explain it to you last night. But don't fret—I know he's planning to go. As a matter of fact, I've already packed a lunch for the two of you."

Allison gave Isabel a startled smile. The woman's calm practicality was amazing. And she was obviously right. If Allison was going to see Martha today, she would have to go with Brent. In the fresh light of the new day, her reaction to Brent last evening seemed exaggerated and unnecessary.

"How can I thank you?" Allison blurted.

"Nonsense, I'm glad to help." Isabel beamed. "Now, as soon as you're finished eating, I'll take you over to see the school. I think you'll agree, it's the perfect place for your play group."

Chapter Nine

THE SCHOOLHOUSE WAS perched on top of a windswept hill. As Allison climbed through the tall grass behind Isabel, she was struck by a wave of nostalgia, even though she'd never attended classes in a one-room schoolhouse. But something about the location and the feeling of the place seemed so elemental, so American, that she felt instantly satisfied, as if, after wandering, she had come home.

On the wide front porch Isabel turned and pointed down the hill toward the sea. "There's a path that runs down to the swimming beach and on around to the thunder hole. On warm days we always used to run off at lunchtime, and it was all the teacher could do to get us back in the afternoon. Some of the boys played hookey every afternoon." She laughed, clearly relishing the memory. "I'm afraid Abel was one of them. Never could get him to sit inside with a book if it was a good day and the sea was calling. Brent's the same way."

She turned to unlock the schoolhouse door. "You'll find it's quite humble inside. Not much to it by today's modern standards, but it should do for your purposes."

Allison stepped into the building and immediately

smiled with pleasure. It was everything Isabel had promised. There was a large, central room that could easily be divided into different play areas, and a smaller room in the back that would be an ideal place for younger children to take afternoon naps.

"It's fantastic!" Allison cried. "It will be absolutely perfect!"

"I think the children themselves might enjoy having a hand fixing it up," Isabel ventured. "The older ones could be a real help, and it would be an adventure for the little ones."

Allison nodded enthusiastically. In her mind's eye she saw a wall mural sweeping around the schoolroom: island scenes, perhaps, painted by the children themselves. "Maybe some of the parents could put up some swings and a seesaw. Or even a slide."

"Did you hear something?" Isabel stepped out onto the porch.

Allison followed, her heart thumping hard as she followed Isabel's gaze down the hill. There, striding toward them, the tall grass fanning his muscular thighs, was Brent, his face open in a wide grin.

"I thought you were going to sleep all morning," Isabel called. "It's only eleven o'clock."

Brent laughed. "It was all I could do to sleep this long. You know staying in bed after the sun comes up goes against my grain." He glanced at Allison. "What are you two lovely ladies up to?"

Allison forced a smile. "Your grandmother was showing me the schoolhouse. I think it'll be perfect for my play group."

"You're still thinking of that, are you? I thought by now you'd have realized you had better things to do with your summer."

"Brent!" Isabel scolded. "Why in the world would you go and say a thing like that? You *know* how excited she is about this project! What do you mean, she has better things?"

"I mean her fiancé, Gran."

"What has Cabot got to do with it?" Allison asked, her voice oddly thick.

Brent reached into the back pocket of his jeans and withdrew a folded yellow paper. "A telegram came this morning. Pete Hayes asked me to deliver it to you. No easy task, either, I might add, since you seem to enjoy traipsing all over the island with my grandmother." He climbed the porch steps in two long strides and held the envelope out to her.

"We haven't been 'traipsing,' as you call it," declared Isabel. "Although I don't see what crime there is if we were. It's the kind of day God created for traipsing."

Allison took the envelope and opened it slowly. She wasn't eager to read a message from Cabot. She hadn't written to him at all since her arrival; too much had happened. And she really didn't want to communicate with him now. She felt uneasy, reading his telegram with Brent looking on. She wondered if her cheeks were betraying her consternation.

RECEIVED NEWS OF MARTHA'S ACCIDENT STOP WILL COME AT ONCE STOP EXPECT ME FRIDAY JUNE TWELFTH STOP I LOVE YOU DARLING STOP CABOT

"Bad news?" asked Isabel.

"No—good, actually." Allison faltered, intensely aware that Brent was watching her. "My fiancé's coming up here. On Friday."

"That's wonderful!" Isabel said. "He'll be able to help with the play group!"

Allison shook her head quickly. "Oh, no, I don't think so. Cabot's not the type."

"Type?" Brent's voice was cool, amused. "What type does it take?"

Her cheeks blazed with embarrassment. "You know. He's not really that interested in children."

She could read Brent's disgust in the quick shake of his head.

Isabel clicked her tongue. "Now, that's enough, Brent. Leave the poor child alone. We have enough to do to get ready for the cleanup on Saturday. You *are* coming, aren't you?"

Brent grinned at his grandmother. "I didn't know I had a choice."

"You don't. I expect you here at eight o'clock sharp."

"You've already planned the cleanup?" Allison looked at Isabel in surprise.

"Gran doesn't believe in wasting time," Brent put in. "Word was all over town by nine o'clock this morning that there's a work bee at the old schoolhouse. Half the women in the village are already baking pies for the luncheon. The whole island's buzzing."

"I didn't realize things would be happening quite so fast," Allison said faintly. She couldn't imagine Cabot joining in a work bee at the schoolhouse, or anywhere else for that matter. He was the most fastidious man alive. And he probably wouldn't want her to be there, either. She could hear him now, telling her that it wasn't an appropriate thing for his fiancée to be doing.

She wished he wasn't coming so soon. He would disapprove of the whole idea of her being involved with the island children. She'd been hoping for some time to get things firmly established before she had to deal with Cabot.

"None of us could see a good reason for waiting,"

Isabel said, locking the schoolhouse door and going carefully down the steps. "The summer's short enough as it is. Those kids need a program as soon as possible. But if you're having second thoughts . . ."

"Oh no!" Allison assured her. "I haven't changed my mind."

"It's just that Cabot's arrival is going to complicate things for Allison," Brent said.

Isabel gave him a puzzled frown. "Whatever do you mean?"

"You see, Allison's relationship with Cabot is a bit tenuous right now." He grinned at Allison, who gave him a furious scowl, but he seemed unperturbed.

"I didn't realize you were having problems, dear." Isabel looked up at Allison. "But I'm sure it's just a temporary thing. Lovers often quarrel. So don't worry about it. It's best that he come sooner rather than late, under the circumstances. That way you can get things all straightened out." She smiled encouragingly. "Now, we'd better get a move-on. If you and Brent want to be back from the mainland before dark, you'll have to hustle."

Less than an hour later Allison was sitting in the pilothouse of the *Blue Lady*, watching Brent guide the boat out of the island's little harbor. To his credit, he hadn't said a word about her earlier refusal to ride with him. He'd apparently taken it for granted all along that she'd go. She was grateful that he hadn't made an issue of it. But inwardly it irritated her that he'd ignored her statement and arrogantly assumed that she would change her mind.

After a time, Allison moved to the stern of the boat, where she could get a better view of the white sea gulls wheeling in the clear blue sky. There was something exquisite about the arcs they made, a graceful but contained energy that spiraled above her head. They seemed to possess a freedom that she, watching them, wanted for herself.

She held up a hand to shield her eyes from the sun and saw the diamond flash on her finger. She had a sudden fantasy of pulling it off and dropping it over the side of the boat into the ocean. She imagined it falling slowly through the dark water to settle into thick, gray silt. She wondered where that thought had come from. Of course, she would never do such a thing. She could never do anything to hurt Cabot. Besides, she knew how valuable the ring was; she certainly wasn't going to throw away ten thousand dollars on a whim. She'd been raised to know the value of things.

Allison returned to the pilothouse. Brent was standing at the wheel, watching the water ahead. She glanced at his rugged profile and tried to imagine him in a courtroom, wearing a suit, delivering closing remarks to a jury. She had never seen him in anything more formal than a clean, knit shirt, and yet she sensed that he was the kind of man who could be comfortable in whatever he chose to wear. His presence in a courtroom would be compelling; he had undoubtedly won many cases.

She stepped up to the wheel beside him, smiling cheerfully. "It's beautiful out here," she said. "I can see why you like it. But I was wondering about what you said last night. Isn't it kind of risky to give up law to become a fisherman?"

"Sure." He glanced at her and smiled.

She looked down at his hands on the wheel, the brown knuckles and strong wrists. She looked back up at him, suddenly aware that he was studying her carefully. "I'm surprised you didn't like law. I would think it would be very interesting."

He shifted his glance back to the water. "It is interesting. And yes, I did like it. For a while. Then I got caught up, like a lot of people, in earning money for the sake of earning money. I took cases I didn't believe in. I worked all the time, day and night. I went for the big bucks, just like everybody else. But something was drying up inside me; I was growing hard and cold and bitter." He paused; his eyes were almost as dark as the sea. "I went to visit my grandparents, and one day, when I was fishing with my grandfather, I just broke down. Cried like a baby right out on the water under the gulls and the sun."

Allison stared at him. She had never in her life heard a man admit that he cried. She couldn't even imagine Cabot crying. Yet somehow she could envision Brent weeping silently against the wall of Abel's boat, his handsome features enhanced by his tears. She felt something thicken in her own throat. She reached out and touched the sleeve of Brent's jacket, but couldn't think of anything to say.

Brent looked down at her. "Abel's a smart man; he let me cry, didn't try to stop me. When I was finally finished, I knew that I had to find a way to get out on the water where I belonged." He covered her hand with his own. "Abel didn't say a word, but I don't think he was surprised when I quit the firm and bought a place on the island."

"Do you ever miss the city?" His hand was still on hers. She felt the warmth as a blessing. Part of her wanted to lean against him, slide under his arm.

He shook his head. "My place is here. I think I knew it even as a kid, only I was too stubborn to admit it." He smiled down at her. "You see, I believe that there's a right place for everybody. When you find that place, it's like coming home, even if you've never been there before in your life."

Allison shivered at the sudden memory of her initial reaction to Harper's Island. She remembered seeing the little village for the first time and experiencing a strange, delightful feeling of being in the right place. It was something she'd never experienced before, and she had dismissed it quickly at the time. But now she recognized the experience in Brent's quiet words.

She was suddenly aware that Brent was gazing at her with an odd, haunted expression on his face. She withdrew her hand from his sleeve and tucked it down into the pocket of her slacks. "What's the matter?"

"Do me a favor," he said quietly.

"What?" She looked up at him warily.

"Take that ribbon out of your hair. Let it go free. It's too beautiful to tie up that way."

Her hands went slowly to the back of her neck and she loosened the ribbon that held her hair. Immediately the wind caught it, lifted the dark red curls into the air and sent them spinning around her face.

"That's much better." Brent reached out and caught one of the strands between his fingers. "You look like a goddess in the sunlight—regal, and at the same time wild."

She could think of no reply. She licked her lips and tasted a delicate film of salt.

He frowned. "When I woke up this morning, I had every intention of apologizing for my behavior last night. Now . . ." He shook his head. "Allison, I might as well warn you that I find you very attractive. I'm also very aware that you're engaged to Cabot, so I'll do my best to keep my hands off you.

But it won't be easy. Especially since I know how little you really feel for the man."

She backed away from him, bumping into the pilothouse wall. "You don't know anything about how I feel," she said hoarsely. "I've told you that I love Cabot. Why can't you believe me?"

His eyes narrowed. "Because you've only told me that with words. Your heart isn't saying that."

"You don't know anything about my heart!"

"Your body, then. It's saying something else entirely."

She felt her legs tremble. She was grateful to have the wall to lean against.

"But I didn't start anything with you, Brent! *You've* taken advantage of me! First, you told me there was some silly tradition about kissing the captain on a boat—"

His expression darkened. "There is. And if I wanted to take advantage of you, Allison, I'd have done a lot more than give you a few kisses."

"It's obvious that you don't want to hear my side of things!" She felt hot tears rising, and her voice shook with frustration. "You won't believe me no matter what I say, so why should I bother?"

"Because it's very important to you to convince me. Then maybe you can convince yourself." He gazed at her, his eyes clear and penetrating. Allison felt an ache in the pit of her stomach. "Only it won't happen, Allison. You don't love him, and all the talk in the world isn't going to change that."

"And I suppose you know all about love! I suppose your affair with Tracy Lawton has made you an expert on the subject!"

He flushed suddenly. "All right," he said quietly. "You win. I'll pretend along with you and everybody else that you really love Cabot Wilder. On one condition."

"What's that?" She knew her words had upset him, and she felt strangely remorseful.

"That you let me be the first to know when you come to your senses."

She stared at him, her face reddening with anger. For a moment she couldn't find words strong enough to shape a reply. How could she have felt sorry for him just a moment ago? He was quite clearly trying to manipulate her feelings, as if she were a naive child. She lifted her chin. "You're the most arrogant man I've ever met!" she hissed. She turned and stalked out of the pilothouse, vowing to herself that this would be the last time she'd ever ride aboard the *Blue Lady*.

She didn't speak to Brent again for the duration of the trip. When he tied up at the large mainland wharf, she deliberately looked in the opposite direction. And when he held out his arm to help her onto the dock, she pointedly refused his hand and climbed clumsily over the gunwale on her own.

She ignored his chuckle and marched ahead of him up the ramp to the sidewalk, her head high. Let him think what he liked; it made no difference to her. Her life was her own, and she could certainly live it without Brent Connor's approval.

When she entered Martha's hospital room, Allison was struck by how much better her friend looked. Martha was sitting on the edge of the bed, eating an apple, chatting on the telephone. When she saw Allison and Brent, she hung up and threw open her arms.

"I've been so lonely! You can't believe what it's

like here! You are absolutely the most wonderful friends!"

Martha embraced each of them warmly and then turned excitely to Allison. "Have you heard from Cabot?" Without waiting for an answer, she continued. "Never mind, I know you have. Would you believe he called here and talked to me this morning? Twice? He says he's coming Friday! You must be thrilled! You see, everything's going to be fantastic, just like I said."

Allison was all too aware that Brent was leaning against the wall, watching her with a look of pure amusement on his face.

She forced her brightest smile. "Yes, I just got his telegram this morning. I'm so happy! I can hardly wait until Friday. I'm staying at Isabel's now—"

"Oh, I didn't tell you! Friday's my big day, too! They're letting me out of here!" She sent Brent a pleading look. "I'll die with embarrassment if I have to use a wheelchair on the ferry!"

"I'll pick you up," he offered, still smiling. "Maybe we can even beat the ferry, so you'll be there to welcome Cabot, too."

"That would be wonderful! You won't believe how excited I am! Of course, I'm sure it's nowhere near as excited as Allison . . ."

"Oh well, you know Allison," Brent drawled. "She's hardly been able to contain her enthusiasm since she got the telegram. Have you, Allison?" He looked at her directly, challenging her with his eyes.

She glared back at him. "You can come along with me Friday, you know," he continued. "I'm sure Martha would appreciate it."

"No," she said stonily.

"Of course not," he nodded. "You'll need to prepare yourself for Cabot's arrival."

"Wait until you meet Cabot!" Martha put her hand on Brent's arm. "He's the most charming man! And thoughtful! Who else would drop everything and come to Maine just because of his fiancée's whim?"

Brent smiled. "Oh, I don't imagine he's as rare as all that, Martha. After all, look who his fiancée is."

Allison blushed hotly and turned away.

"Look, you've made her blush! You bad boy!" Martha giggled and slapped Brent's arm playfully.

"If only it were possible to make you blush as easily. Let's see—"

"Don't even try!" Martha squealed. "Now get out of here, and let me talk to Allison alone."

He gave her a mock bow. "As long as I get equal time."

Allison saw the color rise in Martha's cheeks. She couldn't forget Martha's declarations of love for Brent. It was all too obvious how she felt about him. She wondered what her friend would think if she knew of Brent's behavior in Isabel's kitchen last night. Or his blunt words about Martha's infatuation with him.

"I'll go get some coffee, then. And don't worry, I'll take my time. I know Allison has a lot to tell you." Brent grinned wickedly at Allison as he left the room.

"What is it?" Martha turned to Allison eagerly, her eyes round with curiosity.

Allison shook her head. "Brent's exaggerating. I had an idea about starting a play group for the island children, and it seems to have taken off before I really expected it to." She went on to describe her plans. "The thing is, it'll mean I'll be staying through the whole summer, instead of just a month," she finished. "I hope that's all right with you."

"That's wonderful!" crowed Martha. "But do you think Cabot will go for this idea? I mean, won't he want you to spend most of your time with him?"

Allison shrugged. "Maybe you can keep him company while I'm with the children."

Martha nodded. "Kids are definitely *not* his thing. I'll be glad to help out with Cabot. It'll give me someone to talk to while I'm laid up." She laughed and patted her leg.

"Thanks. I'm really excited about working with the kids. And you were right about Isabel and Abel—they're both wonderful. They've taken me in and treated me just like family." She got to her feet. "Now I'd better get out of here and give Brent a chance to talk to you. I'll see you Friday." She hugged Martha and went into the hall, walking so swiftly that she collided with Brent, who was standing a few feet from the door with an empty plastic cup in his hand.

"Good thing this wasn't full." He steadied her with his hand as he tossed the cup into the waste bin beside the door. "You don't need a nasty burn to add to your list of grievances against me."

She pulled away and gave him an icy smile. "I'm sure you don't want to keep Martha waiting. And please feel free to spend as long as you like. I'll wait for you in the lobby."

She swept past him and headed down the long white hall to the lobby. She certainly wasn't going to stand outside the door and hear the little innuendos between Brent and Martha. No doubt he used the very same lines on Martha that he used on her—and on every other woman he had his eye on—which would certainly explain why Martha believed he cared for her.

She stalked into the lobby and flung herself into one of the chrome and vinyl chairs that faced the street. Outside, fog was rolling in across the water. A tall sailboat slid out of the mist and eased through the thicket of moored ships, furling her sails as she went. The scene was idyllic and peaceful; Allison felt a million miles away from Boston and Cabot and all the craziness of her recent life.

In only three days Cabot would arrive on Harper's Island. The thought didn't bring the sense of relief she expected. Instead she felt a strange, gnawing despair, as if his presence would cast a shadow of gloom over her life. She tried to shake the feeling away, but it persisted.

She closed her eyes and tried to imagine herself in Cabot's arms. What would it be like if he were to become sensuous and bold? She pictured his dark hair, the thin line of his lips, but some quirk of her imagination kept turning Cabot into Brent, and all she could see was blond hair, penetrating blue eyes, and an arrogant smile.

Maybe it was good that Cabot was coming so soon. The sooner the better. Isabel was right; it was just a temporary feeling, a problem that would easily and quickly be resolved in Cabot's presence.

Someone touched her shoulder. She jumped and turned, to find Brent looking down at her with a troubled expression.

"We have a problem."

"What is it?" Her heart in her throat, she stumbled to her feet.

For answer he pointed to the window. Allison turned and gaped. The world had disappeared.

Only moments ago she had been able to see boats rocking on their moorings. Now the harbor was completely gone and the cars parked across the street from the hospital were wrapped in a soft, white haze. The fog had rolled in with incredible speed, obliterating visibility and making the return crossing to Harper's Island impossible.

 *Chapter*
Ten

"**W**HAT ARE WE going to do?" Allison stared up at Brent in horror. She'd always thought of fog as insubstantial and artistic, but the phenomenon was clearly all too real and potentially dangerous.

Brent shook his head. "There's nothing we can do but wait it out."

"How long will that be?" She had visions of sitting in the hospital lobby for hours, staring out at nothing.

He shrugged. "Could be an hour. Could be days. I've seen it roll in and sit for a week at a time. But most likely it'll be gone by morning."

"Morning!" Allison groaned. "Are you sure there's no way to get back to the island this afternoon?"

"Nobody in his right mind would take you out in this pea-soup fog. And I wouldn't let you go if they offered."

She ignored the possessiveness of his words. "Then we'll wait here at the hospital."

"Afraid not. Visitor's hours end at nine. Of course, we can stay until then and hope that it rolls out. But to tell you the truth, Allison, I'm not too optimistic. This looks like it plans on staying awhile." He sat down in a nearby chair. "If it were me, I'd just roll up in a blanket and sleep aboard the *Blue Lady,* but I don't think that'll do under the circumstances." He grinned. "You're used to more elegant accommodations."

She lifted her chin. "If you're implying that I'm the delicate type, you're wrong. I've been camping before." She thought of the dry, roomy tent and comfortable sleeping bag she'd slept in with her friends on her one camping trip to the White Mountains. "I can do it, if you can."

His grin broadened as he shook his head. "Uh-uh. I'm tempted to let you try, just so I could have the satisfaction of hearing you admit you were wrong. But I have no desire to spend the night listening to your moans and groans. We'll go to a motel."

"A motel?" Allison gasped. "Not on your life!"

"Hey, take it easy." He held up his hands in a gesture of surrender. "I never said we'd share the same room. You sure do have a talent for jumping to the wrong conclusions about me." He stood up and came toward her.

"I absolutely refuse to go to a motel," Allison said staunchly. "I'll take my chances on the boat."

His mouth quirked into a slow smile. "If you want a good night's sleep, then the *Blue Lady*'s the wrong choice. There's very little sleeping space on board, believe me."

She felt confused and uncertain, sensing that Brent had somehow maneuvered her into making the most compromising choice. And the way he was smiling at her told her that he was clearly amused at her predicament. If she insisted in staying on the boat, she would probably be cramped and uncomfortable. Yet if she changed her mind and agreed that they should go to a motel, it would send exactly the wrong kind of message to him, as well as characterizing her as weak-willed and fickle.

She stood up. "We'll stay on the boat," she said firmly.

He raised one eyebrow. "That's fine by me. If you're sure."

"I'm sure."

They walked along the fog-shrouded streets, enveloped in the blanketing silence. Something about the fog and the growing darkness made Allison reluctant to speak.

Brent turned down a side street, and Allison saw that they were heading toward a small restaurant. The Blue Lobster was written in large turquoise letters over the door.

"Well, isn't this a surprise," Allison said, her voice tight with irritation. "I thought I made it clear yesterday that I wasn't going to eat out with you."

Brent shrugged. "Just thought I'd give you a second chance. I promise you, it'll be much more enjoyable than eating soggy sandwiches on the *Blue Lady*."

Allison glanced through the window and caught a glimpse of a warmly lit room full of well-dressed, smiling people. For a moment she considered giving in. She was hungry, and the delicious odors emanating from the restaurant were extremely enticing. She pushed her desire away quickly. Once again she was playing right into Brent's hands.

"No." She shook her head. "Isabel packed us a supper, and I intend to eat it."

He shrugged. "Have it your way. But I don't understand why you're so determined to make everything hard on yourself."

Allison turned to face him. "You'd like me to eat

dinner with you, wouldn't you? You have it all planned out—a delicious meal, a bottle of wine, then off to your little motel, where you'll discover that only one room is available and we'll have to share a double bed. Well, you can just forget your neat little plan. I want you to take me back to the boat right now. And we'll leave for Harper's Island the minute the fog lifts!" Her cheeks were burning, but she felt good. At last she had put him in his place.

But there was no surprise in his keen gaze, only a subtle amusement. "We'll do it your way," he said quietly. He held up a warning finger. "But no complaints in the morning."

Allison clamped her mouth shut, unable to think of an adequately stinging reply. This night was something that would simply have to be gotten through. But she was determined that nothing Brent said from now on would upset her.

Moments after they climbed aboard the *Blue Lady*, Brent produced Isabel's supper, and Allison sat on a crate in the stern of the boat, eating her tuna sandwich in silence and drinking the mug of hot coffee that Brent handed to her. She didn't look at him; she was careful to keep her gaze focused on what she could see of the water. The air was darkening around them; the fog had turned a murky, opaque blue. Staring around her, she had the dizzy sensation that the entire world had vanished and there was nothing left but the *Blue Lady*, Brent, and herself.

Brent finished his meal and disappeared into the pilothouse. She could hear him rattling around and banging on something, and when she stole a quick glance at the shelter, she saw that he'd disappeared through a little door to the left of the wheel. There must be a room there, perhaps a cabin, she thought, where she was going to sleep. She shivered, suddenly chilled in the damp, dark air; she pulled her jacket tighter around her. She wondered what time it was, but it was too dark to read her watch. Her eyes strained to discern some indication of light shining through the fog, but there was nothing. They were alone, at the end of the world.

"Your bed is ready when you are." Brent's deep voice came as a shock in the silence. Allison jumped to her feet.

"Isn't it kind of early?" It struck her suddenly that she should have gone to a motel after all. Even sharing a room with Brent would have been less disturbing than the prospect of sleeping hidden in the depths of his boat.

"It's after nine. But if you want to stay up, I'm willing." He came to her and casually slid his arm around her shoulder. Her mind warned her to shrug him away, but his touch was so comforting and warm in the cold, thick darkness that she didn't move.

The plaintive moan of a foghorn sounded in the distance.

"Lonely, isn't it?" His voice was soft. "Makes you feel like you're all alone in the world. There's not a sadder sound on God's earth." He touched the back of her neck, massaging it gently with his fingertips.

Every nerve in her body responded to his touch, and Allison had no desire at all now to move away from him. Instead she felt a powerful, physical yearning to lean against him, to fit her body against his, feel his arms surrounding her. With a shudder, she lurched away from his hand and walked quickly across the deck to the pilothouse. It seemed infinitely safer to go to sleep than to stand beside Brent in the fog-haunted darkness.

"I'm more tired than I realized." She tried to keep her voice even. "If you'll show me my bed, I think I'll turn in, after all."

He nodded as he came toward her. "Watch your head when you go down." He entered the cabin, brushing her arm as he moved past her. Again the molten flow of her own desire welled through her body. He glanced over his shoulder. "Just remember, this was your choice."

She ignored his grin and followed him through the door, stepping down two rickety steps into a small room lit by a battery-operated fluorescent lamp that swung from the low ceiling. In front of her, extending into the pointed bow of the boat, was an oil-stained wooden floor. Along one short wall under the light was a large toolbox and a battered steamer trunk. On the opposite wall hung pieces of fishing equipment: long poles with strangely shaped hooks on the ends, nets, bright round orange floats, lobster buoys, life jackets. Between the two walls a large, faded quilt was spread out on the floor, with a blanket folded neatly at the far end.

"Pillow," Brent said when he saw her frown. He turned and rummaged in the steamer trunk briefly, then produced a second blanket. He tossed it onto the quilt and looked at her expectantly. "Well?"

"Thanks." Allison wondered if he was expecting her to lie down and go to sleep while he stood watching. "I'll just turn out the light when I'm done."

He tilted his head, a slow smile lifting the corners of his mouth. "You expecting me to sleep somewhere else?"

"I thought . . . I assumed that you'd be sleeping on deck. . . ." Her voice trailed away.

"Not unless I want to wake up wetter than a polly-wog." He gave her a broad grin. "No, ma'am, that fog will soak me to the skin long before morning. I plan to bed down right here."

"You mean we're both going to sleep here—together?" She gaped at the small, quilt-covered space on the floor.

"You were the one who didn't want to go to a motel."

"But I can't . . . I can't sleep here with you!"

"Have you changed your mind, then, about the motel?"

She hesitated. Sleeping on the hard floor of the tiny cabin, she'd be wedged up against Brent as if they were a couple on their honeymoon. It was clearly an impossible situation. She turned to him and saw his wide smile of satisfaction. She stiffened.

"No." She shook her head firmly. "I haven't changed my mind."

"Good." He yawned and kicked off his shoes. "I guess I'll go ahead and turn in, then." He plopped down onto the quilt, pulled the second blanket over him, laced his hands behind his head and lay grinning up at her. "You want to kill that light, please?"

Hastily she reached up and flicked the switch on the hanging lamp; the tiny room was immediately plunged into darkness. She could hear Brent's breathing, but she could see nothing. Carefully, she removed her shoes and knelt down, gingerly feeling her way along the edge of the quilt to the empty space beside Brent. He didn't speak as she lay down. She turned on her side so that her back was to him and there was as much space as possible between them. But she knew, by the warmth behind her, that there wasn't much.

"Good night," he said softly.

"Good night."

The quilt provided very little comfort; Allison felt as if she were sleeping on rocks. She moved gingerly, to find a more comfortable position, and her leg brushed Brent's. Instantly she jerked away. How in the world would she ever be able to sleep tonight, with Brent Connors lying beside her like a lover? No, she couldn't think such thoughts. They were wrong, and disloyal to Cabot. What she felt for Brent was merely physical attraction. And that was all.

She tried to sleep. She listened to Brent's long, slow breathing, the gentle slap of the waves against the hull, the distant wail of the foghorn.

She rolled onto her back, fidgeting for space; her arm touched Brent's, but she didn't pull away. She was certain that he was asleep, and the contact was soothing and strangely relaxing. She closed her eyes and finally started to drift into a deep, blissful sleep.

Allison woke slowly, wondering what was causing the vague, rocking sensation she felt. Was she in a waterbed? A boat? She remembered, and blinked awake, her eyes probing the dim interior of the *Blue Lady*'s cabin. Brent was not beside her; the door to the deck was closed.

For a long time she didn't move, listening for clues as to Brent's location. But there was no sound except the lapping waves, and at last she got to her feet and folded the quilt and blankets carefully before placing them on the steamer trunk.

"Brent?" She opened the door and stepped out into brilliant sunshine. The air was crystal clear. Light glinted off the surrounding water, making it look as though thousands of tiny diamonds rode the sea. The fog had disappeared overnight. In the far distance she could even see the tiny bump on the horizon that was Harper's Island.

But there was no sign of Brent.

She walked the length of the boat and sat on a crate in the stern. She glanced casually at her watch and her eyes widened. It was ten o'clock! Where in the world was Brent? He surely hadn't forgotten that she wanted to get back to Harper's Island as soon as possible. The fog must have been gone for hours. Had he walked back to the hospital to see Martha?

She sighed. There was nothing she could do but wait. When she heard a low whistle a moment later, and Brent's blond head appeared over the top of the pilothouse roof, she felt a distinct wave of relief.

"Good morning, Sleeping Beauty!" He flashed her a broad grin, stepped onto the gunwale and easily walked along it to where Allison stood, gaping up at him. "I trust you slept well last night?" His voice was gently mocking, as if he were treating her like royalty. She remembered, with chagrin, her high-handed dismissal of his suggestions the evening before.

"I slept very well, thanks."

"The bathroom's in the second building on your right. Around back." He nodded at a small green shed.

She ignored his outstretched hand and climbed over the *Blue Lady*'s gunwale on her own, then hurried quickly along the wharf to the building he'd indicated.

When she returned to the *Blue Lady*, he was still grinning.

"It was a wonderful night, if I do say so myself." His blue eyes twinkled.

Allison looked pointedly at the horizon. "I'm ready to go back to Harper's Island now."

"Are you?" He chuckled. "I'm beginning to think you've forgotten who's the captain on this ship."

She looked at him. What was he trying to pull now? Had he planned some new ploy to keep her from returning to the island? "I thought we had an agreement," she said tightly. "You'd take me back as soon as the fog lifted. Well, it looks like it lifted hours ago, and we haven't moved. What exactly is going on?"

"Your good night's sleep certainly didn't improve your disposition. I thought maybe you'd like a bite to eat before we shoved off."

"I'm not hungry."

"Okay. I'll eat by myself." He disappeared into the pilothouse and emerged with a small plastic box and cup. Allison's mouth watered as she smelled the egg sandwich and the hot coffee, but she wasn't about to reveal her ravenous appetite. She stalked to the far side of the deck and sat on the gunwale in the corner, her arms crossed in front of her, her foot tapping the deck impatiently.

"Change your mind?" Brent grinned at her. "There's more where this came from."

"No thank you."

He took his time eating, apparently savoring every bite, and when he was finished, he retrieved a second sandwich, offered it to her again. When she icily refused, he ate that as well. Slouched comfortably against a lobster trap, he watched her with amusement and a trace of curiosity.

"I guess I'll never understand summer people," he said, shaking his head thoughtfully. "They don't seem to be able to take life as it comes. Always want to control everything. The weather, other people. Even their own feelings."

Allison felt her back muscles tighten. "If you're

trying to goad me into an argument, you can forget it. I'm not interested in anything but getting back to Harper's Island."

"Cabot's not coming until Friday. What's the rush?"

"It has nothing to do with Cabot! I don't want to talk about Cabot!" She felt her cheeks redden, and she lifted her hands to them.

He crumpled his empty breakfast things in one hand and stood up slowly. "I know you don't want to talk about him—with me, especially. And I know why, Allison."

She closed her eyes against the hot tears that burned them. She heard him come toward her, felt every muscle in her body stiffen as he stood over her. When he touched the side of her neck, it was all she could do not to cry out.

"Look at me, Allison."

She was surprised to find herself obeying him. His thumb continued to caress her neck. Something warned her that she was in grave danger. Something else told her that she didn't want him to ever stop touching her.

"Why are you so determined to deny the obvious?" His voice was low.

She jerked away from his hand and stood up, then realized instantly that she'd made a mistake, because she now stood so close to him that her breasts were almost touching his broad chest. He blocked escape with his massive body. Unless she wanted to dive off the boat and swim for shore, she couldn't move.

"I don't know what you're talking about," she said tightly. "I thought you were going to take me back to the island."

"You're avoiding the issue," he murmured, lifting a

long strand of her hair between his fingers and bringing it to his lips. "We were talking about you."

He bent his head slowly toward hers, and she didn't turn away. As his mouth claimed hers, a sweet fire rose within her, burning away every reality but one: her desire for him. His arms enclosed her firmly, and her own hands lifted to curl around his neck, her fingers stroking the powerful muscles of his upper back and the thick hair at the base of his neck. She had no will of her own, only an aching hunger that made her cling weakly to him, even when he had stopped kissing her and was gazing down at her with bright, knowing eyes.

It took Allison a full minute before she shook herself violently and lurched out of the circle of his arms.

"Why did you do that?" Her voice was thick.

His lips curled into a slow smile. "Because you wanted me to."

"I certainly did *not*!" She was trembling with fury, and with a deeper emotion as well: fear.

His smile disappeared. "I'm not going to apologize because you can't bring yourself to recognize the truth of what's going on between us, Allison."

"Nothing's going on between us! And nothing will! I'm engaged!" Her voice rose, close to hysteria. She shoved her left hand toward his face. "I've promised to marry Cabot Wilder. I love him! Don't you understand?"

"No, I don't understand. And I don't think you do, either. But you keep trying to convince yourself that what you feel for Cabot is love, even though the truth is staring you right in the face."

Her eyes narrowed. "You told me you wouldn't harass me about Cabot anymore!"

He frowned for a moment, and then his face softened. "You're right. I was pressing the issue. I'm sorry." He shook his head. "I don't seem to be able to help it. You're more than I bargained for, Allison."

"If you mean I won't jump into bed with you like every other woman you smile at, then you're right! I happen to have standards. When I commit myself to someone, I mean it. And I'm committed to Cabot." She took a deep breath. "No matter what you may think, every woman in the world isn't dying to melt into your arms, Brent Connors. Not all of us are so easily manipulated."

He was frowning again. "What gave you the idea I was manipulating you? Or any other woman?"

"It's obvious! The way you treat me. And Martha. And there's that other girl—Emily somebody."

"What do you know about Emily?"

"Nothing! I heard Abel mention her. She's someone you're seeing, isn't she? Well, I suggest you keep seeing her and leave me alone!"

His face hardened suddenly. He seized her shoulders, the pads of his fingers digging into her soft flesh. "I'm not trying to manipulate you, Allison. I just want you to wake up and face the facts. Before it's too late." His jaw muscles worked tightly and Allison felt a flash of alarm. She had clearly roused some deep emotion within him; he was close to anger. She tried to shift away from his grasp, but his hands held her tightly.

"Why does it matter to you?" she said, her voice strangely hoarse.

His blue eyes darkened. When he spoke, his voice was very low. "Because I came very close to making the same kind of mistake you're making. Last winter, I thought I was in love. If it hadn't been for one incident that opened my eyes to what I was *really* feeling, I might have made the biggest mistake of my life."

"You're talking about Tracy Lawton again." She spoke through dry lips.

His hands slid slowly off her shoulders as he nodded. "I know what I'm talking about, Allison. Believe me."

"What happened?" Strangely, she wanted to touch him, to put her arms around him. She pressed her hands together at her waist. Her heart was pounding much too hard.

"I woke up. I saw who she really was. For almost four months I was enchanted by her intellect and her beauty. I didn't even realize that it was the *idea* of her that captivated me, not the reality." He sighed, and raked a hand through his hair. "I should have known better. Gran had warned me about her, but I didn't listen until I saw her with a group of kids."

Allison saw his shoulders sag and a look of pain cross his face. Something warm opened in her chest. She touched him, very lightly, on the arm.

"I took her to a skating party down at the old ice pond," he continued. "Everybody was there, the whole island." He swallowed, glanced past her at the water. "I knew Tracy didn't like kids, but I didn't realize how much until I saw her push a little boy down. He was having trouble staying on his feet; he kept wobbling around the pond, grabbing at people for support as they skated by. Tracy just brushed him off like an annoying insect." He sighed. "The thing is, I knew all along, deep down, that she had this cold, iron center, but I closed my eyes to the truth. Until I couldn't ignore it anymore."

Allison stared up at him. Something about the tone of his voice and the look on his face made her own eyes burn. He glanced down at her again. "Do you see what I'm saying about Cabot? You have to open your eyes, Allison. You have to listen to your heart."

She swallowed hard, trying to find words that would express what she was feeling. But there were none. He seemed to be waiting for her to say something, to acknowledge the truth of his statement. But that was something she couldn't do, not without betraying Cabot and her parents, not to mention herself and her whole frame of reference for the past twenty-four years. She cleared her throat.

"I'm sorry you were hurt, Brent, but it doesn't have anything to do with me. I trust Cabot completely. He's never done anything to make me doubt my love for him." She straightened her shoulders. "And I don't think I should have to keep saying this again and again. I love Cabot and I'm going to marry him. I wish you'd just leave me alone." For some reason, she couldn't look at him directly, and it was only after she had finished speaking that she became aware that he was gazing at her with an expression she'd never seen on his face. It seemed to be a combination of pain and bewildered resignation, and it kindled something sorrowful inside her.

"All right," he said softly. "You win. I'll leave you alone." He turned abruptly and crossed the deck to the pilothouse, leaving her standing alone in the stern, startled and strangely sad.

They didn't speak again for the entire trip back to Harper's Island.

Chapter Eleven

WHEN BRENT TIED HIS SKIFF UP at the village wharf, Allison quickly climbed ashore and walked alone down the road to Isabel's house. The trip from the mainland had been painful. Brent's silence had cut into her like a knife.

She entered the kitchen nervously, wondering if Isabel would question her about her absence during the night. The older woman was sitting at the table with a cup of tea, reading a newspaper. She glanced up at Allison with a smile.

"Help yourself, dear. The teakettle's still hot." Isabel waved her hand in the direction of the refrigerator. "Feel free to eat anything you want. I don't imagine you've had lunch yet." She smiled over the rim of her teacup. "You got more than you bargained for last night, I reckon. Fog doesn't get that thick more than once or twice a year, but when it does, you'd best stay put. I'm glad Brent didn't try to make it across in that pea soup."

Allison smiled weakly. She opened the refrigerator and located bread and some cheese slices. She'd never realized such simple fare could look so delicious.

"I've been thinking about this whole play group

135

idea," Isabel said. "Maybe we've been too hasty. You probably don't want to start up something like that with your fiancé coming and all."

"I don't want to give it up!" Allison took her sandwich to the table and sat down across from Isabel. "I'm really getting excited about it."

"It's a big project, and it'll be a real headache at times, especially with those Flory children to manage. I talked to their mother this morning, and she's all for it, but it may not be a good idea for you. Ricky—he's the oldest—has been a trouble to her since the day he was born."

"He sounds like a challenge." Allison smiled and took a bite of her sandwich. "I don't think you know how much I'm looking forward to doing something useful."

Isabel's voice softened. "Well, to be honest, Brent mentioned to me that you and your fiancé were having some problems. This may not be the best summer for that sort of project."

Allison flushed. "I'm afraid you have the wrong impression. Brent has some strange idea that I don't love Cabot, and he—"

"So Brent is behind this." Isabel nodded thoughtfully. "Well, I'm not surprised. I've never seen him look at a woman the way he looks at you. Not even that Lawton woman. And I'm afraid he's the kind of man who goes after what he wants." She took another sip of tea and smiled apologetically at Allison. "I wish there were something I could say to help, but where Brent's concerned, I don't dare to give advice. He's always been his own man, even when he was a little boy."

"I think he understands my position," Allison said. "We had a long talk this morning."

"Good." Isabel put down her teacup and stood up.

"And I'm glad to hear that nothing's wrong between you and your fiancé. If you're absolutely certain about wanting to go ahead with the play group, I thought I'd invite a few of the parents over after supper, and you could get acquainted."

"I'd like that."

"I'll be out, then, for the afternoon." Isabel turned in the doorway and smiled. "By all means, fix yourself another sandwich. You looked famished."

Allison spent much of the afternoon in the tiny guest bedroom, staring out at the harbor. It was impossible for her to avoid seeing Brent's house, and now she was beginning to regret having accepted Isabel's offer of a place to stay during Martha's absence. She knew she should be as far away from Brent Connors as possible.

By evening she was looking forward to meeting with the parents of the island's young children. Isabel served a nourishing supper of corned beef hash and fresh peas from Abel's garden. After dinner, Abel left for his weekly pinochle game at Peter Hayes's house, and Allison washed the dishes. Isabel bustled around the kitchen and the living room, busily arranging things for the coming guests.

Six women came, and by seven o'clock they were all sitting in the living room, sipping coffee and watching Allison with solemnly curious faces.

"I'm so glad you all could come," Isabel said, settling into a chair at last. "This is Allison Curtis, and she's starting a summer play group up at the old school."

As Isabel introduced the guests, Allison studied each face carefully, hoping to read some hint of acceptance in the noncommittal glances. She was particularly struck by the weary expression on the face of Natalie Flory. The woman, whom Allison guessed to be in her mid-thirties, had a hint of gray in her limp brown hair, but her sculpted cheekbones and wide mouth indicated that she had once been quite a beauty. She was sitting in a corner of the couch, a tiny infant cradled in her arms. When Allison asked about the baby, a thin smile came to her lips.

"Charlene's four weeks old today. She's the best baby in the world." She held her out for Allison to admire. Allison saw a wisp of blond hair on the rounded head, and a red face with the eyes squeezed tightly shut. "She's my fifth."

Allison caught the pride in the woman's voice and smiled. "She's beautiful. May I hold her?"

Natalie nodded, beaming. It struck Allison that Natalie was probably a woman who had little time for pride or pleasure of any kind.

Allison cradled the baby against her chest, and felt a serene softness spill through her. Something about the tiny life she held made her feel gentle, maternal. She wondered what it would be like to rock her own children.

She tried to imagine that it was Cabot's daughter she was holding, but something blocked her. The wisp of blond hair, perhaps? No child of hers and Cabot's could possibly have hair that light. Perhaps Brent Connor's child . . . What was she thinking? She felt a deep pinch of dismay and quickly handed the baby back to Natalie, as if her thoughts might contaminate the child.

The meeting went smoothly. The parents all seemed friendly and responsive to the idea of a play group. They promised to help as much as possible. They all agreed to meet again on Saturday morning, to help clean out the old schoolhouse.

"I'll start next Monday, then," Allison said. "I'll be

there from eight until two, and you can send your children anytime between those hours. Make sure to pack a lunch."

The women left with broad smiles, talking happily among themselves. Isabel patted Allison's shoulder.

"Well, what did I tell you? The nicest people in the world live on Harper's Island!" She grinned, and Allison felt a little shock of recognition go through her; the older woman's expression was exactly like Brent's when he was pleased with something he had said.

"They're wonderful," Allison agreed. "And I'm really looking forward to working with their children."

"You'll enjoy it, dear. You know, I really feel as if I've known you for a long time. There's something special about you, Allison. It makes me feel as if you belong here."

Allison laughed. "The funny thing is, it's just a fluke that I'm here at all. I was planning to go to California until Martha talked me into coming up here with her."

"Well, thank goodness for Martha, then. We're all lucky you decided to come to Maine."

Allison felt bathed in Isabel's big smile. She wished she could tell her how much she enjoyed being here, how at home she felt. The only problem she faced on Harper's Island was how to deal with Brent. Perhaps, after this morning, that problem would stay resolved. She certainly hoped so.

"I think I'll take a little walk," she said cheerfully. "I could use some fresh air before I turn in."

"That's a wonderful idea, dear. You go right ahead. It's a lovely, clear night. And one thing about Harper's Island—there's not a safer place on earth. As long as you don't run into any ghosts." Isabel smiled and stifled a yawn.

"Ghosts?"

The older woman nodded. "There's a legend about a sea captain who haunts the island on summer nights. Tourist stuff, is my guess. It's the kind of thing they eat up. I've lived here almost seventy years, and I've never seen anything myself."

Allison laughed. "I guess I'll take my chances, then."

"Have a nice walk, dear." Isabel yawned again. "I'll go on to bed. Abel's already asleep, and if I don't join him soon, I'll be nodding over my oatmeal tomorrow morning. Just make sure the lights are out when you come to bed."

Allison went to her room for a sweater and slipped quietly out the kitchen door. The night sky was shimmering with stars, and a crescent moon hung low over the water. She walked slowly down the street toward the harbor, breathing the pure air with delight. How different it was from the city, and even from the suburbs! As she passed Brent's house, she studiously avoided looking at the lighted windows, but she couldn't stop her mind's eye from seeing Brent at his kitchen table, reading a book, perhaps, or eating a late night snack.

She walked on quickly. Her heart was beating in her ears as she continued down to the harbor and stood at the top of the wharf, gazing out at the still water of the little cove. Silence enveloped her, settling around her like a cocoon. Her heartbeat slowed; she began to feel calmer.

All this foolishness was just that. There was no reason in the world for her to respond to Brent Connors with anything but suspicion and distrust. He was an arrogant, amoral man. He had probably told her the story of his relationship with Tracy Lawton just to manipulate her, to make her feel sorry for him. Well, it wasn't going to work.

A small sound behind her made her start. Someone was there, hiding in the bushes beside the fishing shack. The muscles in her legs tensed. She turned to look, but her eyes couldn't penetrate the darkness.

Years of city and suburban living had taught Allison never to trust the darkness. Nervously, she turned and started to walk quickly back to Isabel's house. The sound came again, closer this time. She looked back over her shoulder, but there was nothing there.

She was afraid to run. If someone or something was stalking her, it would sense her fear and leap to attack, like a vicious dog. She glanced at Brent's lighted kitchen window. A few more steps, a quick turn, and she'd be at his front door. She imagined herself knocking, imagined Brent opening the door and gathering her into the safety of his arms. It was a fantasy, she knew, something she couldn't do no matter how much she might want to. She'd told Brent she wanted him to leave her alone. What would he think if she came knocking on his door in the dead of night?

She heard the sound again, closer now, and her resolve evaporated. She was in danger. Pride be damned. She turned into Brent's driveway and ran up onto the porch. She was about to lift her hand to knock when a sound made her freeze. It wasn't behind her this time; it was inside the house. It was the sound of a woman's laugh, soft but distinct.

She whirled away from the door, stumbled back across the porch. And stepped into thin air.

The porch step wasn't where she'd expected it,

and she fell heavily onto the ground, twisting her ankle under her.

Her cry was involuntary, and she bit down hard on her lip to distract herself from the pain. The door opened and she looked up to see Brent standing, framed in the soft, interior light. His arm was around the shoulder of a beautiful, dark-haired woman.

"Allison? What in hell . . . ?" He was wearing tight jeans and a tank shirt. He held a beer can in his free hand.

"I'm sorry," she moaned. "I didn't mean to bother you."

She grasped the porch rail and pulled herself up, wincing painfully. "I was just leaving." She started to limp away.

His hand caught her upper arm. "Hold it. You're not going anywhere. You're hurt!"

"Please, just let me go," she said. "Go back to your guest."

He released her arm and squatted in front of her, his fingers gently probing her throbbing ankle.

Allison glanced over Brent's head at the woman in the doorway. She had shoulder-length black hair and the longest eyelashes Allison had ever seen. She was wearing a form-fitting red sundress, cut very low in front, exposing deep, full breasts. Her calm smile showed perfect, white teeth.

Brent's searching fingers suddenly hit swollen muscle, and Allison jumped and cried out.

He stood up. "You've sprained your ankle. Come on. We'll put some ice on it." He pulled her against his side, tucked his arm firmly around her waist, and started toward the house. "Emily, get the ice pack out of the freezer."

The woman arched her back and turned in the

doorway. She moved away with the sinuous, catlike grace that Allison had always envied.

"Take it easy," Brent said quietly. "One step at a time."

Despite her pain, Allison was intensely aware of the pleasure his nearness created in her body. Her skin felt warm and tingled with joy at his touch. Her heart was beating fast; she felt slightly dizzy. She glanced up at him.

"I'm really sorry about this. I didn't mean to intrude. I didn't know you had company until I heard . . . when I came up on the porch . . . I feel terrible," she finished lamely.

"You should." There was a trace of laughter in his voice.

She felt a hard knot in the base of her throat. She hated her body for wanting to be close to him.

Emily appeared in the doorway, holding a blue ice pack. "Is this what you wanted, Brent?" Her voice was languid and seductive.

"Yeah. Thanks." He gave her a quick grin, and Allison felt a wrench of pure white jealousy blossom in her chest. She took a deep breath.

"I'm feeling better. I think I'll run along home now." She lurched away from Brent, steeling herself against the protesting pain shooting up her leg.

He grabbed her arm. "Just a minute. You're not in shape to run anywhere." With a sudden lunge, he lifted her in his arms, carried her up the steps, through the door and into the living room, where he deposited her unceremoniously on the couch.

He took the ice pack from Emily and wrapped it around Allison's throbbing ankle. "Now, stay put. I'll be right back." He gave her a warning frown and touched Emily's shoulder. Together they crossed the room and went into the kitchen. When the door closed behind them, Allison shut her eyes against hot tears.

She'd never felt such embarrassment in her life. Nor such raw jealousy. How was it possible for her to be jealous of this woman? She was Cabot Wilder's fiancée. She leaned back against the arm of the couch and tried to focus on the pain in her ankle, hoping it would distract her from the pain in her heart.

She heard the sound of voices from the kitchen, the low rumble of Brent's tone, then a silence, then Emily's voice, high and sweet. "Call me as soon as she leaves, Brent. I'm free all evening." The back door opened and shut, and then light footsteps crunched on the driveway. A moment later Brent came back into the room, closing the kitchen door behind him. His expression was grave, his eyes narrow.

"I'm really sorry. I feel terrible about this." Allison sat up, reaching for the ice pack.

"Don't touch it!"

He stood over her, his hand blocking her reach. Every bulge and muscular ripple was exposed in the blue tank shirt. "Now tell me why you're here. And no lies this time, Allison. I want the truth."

"I told you the truth!" she said hotly. "I was on my way back to your grandmother's house."

"That doesn't explain what you were doing on my front porch." His piercing gaze was deeply unsettling.

She swallowed. "All right, but I feel pretty foolish. I was taking a walk down to the harbor when something frightened me. A noise in the bushes." She licked her bottom lip. "I thought maybe someone was there, so I started back home. Then I realized it was following me. I was frightened."

The corners of his mouth lifted. "Sounds like you flushed a raccoon."

She blinked at him. "It sounded like a person, or something awful. Isabel said something about a ghost before I left the house. I guess my imagination ran away with me."

Brent nodded. "I would say so. I'm afraid you won't be going on nighttime walks for a while now, not with that ankle."

She grimaced. "I really am sorry. The last thing I wanted to do was to spoil your evening."

"Well," he grinned, "you do seem to have a talent for playing havoc with my life. Ever since you've come to the island, I've hardly had a moment's peace. And I'll be damned if I'm going to interrupt my grandmother's good night's sleep by stumbling in with you in my arms."

"You won't need to. I can walk." She started to swing her legs off the couch, but Brent clamped one hand onto her shoulder and pushed her back down.

"You're not going anywhere tonight."

She stared up into his eyes and for a moment felt herself yielding to his will once again. She shook herself slightly, glanced away and caught a glimpse of two beer cans sitting side by side on the windowsill.

"No," she said quickly. "I can't stay here. Emily's waiting for you."

He sat beside her on the edge of the couch. "You're jealous!" His face opened into a broad grin. "My God, you're jealous of Emily!" He cupped her chin in his hand, turned her face toward him. "Doesn't this prove it to you, Allison? What I've been saying all along about you and Cabot? It's not Cabot you're in love with."

She wasn't aware of the fury inside her until it

burst from her mouth. "I certainly am! And this proves nothing to me except that I'm not staying *here* all night!"

She slapped his hand away from her chin and kicked the ice pack to the floor with her uninjured foot. To her surprise, he didn't try to stop her. Instead he sat watching with a bemused smile as she struggled to her feet.

"You won't get out the door," he said, shaking his head.

Painfully, she hobbled a few steps, gritting her teeth as she forced herself forward. The only thing she wanted in the world was to get out of Brent Connors's house. A sudden, jagged pain shot up her leg; she moaned and sagged against the wall. Tears jumped into her eyes.

She knew that Brent was still watching her, and it was his self-righteous grin that goaded her on. She took a deep breath, lurched forward and finally reached the door. Yanking it open, she pitched forward into the darkness. Only then did she feel Brent's hand on her shoulder.

"Allison, stop." His voice was as gentle as his hand, and for a moment all she wanted was to turn and sink into his arms.

"You don't have to do this, you know," he said softly. "You're only hurting yourself by pretending. Can't you at least be honest with yourself about this?"

She felt his words like a knife; he wasn't talking about her ankle; he was talking about her feelings for Cabot again. She shook his hand off angrily. "Leave me alone!" she hissed. "And stop telling me how to live my life!" She wrenched away from him and limped across the porch and down the steps.

She tried to make herself hurry down the driveway to the street, each step a sharp spasm of pain. She didn't have any courage left to look back over her shoulder and watch Brent go into his house and shut the door.

Chapter Twelve

No ONE INTERRUPTED Allison's slow progress down Brent's driveway and up the road toward the Cutler house. It began to rain as she started up the hill, big, soaking drops, but the vague discomfort of being wet helped to distract her from the pain in her ankle. She limped on, up the slight hill, around the bend, and then Isabel's house was in sight. It seemed like an island of safety in a world fraught with danger. But the real dangers were all in her own heart, she thought grimly.

She was only a few yards from the front door when she slipped and fell in a patch of slick mud. Her ankle twisted clumsily under her, and pain went through her leg. She groaned and tried to stand, but her ankle buckled and she sprawled facedown in the mud. For a moment she lay there, moaning softly. The house in front of her was dark; Isabel and Abel were peacefully asleep. If she screamed for help, she would probably waken not only them, but the whole neighborhood. There was only one thing to do. She pulled herself up on her hands and knees and crawled to the house.

At the front door, she dragged herself to a standing position and tried the knob. It swung open, and she stumbled into Isabel's immaculate front hall. She was in too much pain to care about the muddy prints she was leaving with her hands and knees. Slowly, painfully, she crawled up the stairs to the little guest bedroom. With a sigh of relief, she dropped onto the bed. She was aware only of her throbbing ankle, until sleep mercifully claimed her.

When Allison woke at dawn, chilled and groggy, she knew that a sound had roused her. It came again, a sharp, thumping noise, a deep, familiar voice. She heard scuffling feet, Isabel's worried tones, then quick footsteps on the stairs.

"She sprained her ankle last night, Gran. She wouldn't stay put at my house. Insisted on going back on her own."

A light knock sounded and then the door to the room opened. "Oh my Lord! What in the world happened, dear?" Allison looked up into Isabel's worried face.

Allison lifted her head, but an angry throb of pain forced her back onto the pillow. She tried to smile as Isabel hurried into the room.

"I had an accident. I'm all right. I just need to get some sleep." She was dimly aware of Brent's form looming in the doorway. She closed her eyes, welcoming the cool touch of Isabel's palm on her forehead.

"Why, she's burning up with fever! Poor child! I'll get you out of these clothes and into a warm tub right away. Brent, go get Dr. Johnson. He's summering at the old Andrews place."

"I don't need a doctor." Allison winced and tried to push Isabel's hands away.

"Nonsense." Isabel clicked her tongue. "Hurry, Brent. I don't know why in the world you let her come home all by herself. What on earth were you thinking?"

"It was my idea," Allison said quickly. "I can be very stubborn sometimes."

"Well, no sense crying over spilt milk. Let's get you clean and warm."

Isabel alternately soothed and chided as she helped Allison out of her mud-caked clothes and into the bathtub of warm water. Allison gradually relaxed under the older woman's comforting ministrations.

"You really should have listened to Brent, dear," Isabel said, helping her into her nightgown. "A sprained ankle isn't anything you should be walking around on. How did you hurt it in the first place?"

Allison briefly explained the events of the previous evening, omitting the presence of Emily. She tried lamely to justify her own return to the Cutlers' house. "I just didn't want to burden Brent any more than I already had," she said. "And it didn't seem like it was that far to your house."

"Oh pooh!" scoffed Isabel. "Brent's never happier than when he's helping someone out. That boy has the softest heart in the world, though he'd never let it show on purpose. Now, you get back under those covers. If I know Brent, he'll have Dr. Johnson here within the hour, even if he was to drag him kicking and screaming."

Allison closed her eyes as she slid gratefully between the cool, clean sheets that Isabel had put on the bed. How in the world had she come to this state of affairs? She couldn't remember the last time she'd been sick or injured. She was someone who took excellent care of herself. She hadn't seen a doctor, except for her annual checkup, in years.

She dozed briefly, lulled by Isabel's calm voice,

and her pain lessened as her body relaxed. The sound of the front door opening and closing in the hall below roused her back to wakefulness. She started to sit up, but Isabel's hand urged her back onto the pillow.

"Just relax, dear. Art Johnson's a wonderful doctor. We'll have you fit in no time."

Brent appeared in the doorway, followed by a towering man with white hair and a neatly trimmed beard. The doctor quickly shooed Isabel and Brent out of the room and bent over Allison with a concerned smile on his large face.

"Well, it seems you've been overdoing it," he said, as he finished his examination.

"I'm just a little tired. Except for my ankle, I'm fine."

"I'm afraid not, little lady. You've got the flu. You're going to need a few days in bed before you even *think* about getting back on your feet."

"But I can't!" She felt a sudden wave of panic as she thought about the play group and then of Cabot's imminent arrival. And she wanted to be ready to help with the cleanup on Saturday. "I have too much to do!"

The doctor shook his head sternly. "I'm afraid you don't have a choice. I'll give you Motrin for your ankle—it'll relieve the pain and reduce the inflammation—but you're under strict orders to stay in that bed until Monday."

When she opened her mouth to protest again, he frowned and held up a warning finger. "I'm putting you in Isabel's care, so I suggest you don't disobey orders. You've never seen wrath until you've seen Isabel Cutler crossed!"

He turned to open the door. Allison caught a glimpse of Brent looming in the hall.

"Just leaving," Dr. Johnson said, giving Brent a pat on the shoulder. "Don't bother about the ride back. I'm headed over to Edie Chaney's for a fisherman's breakfast." He winked at Brent. "You ought to take better care of your girlfriend. Looks to me like she needs a firm hand."

Allison reddened with embarrassment, but the doctor was gone before she had a chance to explain that she wasn't Brent's girlfriend, not by any stretch of the imagination.

Brent grinned down at her. "You heard what the doctor said, Allison. Bed rest and a strong hand." He sat next to her on the bed. "*My* strong hand."

Allison bristled. "He didn't mean it that way! Anyway, he put me in Isabel's care."

Brent nodded, his eyes twinkling mischievously. "Don't get excited. I just came up for a minute—with Gran's permission, incidentally—to make a couple of arrangements with you." He shifted closer; she felt his hip nudge hers through the thin blanket. "Then I'll leave, if that's what you want."

"It's what I want," she muttered, trying to slide away from him and finding, to her chagrin, that her movement merely brought her face closer to his.

His smile disappeared and his eyes sobered. "It's about Cabot. I wanted to let you know that I've wired him about your injury. When he comes, I'll pick him up at the ferry and get him settled in at the guest house. Just so that your mind's at ease."

She swallowed. "You don't have to do that, Brent."

He shrugged. "I'm the logical greeting party, with both you and Martha out of commission."

"I know how you feel about him," she whispered.

"Do you? I haven't even met the man. Maybe I'll think he's terrific." He stood up. "Get some rest now." He went to the door, turned and looked back at her. "About last night, Allison. I thought it was pretty courageous of you to come all the way back here on your own. I'm just sorry you felt you had to do it."

Then he was gone.

Isabel appeared in the doorway, and Allison looked up at her bleakly.

"What's wrong, dear? You look like you're about to cry! Did Brent say something to upset you?"

Allison shook her head, but the tears welled up anyway and soon she was sobbing openly. Isabel put her arms around her, and Allison rested her head on the older woman's shoulder.

"Now, why don't you tell me what's the matter. It can't be as hopeless as you imagine."

"I'm just so confused! My fiancé's coming and Dr. Johnson thought I was Brent's girlfriend and Brent said he was sorry I felt I had to come back here—" Sobs choked her.

"Shhh, dear." Isabel lowered her gently onto the bed. "It's just the fever talking. Now close your eyes and get some sleep. You'll feel better when you wake up."

Waves of heat and fatigue washed over Allison as Isabel covered her with the blanket and drew the curtains across the window At the door she turned and smiled.

"You mustn't worry, you know, dear. Things will work out for the best. They always do."

Allison tried to smile back. Isabel closed the door softly and Allison felt herself slide toward sleep. In the dim light of the curtained room, she thought she sensed a strong, loving presence, as if Brent were standing beside her, watching over her.

* * *

Allison slept all day and well into the next. When she woke, at noon on Friday, she felt refreshed and at peace. Her headache was gone; her ankle no longer throbbed. Sunlight streamed into the little room, lying in oblongs on the polished hardwood floor and across the narrow bed. She could hear the low voices of Abel and Isabel in the kitchen below. She realized, with pleasure, that she was hungry.

She sat up and swung her legs over the side of the bed. A wave of dizziness swept through her, then passed, and she stood up, testing her weight on her injured ankle. It was still sore, but the pain had eased considerably. If she leaned against the wall, she could go down the stairs without putting more strain on it.

She found her brush and forced it through her tangled hair, then slipped into her bathrobe and limped through the door and into the hallway. She was surprised at how giddy she felt, as if she'd just had three glasses of champagne. She sagged against the wall for a moment, taking deep breaths of warm, summer air. A door opened below; she heard a thumping sound and then the scrape of a kitchen chair. She loved the sounds in Isabel's house. They made her feel comfortable, content. More relaxed than she'd ever felt in Cabot's home, she thought suddenly.

She tottered her way down the stairs and stepped into the kitchen. Her eyes widened. Brent was seated at the table, bent over a plate heaped with pancakes.

"Allison!" Isabel turned from the stove and rushed across the room to embrace her. "What in the world are you doing up? You're supposed to stay in bed!"

Allison knew that Brent's head had come up and swiveled toward her, but she couldn't bring herself to return his glance.

"I wanted to get up. I'm starved."

Isabel touched her forehead and nodded knowingly. "Well, your fever's gone, dear. You probably are hungry." She scurried to the table and pulled out the chair next to Brent's. "Come on, then. Sit down and have some pancakes."

From his chair, Abel fixed her with a long, approving stare. "You look prettier than a spring morning, Allison. The rest has done you good."

"Thanks." She smiled past Brent, aware of the clean, masculine scent emanating from him. She couldn't look at him, couldn't bring her eyes to meet his. If only she'd known he was here, she would never have ventured downstairs.

"Allison." Brent's voice, low and serious, forced her to turn toward him. He was looking at her with a gravely earnest expression. She felt another wave of dizziness and swayed away from him slightly.

"Oh, for goodness' sake, Brent! Let the poor girl eat first." Isabel placed a huge plate of pancakes in front of Allison and handed her a blue pitcher brimming with maple syrup.

"Eat first? Before what?" Allison felt a wave of panic. She looked first at Isabel, then Abel. "What's wrong?"

"See," Isabel chided, sitting in the chair beside Abel, "what did I tell you? You've got her all upset over nothing."

"Tell her, boy. Get it over with." Abel's low growl was muffled as he took a bite of pancake. He pointed his fork at Brent.

Allison turned to Brent. His face had become even more somber, almost sad. Her throat knotted; she put her hand to her chest.

"It's Martha, isn't it? Something awful's happened."

"Oh, goodness no, child," Isabel snorted. "No one's hurt. Will you get on with it, Brent? Deliver your message."

"I will, if I can get a word in edgewise." His voice was tight, hard. He reached for Allison's hand and tucked it peremptorily into his own. "I wired Cabot yesterday about your illness. This morning I got word from him. A telegram, actually." He jammed his free hand into the front pocket of his jeans, pulled out a yellow slip of paper, handed it to her. "I'm afraid he's not coming."

She took it with trembling fingers. She felt a strange bubble of gaiety form in her chest.

"He says he's 'unavoidably detained.' I'm sorry."

She opened the telegram, scanned it quickly. She could have predicted it, down to the exact wording. The business merger was in its final stages; he couldn't get away for another week. But she knew it was more than the merger; Cabot didn't like awkward situations. And her injury and illness were certainly awkward, something that he wouldn't want to face.

"Well, I'm sure he'll come as soon as possible, dear." Isabel pushed a plate of fresh butter across the table toward her. "In the meantime, your job is to get well."

Brent squeezed her hand under the table. She glanced at him, saw his pitying smile. A jolt of anger went through her. She resented his sympathy. It was all an act, to prove to her how little she wanted Cabot's presence on the island. Brent wasn't really sorry at all, and he didn't expect her to be.

She yanked her hand out of his and reached for the butter. "It shouldn't take me long to get better with this kind of down-home care." She gave Isabel her brightest smile.

"You show 'em, girl," Abel said. "That boyfriend of yours ought to know better than to leave a beauty like you unprotected. If I was thirty years younger, he wouldn't stand a chance."

"Abel Cutler!" Isabel gave his arm a playful swat. "You just keep your thoughts to yourself!"

"Yes, ma'am." He poked his fork into another layered chunk of pancake, his blue eyes dancing merrily.

Allison poured syrup over her pancakes, watching the clear dark liquid roll over the pile and across the plate. She sensed that Brent was still watching her. Was he gloating, amused?

But he didn't say a word to her for the rest of the meal, and before she finished her own pancakes, he had excused himself from the table, kissed his grandmother good-bye, and left the house.

She felt an immediate sense of loss, as if some vital ingredient had been abruptly removed from the air. She pushed the feeling away and smiled across the table at Isabel. "These pancakes are absolutely delicious. I wish I could cook like this."

"Oh, you will, dear. It just takes practice. And an appreciative man." Isabel grinned at Abel and stood up. "Now you'll have to excuse me. I've got a lot to do before Martha gets here."

"Martha? Oh, that's right! She's coming home today!" Allison took a final bite of pancake, pulled herself to her feet. "I'd better go pack my things and get moved back to the Hollingsworth house."

Isabel's hand was instantly on her shoulder, pushing her back down into her chair. "Nonsense! You're doing no such thing! Martha's staying here with us until you're both back on your feet. I've already fixed up the back bedroom."

Allison opened her mouth to protest, then shut it when she caught sight of Abel's knowing grin.

"No use fighting with her, girl," he said. "When my wife makes up her mind, there's no moving her. It's like trying to set a mast in a hurricane. Can't be done."

"I don't know what to say," Allison murmured. "I've imposed on you both so much already."

"There's nothing *to* say." Isabel took Allison's empty plate to the sink. "And it's never an imposition to have young people around. It keeps *us* young."

Abel lounged back in his chair, pulled his pipe out of his pocket and regarded Allison with a bemused smile. "If I didn't know better, I'd swear you grew up on this island. You fit right in, smooth as a hand in a glove."

"Enough of this jibber-jabber." Isabel's hand descended on Allison's shoulder once again. "This girl belongs in bed if she's going to be well enough to mind those children come Monday. And *you*, Abel Cutler—go take that stinking pipe *outside* if you intend to smoke it!"

Chapter Thirteen

AT FOUR O'CLOCK Allison was lounging in bed, trying to make herself believe that the hero of the romance she was reading didn't look anything like Brent Connors. When she heard Martha's excited voice in the kitchen below, she dropped her book, got to her feet and limped quickly into the hall.

"Martha!" she called, leaning over the rail at the top of the stairs.

She heard Martha's answering whoop of enthusiasm, and then Isabel's voice.

"Brent, go get Allison. She shouldn't come down those stairs all by herself again today."

Brent instantly appeared at the bottom of the steps. "My pleasure, Gran." He grinned up at Allison, then took the stairs two at a time and scooped her quickly into his arms. When she started to protest, he shook his head. "If you're going to be in shape by Monday, you can't keep running up and down these stairs. Sprained ankles don't heal by themselves, you know. Besides, these are Gran's orders."

As he carried her down, Allison felt her body relax instinctively into his strong arms. He brought her into the kitchen and deposited her in the chair beside Martha.

"There," he said. "The two beautiful invalids. Happy once more."

"Invalids!" Martha shrieked. She leaned over to hug Allison. "We're both healthy as horses!"

"Right." Brent dropped into the chair opposite them. "And crazy as loons."

"I'll have you know that I'll be the life of the party by the Fourth of July Social this year, Brent Connors! So there!" Martha stuck out her chin defiantly.

"You must be dreaming. The fourth is only three weeks away. You're going to be on crutches for the rest of the summer, my sweet."

"Want to bet?"

"Sure." Brent leaned toward Martha, his hands stuffed deep into his pockets, his eyes dancing wickedly. "If you're on your feet by the fourth, I'll escort you to the dance. Personally. How's that?"

"It's a date. You can mark it on your calendar."

He chuckled. "We'll see about that."

Allison looked down at her hands, aware of a sudden tightness in her chest.

"Cabot should be here by then," Martha said, putting her arm around Allison's shoulder. "We'll double date."

"Great idea." Brent looked at Allison, grinned. "We'll paint the town red."

Allison smiled weakly. She tried to imagine dancing with Cabot while she watched Martha in Brent's arms. A wave of hot jealousy spilled through her. She looked at Martha, noting the bright pink spots on her cheeks. Going with Brent would give her plenty of incentive to be ready to dance by the fourth.

Still, there was one consolation. Allison loved dancing, and Cabot was a fantastic dancer. Together, they were graceful and fluid, the envy of onlookers.

Maybe Brent was passionate and handsome, but she doubted he could hold a candle to Cabot when it came to dancing.

Isabel bustled in from the living room, waving a disapproving hand at Brent. "Now, shoo. I told you I didn't want you hanging around this afternoon, tiring these girls out. I've got Martha's room all fixed up and she needs to rest. So does Allison. I intend to keep things strictly under wraps around here until everyone's hale and hearty."

"Yes, ma'am." Brent got to his feet and headed for the back door, grinning broadly. "I'll see you tomorrow, bright and early, at the schoolhouse."

"You certainly will." Isabel gave him a quick peck on the cheek. "And don't expect to be socializing all day with that Potter girl. You're coming to *work*, make no mistake about it."

He gave a mock sigh. "You sure do drive a hard bargain, Gran."

"Shoo! Out!" She waved her hand at him again, and he laughed out loud, winked over her shoulder at Allison, and left the house.

"Now," Isabel said briskly, handing Martha's crutches to her. "Off to bed with the two of you until suppertime."

"Oh—but we have so much to talk about!" Martha wailed.

"You'll have plenty of time later. Now, I've got the back bedroom all fixed up. You just go through the living room—"

"I know where it is." Martha pulled herself to her feet, adjusted the crutches under her arms, gave Allison a beleaguered look. "Guess we don't have a choice, amigo. When Isabel Cutler says jump, you jump."

Allison laughed and stood up. "I've found that

out." She appreciated the chance to retreat to her bedroom; her feelings were in such an uproar, she wondered if she would ever feel calm again.

By suppertime she felt better able to face the onslaught of Martha's probing questions. After Abel had helped her slowly down the stairs, Allison sat across the table from Martha, thoroughly enjoying the pot roast and vegetables heaped on her plate. When she offered to do the dishes, Isabel refused and shooed the two girls into the living room for a "real heart-to-heart." Allison curled up in the easy chair, while Martha stretched out on the couch, and soon they were giggling together like old times.

When Allison finally fell into bed, it was past one in the morning. Exhausted, she lay thinking about the day ahead; it was Saturday; the big cleanup was scheduled at the schoolhouse. She realized, with a start, that no one expected her to go. Everyone was assuming she wasn't up to it.

Yet it was exactly what she needed. All this bed rest and relaxation was wearing her out. What she needed was exercise and fresh air, not more lazing around and enduring gossipy conversations about Martha's love life. Her ankle was much better. A little stiff, maybe, but the pain was almost completely gone. And she wanted to be busy doing something, to get her mind off the whirling confusion within.

She couldn't forget the pitying look Brent had given her when she heard the news about Cabot's delay. If she didn't know better, she might almost have believed he was sincere. But he had spoken too many times about how he believed she didn't truly love Cabot, so clearly his expression of sympathy was intended to mock her. And then there was her own strange reaction to his flirting tone with Martha. Her odd twinge of jealousy didn't make any sense. It was Cabot she was in love with. She didn't care who Brent flirted with or took to the dance. What she was feeling, she assured herself, was disappointment over Cabot's telegram. She had let it color her feelings about everything throughout the day.

She yawned, rolled over and tucked her hand under the pillow. She had to get a good night's sleep if she were going to work at the schoolhouse in the morning.

Allison was up at dawn. She dressed quickly in jeans and a short-sleeved green knit shirt, went to the window and opened the screen. She leaned out over the dew-splashed sill, gazing down at the row of rooftops that led down to the harbor. The tide was out; it was a clear, cool day. Brent's boat waited at its mooring, its blue and white curves reflected in the still water. She had never thought of boats as being beautiful before, but the *Blue Lady* had a grace that seemed to belong to nature, just as surely as the big white pine that towered over the general store. Her eyes picked out Brent's house. His truck was parked in the driveway; she wondered if he was eating breakfast. She remembered the morning she had eaten with him, the deliciously spiced scrambled eggs, the comfortable coziness of his kitchen.

Her heart lurched. She couldn't think about such things. She deliberately brought Cabot into her mind, concentrating on his fine features, his slim shoulders, the refined carriage of his head.

She took a deep breath and closed the screen. Good hard physical labor was exactly what she needed to take her mind off her confusion. She went to the door of her room, opened it. There was no sound from the kitchen below. Apparently Isabel and Abel weren't up yet. Instead of waiting for them, she'd grab a bite and start out for the schoolhouse right away. The early morning walk would do her good.

Allison was surprised at how vigorous she felt as she walked up the hill toward the school. She munched an apple as she went, its crisp, pungent scent filling her nostrils. Her ankle was only mildly noticeable; an occasional dull throb reminded her that she had injured it just three days ago.

She was watching three white gulls circle overhead when the sound of a truck made her turn and step onto the shoulder of the road.

It was Brent. He slowed the truck to a crawl and leaned his head out the window. "What are *you* doing out here?" He was frowning. The truck shuddered to a halt.

"Taking a walk." She forced a cheery smile and took another bite of her apple.

"Get in." He reached across the passenger seat and yanked open the door.

"Excuse me?"

"Get in. I'm taking you back home."

She straightened her shoulders. "I'm not going back." She turned away from him and started to walk on up the hill.

She heard the truck door open and slam shut, then the hard crunch of his boots on the road behind her. It was only the tenderness in her ankle that kept her from running.

He spoke just before his hand fell on her shoulder. "Where are you going?" He spun her to face him. She was startled at the concern in his eyes; she had expected to see anger and criticism reflected there.

She lifted her chin. "To the schoolhouse."

"Didn't Gran tell you to stay put today?"

"Yes, but I feel much better. I want to help with

the cleanup. I'm not an invalid, you know. I don't like being treated like one."

"I can see that." There was the hint of approval in his eyes. His hand drifted down her arm. "Okay, then at least let me give you a lift."

For a split second she was tempted. His fingers on her skin were sending little jolts of delight along her arm. Which was, she realized, precisely why she couldn't accept his offer. "No thanks," she said firmly. "I'd rather walk."

His hand slid down to her wrist, curled around her palm. "You don't need to be afraid," he said softly. "I'd never do or say anything to hurt you."

Something choked her suddenly, as if a stone had fallen into her throat. She jerked her hand away. "Yes you would," she declared. "You say things all the time that hurt me, that are *meant* to get me confused and upset."

He shook his head and touched her cheek lightly with his palm. "No, Allison, you've got me all wrong."

She whirled away from him and stalked up the hill, but her whole body was trembling. She felt his eyes on her back, raking over her, and she forced herself to concentrate on putting one foot down in front of the other, very precisely. After what seemed like hours, she heard the sound of the truck door banging shut and then the engine starting. A moment later Brent's truck roared past her up the hill.

She stopped and stared after him. It was several minutes before she started walking again. When she finally got to the top of the hill, it took all her willpower to traverse the last hundred yards to the schoolhouse.

There were several trucks parked on the lawn behind the school, but she saw with relief that Brent's wasn't among them. Perhaps he had decided not to go to the cleanup. Perhaps, finally, her words had gotten through to him.

Work had already started. As she climbed the front steps, two men carried out a broken desk. They were dressed similarly, in jeans and plaid shirts and dark blue baseball caps.

"Hello there! You must be Miss Curtis." The taller of the two men took off his cap and smiled at her. "I'm Matt Flory. It sure is good of you to do this for our kids."

"Sure is," agreed the smaller man. "My name's Newt Emory." He stuck out his hand for Allison to shake. "Come on in. Some of the ladies are inside, scrubbing down the walls."

Allison followed them into the building. The pain in her ankle had vanished. She'd been right; all she needed was fresh air and exercise. And the absence of Brent.

Soon she was busily scrubbing the worn woodwork of the little schoolhouse, happily plunging an old rag in and out of a bucket of suds as she listened to the gossip of the women mopping the grimy walls. Before long she'd worked up a sweat, and then she began wishing she'd brought a comb. Long tendrils of hair kept loosening from her ponytail and hanging over her face. Once, she caught sight of herself in the cracked mirror behind the door, and almost laughed out loud. Her face was smudged with dirt, and her hair stuck in lengthy curls to her forehead and temples. She was a mess.

More people came; by the time Isabel and Abel appeared, sheepishly apologizing for having overslept, Allison felt as if she'd been working for hours. When Isabel caught sight of her, she bustled over and pointed an accusing finger.

"You belong in bed!"

"Oh, Isabel, I'm fine! I'm having the time of my life!" Her grin was contagious, and she soon had Isabel laughing as they worked side by side on their hands and knees scrubbing the floor. The sound of hammering on the roof above didn't daunt the women's conversation; they just talked over the noise.

"What's going on up there?" Allison asked Natalie Flory, who had taken a break and was nursing her baby in a corner of the room.

"Some of the men are fixing the roof. When it rains, this place is as leaky as a colander."

Allison smiled at the baby. "Where are your other children? I'd like to meet them."

"Outside, I expect." Natalie waved an arm vaguely. "They're usually all over the island on a day like this."

The door burst open and a thin boy ran in and slid to a stop in front of Allison.

"Ricky, look what you did!" Natalie pointed to the muddy footprints crossing the freshly scrubbed floor. She gave Allison a wry grin. "You wanted to meet them—Ricky here's my oldest. Say hello to Miss Curtis, Ricky."

Ricky peered at Allison from under a thatch of red curls. "Hi." He gave her a shy grin.

Allison held out her hand. "Nice to meet you, Ricky. How old are you?"

He shook her hand. "Nine," he said softly.

"Ricky's small for his age." Natalie put her hand on her son's shoulder. "Now you get on out of here, Ricky. You're messing up the place. We want it nice and clean for Monday morning."

"I'm hungry!" he whined.

"Out!"

Isabel appeared at Allison's side. "It's almost lunchtime. What do you say we go set things out, ladies?"

Allison followed Isabel out into the brightest day she'd ever seen. The sun was pouring down from a crystal blue sky. The ocean gleamed green and gold in the distance. She squinted and raised her hand to shade her eyes.

Isabel touched her arm. "The tables are stashed in Brent's truck. If you'd go find him and ask him to round up a few men to set them up, I'd be grateful." She hurried away before Allison could shake her head in refusal.

Allison looked at the line of trucks and spotted Brent's, but he was nowhere in sight. She sighed and descended the steps to the grass. A low whistle made her turn and look up. Brent was standing on the porch roof, grinning down at her.

"Brent?" She put her hand to her throat, as if it would steady her voice. "Isabel wants the tables set up for lunch."

He jumped from the roof, landing lightly on the grass in front of her. A slow smile lifted the corners of his mouth. "You're a mess, Allison. I don't think I've seen a dirtier woman in all my life." His smile broadened. He stuck his hammer into his belt and stepped closer to her. "If I didn't know better, I'd swear you've been floating around in the bilge water of the *Blue Lady*."

He ran his finger the length of her cheek and shook his head in mock disgust. She took a step backward, wary of his mischievous grin.

"I ought to give you a saltwater bath right now."

"You keep your hands off me!" She took another

step backward. "Isabel wants the tables set up *now*, Brent."

But he didn't hear her. Laughing, he scooped her up over his shoulder and started running down the lawn toward the water.

"Put me down!" she screamed. She felt strangely excited, even as she struggled to right herself and twist out of his arms. Long strands of hair caught on her lips and she brushed them away. "Stop, Brent! Please!"

He carried her over the ridge of the lawn down to the little beach. She could no longer see the schoolhouse, or the crowd of people that had watched their dash down the hill. He dropped her onto the beach and grinned down at her, laughing. She stumbled to her feet and started to run clumsily up the beach. Her heart hammered wildly in her ears. When he tackled her, she turned as she fell, so that she was lying face-to-face with him on the sun-warmed sand. The length of his body against hers flooded her in sudden longing.

His arms went around her, pulling her tightly against him. He was no longer laughing; his face had taken on a yearning intensity that made her stomach flip-flop.

"Oh God, Allison!" His lips moved against her cheek, down the length of her neck, and then up again to cover her mouth. His kiss was deep and passionate, and she had no will to resist him. She was drowning in his arms.

His hand was in her hair, stroking, cradling her head. His legs moved against hers, hard and muscular. She melted into him, responding to his kiss with a passion of her own she'd never dreamed possible.

When he finally released her, she was weak with desire. He sat up slowly, groaned softly.

She got to her knees beside him, sagging against his arm. "What are we going to do, Brent?" she whispered.

He looked down at her. The expression in his eyes made her want to bury herself in his arms once again. He cupped her face between his hands, kissed her forehead.

"That's up to you, my love."

"I can't," she moaned.

If at that moment he had kissed her again, she believed she would had taken off Cabot's ring and thrown it in the sea. Instead he stood up, brushing the sand off his jeans.

"That's what I figured. I'd better go get those tables before Gran comes looking for me."

She watched him stride up the hill, over the crest of the ridge to the schoolhouse. She got slowly to her feet and walked to the water's edge, where she squatted, dipped her cupped hands into the water and lifted it to her face. She gasped as the icy water touched her cheeks. She scrubbed at them blindly with her fingers, hoping the grime would disappear. When she stood up again, her face felt stiff with salt.

She started back up the long hill to the schoolhouse, suddenly aware of her fatigue. Maybe Isabel had been right; perhaps she should have stayed in bed after all. After lunch she'd go back to Isabel's house and take a nap. The cleanup was almost over anyway, except for a few repairs to the windows and doors. It was important for her to get her act together before Monday morning.

As she came up over the crest of the hill, she saw that the tables had already been set up. People were gathered around them, holding paper plates and cups, laughing and talking. Her eyes searched automatically for Brent, and when they found him, her heart turned to ice. He was leaning against the side of his truck, his arm draped possessively around the shoulder of Emily Potter.

Chapter
Fourteen

ALLISON ATE LUNCH with Isabel, who chatted happily with her neighbor about the rising price of lobster, apparently oblivious to the fact that Allison had been carried down to the beach over Brent's broad shoulder. After lunch Isabel turned to her and patted her gently on the shoulder.

"You ought to go back to the house and give your ankle a rest, dear. I'll get Brent to give you a lift." She stood up quickly.

Allison glanced toward Brent's truck, where he was still talking with Emily. "Thanks, Isabel, but I'd really rather walk."

Isabel's gaze followed hers and she broke into a laugh. "Are you worried about interrupting Brent and Emily? Oh, my dear, Emily Potter's just somebody he's passing time with. She doesn't mean any more to him than a butterfly matters to a dog. A diversion he's better rid of, if you ask me." She turned and looked down at Allison. "I probably shouldn't be telling you this, you being engaged and all. But I'm afraid that the truth of the matter is that *you're* the one Brent's really got his eye on. I've never seen him light up for anyone the way he does around you." She saw Allison's look of dismay and patted her hand. "Now, don't let that worry you, dear. He'll survive; men do. In fact, it'll be good for him to realize for a change that he can't have any woman in the world he wants. Some things have come all too easy to that boy." She got to her feet. "Now, I'll go tell him to give you a ride, so you can get some well-deserved rest for that ankle."

She hurried off across the lawn. Allison watched her approach Brent, saw the way Emily edged away from Isabel, saw Brent's cocked head and quick nod. When Isabel turned and signaled, there was nothing for Allison to do but go. She trailed slowly across the lawn, her heart in her throat.

By the time she reached the truck, Brent already had the door open. She studiously avoided his eyes, accepted Isabel's motherly kiss, and climbed up into the passenger seat. A moment later Brent was beside her. The engine roared to life; he shoved the stick shift into reverse and turned to look over his shoulder, automatically sliding his arm along the back of the seat until his hand rested behind her head. The skin of her neck prickled and she quickly shifted away from his fingers.

"Tired?" His voice was cheerfully distant.

"Just a little. It was fun; I wish I had the energy to stay all day."

He nodded. "I know what you mean. When everybody gets together, it's a great feeling."

Allison glanced back at the schoolhouse lawn. People milled around in small clusters, laughing and talking. She smiled to herself. It was wonderful to be a part of a community like Harper's Island, if only temporarily. It was hard to contemplate leaving at the end of the summer. Perhaps she could persuade Cabot to buy a summer cottage on the island. Something inside her stiffened. It wouldn't be the same, living in one of the luxurious summer residences and meeting islanders only occasionally, when she went to pick up her mail. Not the same at all. She became suddenly conscious of the fact that Brent was watching her. He turned into the Cutler driveway and pulled to a stop in front of the back door. Allison reached quickly for the door handle.

"Allison." His voice stopped her. He turned and touched a lock of her hair, stroked the length of it with his fingers. She tried to control the shiver that was bleeding through her. "I'm sorry about what happened on the beach. It won't happen again. I'll make sure of it."

She gaped at him. His hand slid away from her hair. She lurched out the door of the truck, dropped to the ground, and walked to the door. As she opened the door, she heard the truck pull out of the driveway. She wanted to cry.

"Allison?" Martha's cheery voice sounded from the living room.

"Hi." Allison squared her sagging shoulders and went in to face her friend.

Martha was stretched out on the couch watching a black and white movie on television. She punched a button on the remote control and the screen flickered off. "I'm so glad you're back! I'm *dying* of boredom!" She pulled herself up, making room for Allison at the end of the couch. "Tell me everything! Did you have a good time?"

Allison nodded. Martha's questions reminded her of her mother's interrogations when she came home from a date. "But I'm beat. I haven't been so tired in ages. How are you feeling?"

"If I weren't so set on being ready to attend that dance on the fourth, I would have gone with you. But

I know I don't stand a chance of being able to dance if I don't stay off my feet for another week or so."

Allison grinned. She knew how hard it was for Martha to be sensible, especially when it came to missing a social event like the cleanup. She rubbed the tip of Martha's foot. "Everybody was there, but it was mostly hard work."

"You're kidding! No fooling around at *all*?"

Allison shrugged. "Not much. It wasn't exactly a party."

"Wasn't Brent there? I've seen him at work bees before. He usually grabs somebody and throws them in the water before it's over."

Allison wondered if her warm cheeks betrayed her; all she could think about was Brent scooping her up over his shoulder and running down the hill. "Yes. He was working on the roof."

"God, he's so cute! He gets sexier by the day. He's making me forget all about Raoul."

"Well, that should please your parents." Allison forced a yawn and stood up. "I'm going to go take a nap. I've got a lot to do to get ready for Monday morning."

"Allison, you can't really be *serious* about this play group! What am I going to do all by myself?"

"Maybe Brent can take you fishing." She watched Martha's face light up and felt her own spirits plunge. Why had she said that? "See you later." She went to the doorway, waved the tips of her fingers.

Martha flicked the television back on and was immediately absorbed in the flashing images.

As she climbed the stairs, Allison deliberately forced her mind to focus on the play group. By the time she reached her bed, she was eagerly looking forward to Monday morning. The group would give her a chance to feel useful, something she hadn't experienced in a long time. Perhaps it would be the last opportunity of its kind until she had her own children.

How she wished that Cabot hadn't postponed his visit! His presence would put everything into perspective once again. With Cabot on the island, she would no longer have any reason to feel envious of Martha's open attraction to Brent. Cabot would be there, protecting her . . . She frowned. Protecting her from what? What on earth was there to be afraid of on Harper's Island? There was no safer place in the world.

She closed her eyes and willed herself to sleep. But she couldn't escape the truth. It was there, even behind her closed eyelids. The threat to her on Harper's Island was very real. She wanted Cabot's presence because he was the only person in the world who could keep her at a safe distance from Brent.

Maybe if she called Cabot, he would change his mind. If she begged him to come, told him that she missed and needed him, how could he refuse? Surely his attorneys could handle the merger without him. Hadn't Martha told her that? And Martha knew about these things, knew about the world of high finance and big business. She decided to walk down to the store after her nap and place a call to Boston. Cabot would be thrilled to hear from her, and just the sound of his voice would turn her world rightside up again.

She yawned, and felt herself relax. Brent had promised her that there would be no more upsetting scenes between them. Soon Cabot would come, and her love for him would be rekindled. It would be like old times, and she would feel again the excitement of her coming marriage.

* * *

Allison woke just after three; the room was filled with a soft shimmering glow. She realized, as she stood at her window, brushing her hair, that it was the shine of the sun reflected off the water that gave the light its strange, rippling quality. She looked down at the harbor. The water was a bright, sapphire blue; a few boats rode on the gentle swells. She saw that Brent's boat was gone from its mooring. He must have gone out fishing when the cleanup was over.

She found her purse, checked to see that she had her telephone calling card, and went quietly downstairs. Martha had disappeared from the living room; she must have taken Isabel's advice and gone for a nap. Allison slipped out of the house and headed down the road to the general store.

She was quite certain that she would reach Cabot at his office. If the merger deal was as close to being closed as he claimed, he probably spent twelve to fifteen hours a day there. She had been to the office only twice; once, when Cabot wanted to stop and pick something up after a dinner date, and once to a Christmas party. It wasn't like any office she had ever seen; it looked more like an executive hotel suite than an office. It was located on the fifteenth floor of the Wilder Building, a tall, glass and steel structure in downtown Boston. Cabot had asked for his own office shortly after his eighteenth birthday, and his father had given it to him as a gift when he graduated from Groton. Carefully decorated with expensive antiques and custom-made furniture, it didn't strike Allison as a place where anyone would get much work done. Cabot, however, insisted that he couldn't work anywhere else. More than once, he told her, he had slept overnight on the fold-out bed because he wanted to be by the computer if someone should call from Tokyo or Zurich.

She went into the store, found the pay phone in the back corner and placed the call. The clerk at the counter, a large, blunt-faced woman, eyed her curiously as she waited for Cabot to pick up.

At last she heard the receiver lifted, but the voice on the line wasn't Cabot's. It was a woman's voice. "Wilder Enterprises. How may I help you?"

"Oh." Allison felt a flutter of consternation. "May I speak with Cabot, please?"

"Who's calling, please?"

"Allison. Allison Curtis."

There was a long pause. From the dead hum on the line, Allison realized she'd been put on hold. Finally she heard Cabot's voice.

"Allison?"

"Yes. Cabot, who was that woman?"

She heard the trace of a laugh in his voice. "That's Pia. You know, my father's secretary. Did you get my message?"

"I didn't know Pia worked for you, too."

"What did you want, darling?" She sensed impatience behind his meticulously chosen words.

"I was hoping you could come sooner. I really miss you a lot. I need you—" Something choked her. She felt a hot, burning sensation on the back of her neck. She turned to look over her shoulder, and her eyes widened in surprise. Brent was standing at the checkout counter, fishing bills out of his wallet.

"Didn't you get my message?" Cabot's voice was sharp.

Allison swiveled quickly back to face the phone. "Yes, I . . . I was just hoping that you could get away in the next day or two."

Cabot sighed. "I'll come as soon as I can, darling.

You don't seem to have any idea of how delicate this situation is." There was a short pause. "I'm afraid I'll have to hang up now. I've got a call on another line."

"Will you at least think about it, Cabot? I really miss you." Her voice was whiny; it sounded unpleasant even to her own ears.

"I miss you, too, darling. I'll get there as soon as I can." He hung up before she had a chance to tell him how much she loved him.

She slowly replaced the phone in its cradle. She saw that her hand was shaking, and tucked it quickly into the pocket of her jeans before she turned.

Brent was standing only a few feet away from her, holding a large paper bag in his left arm. "Are you okay?" His voice was low. "You look like you just received some bad news."

She forced herself to look straight at him and smile. "No, I'm fine. Honestly."

"I couldn't help overhearing, Allison. I'm sorry."

"Are you?" She felt a bud of anger open in the base of her chest. "I would have thought you'd be quite pleased that I couldn't get my fiancé to come earlier than expected. I would have thought that's just what you wanted." She felt her face reddening. "I suppose I shouldn't be surprised that you seem to know everything about my life! Or that you don't have any compunctions about eavesdropping on my telephone conversations!" Her breath was coming in short, shallow gasps. "Well, if you'll excuse me, I happen to have work to do." She started to move past him, but he shifted to the left, blocking her with his body. She was trapped between the phone console and a shelf of canned vegetables.

He stepped closer. "Allison, don't push me away. I just want to help."

Her eyes stung suddenly. "Thank you very much,

but I can handle things just fine on my own. Now, please let me go."

He moved then, and let her march stiffly past him, but she knew he was watching her all the way down the aisle and out the door. When she returned to Isabel's house, she ran up to her room, flung herself on her bed and buried her face in her pillow. She wept for a long time, and when Isabel called her for supper, three hours later, her face was still red and swollen from her tears.

Allison was grateful that neither Abel nor Isabel mentioned her looks. Martha gave her an occasional curious glance, but was too absorbed in detailing a blow-by-blow description of her hospital stay to ask any questions. By the time the meal was over, Allison felt better. Her overreaction was probably just hunger, she told herself, as she helped Isabel clear the table. That, and the strain of meeting so many wonderful new people in such a short time.

"Let me wash," she told Isabel. "You know where everything goes."

"All right, dear, if you're sure you're up to it."

Abel coughed and stood up. "Guess it's time for me to make myself scarce." He glanced at Martha. "You up for a game of gin rummy?"

"I'd love one." Martha giggled. She grabbed her crutches and pushed herself to her feet.

"Your turn's next," Isabel called after the vanishing pair. She laughed and turned to Allison. "One thing Abel hates, it's washing dishes. Makes him uncomfortable, just watching somebody else do it. Maybe it's because he has to do so much washing down on the boat."

"Well, I'm glad to help," Allison said. "I've always thought it was very satisfying." She turned on the tap in the sink, watched the water splash down onto the white porcelain.

"Yes, it is." Isabel opened a drawer and took out a clean dish towel. "I couldn't help noticing, dear, that you were upset earlier. Do you want to talk about it?"

Allison took a deep breath. She nodded as she squeezed dish soap into the water. "I ran into Brent at the store this afternoon, while I was making a phone call." She swallowed, plunged her hands into the soapy water. "He overheard my conversation with Cabot."

Isabel nodded thoughtfully. "Well, I doubt he was the only one who overheard, dear. Talking on that telephone is as good as broadcasting your business to the world. Anybody on Harper's who wants to have a private conversation doesn't do it by telephone." She touched Allison's arm. "How is your fiancé? Is there any chance he can get away sooner?"

Allison shook her head. "That's just it. I miss him so much, but he's awfully busy. He said he'd get here as soon as he could, but it could be another week or more."

"Well, don't you worry, dear. He loves you; that's the important thing. And who knows? You may get so involved with this play group that the time will fly by just like that." She snapped her fingers. "But what does Brent have to do with it? Did he say something to upset you again?"

Allison rinsed a glass and placed it in the drainer before she answered. "He said he was sorry. He wanted to help."

The older woman nodded. "I told you, that boy has the softest heart in the world."

"Well, it's just that . . . I don't know . . ." She bit her lip. "I don't want his pity or anything."

"Of course you don't, dear. I'm sure whatever he said wasn't meant that way. You have to understand, he just went through a rough time with a woman he thought he loved. He probably feels you have something in common."

"You're talking about Tracy Lawton, aren't you?" Allison turned to glance at Isabel. "What exactly happened between them, anyway? It all seems so mysterious."

Isabel clicked her tongue. "I don't think there's any mystery to it. She's a very beautiful, intelligent woman, and she came to the island at a time when there aren't many available women around. She and Brent started spending time together and things got serious." She picked up a glass and dried it carefully. "I think Brent honestly thought he was in love. Then something happened—I couldn't tell you what it was —and he stopped seeing her. Just like that. A couple of weeks later, she left the island."

Allison remembered Brent's mention of the incident at the ice pond. "Did you like her?"

Isabel frowned. "To tell you the truth, I didn't really get to know her. She didn't mingle with the islanders very much. She went around asking questions, but she mostly kept to herself—and to Brent." She shook her head slowly. "Abel didn't have any use for her at all. Said she was a snob and a sophisticate." She gave Allison a small smile. "Those are about the worst things Abel can say about a person."

"But Brent was really hurt, wasn't he?" Allison kept her eyes on the plate she was washing.

"Well, yes, he was hurt. But to tell you the truth, I think he was also relieved. Once he saw her for what she was, he was glad he hadn't gotten in any deeper." The older woman leaned against the counter, the dish towel tucked into the top of her apron. "He did a lot of soul searching after she left. On the whole, I think he's come out of it a lot more considerate and a sight more sensitive than he was. So it's all turned out for the best." She turned to pick up a plate. "Which is the way I am sure things will turn out for you, too, dear. So don't you worry." She gave Allison an encouraging smile. "How are the arrangements coming for Monday, by the way? The whole island is buzzing over this project. It's the best thing that's happened here in years."

Allison flushed. "I still have a lot of work to do, but I think I'll be ready."

"If there's anything I can do to help," Isabel said, "you be sure to let me know."

Allison spent the entire day Sunday immersed in preparations for the next morning. She didn't have time to think about either Brent or Cabot; she believed if she had encountered either one of them, she would have been too busy to be affected. Before she knew it, it was six o'clock Monday morning and her alarm clock was ringing.

She got out of bed eagerly, dressed quickly in comfortable corduroy jeans, a light green blouse, and a fair isle sweater, and went downstairs to the kitchen. She found Abel and Isabel cutting ripe strawberries into bowls of hot oatmeal.

"You look chipper," Abel observed. "Want a lift up the hill after breakfast? I'm headed that way."

"I'd love one. Don't move, Isabel." She raised her hand as Isabel started to rise, and went to serve herself from the pot on the stove. "I intend to carry my share of the load around here. No more waiting on me, either of you."

"Whatever you say, dear." Isabel smiled. "Are you all ready for this morning?"

"I think so. I'm so excited about this project. I hope the kids like it."

"They will dear, I'm sure." Isabel wiped her mouth with her napkin, coughed lightly. "I thought I'd go along with you, if you like. Kind of introduce you to the children as they come in."

"Oh, would you? That would be wonderful!" Allison beamed.

"I don't want to intrude. But I happen to be free this morning."

"Thanks so much, Isabel. How can I ever repay you?" Allison embraced the older woman happily.

"Just seeing you so happy is payment enough. Besides, I have the feeling there'll be plenty of opportunity to repay me many times over before you leave Harper's Island."

"*If* you do," put in Abel.

Allison blinked at him.

"Hush, you old coot!" Isabel scowled and slapped his hand. "What are you saying? The girl's engaged to be married!"

Abel grunted and stood up. "So were you before I came along, Isabel Murphy. When's that grandson of ours going to wake up and see what's in front of his eyes? What he needs is a good kick in the pants, and I have half a mind to give it to him!" He carried his empty bowl to the sink. "Maybe I'll go haul with him tomorrow, give him a piece of my mind."

"Abel Cutler, you'll do no such thing!" Isabel jumped up and took her own bowl to the sink. "It doesn't concern you. Besides, you're embarrassing Allison. What's she supposed to say, with you acting like some know-it-all matchmaker? You haven't even met her fiancé!"

184

Allison bent over her bowl of oatmeal, praying that her cheeks weren't as red as they felt.

"Don't pay any attention to him, Allison." Isabel splashed water into the sink. "There's no fool like an old fool, you know."

"Brent's the fool around here," Abel muttered. He went to the door and yanked it open. "I'll wait for you two girls in the truck. Take your time. It'll give me a chance to smoke my pipe." The door banged shut behind him.

"Allison, I'm sorry." Isabel came up behind Allison, placed gentle hands on her shoulders. "He really isn't himself today. He got this idea in his head that you'd be the perfect wife for Brent. So now he's riled at the boy for not sweeping you off your feet. It's been eating at him something wicked. Please don't take it to heart."

But Brent *has* swept me off my feet, Allison thought suddenly. She took a last spoonful of oatmeal, forced herself to swallow it. "It's okay," she murmured. "I just don't know what to say."

"Of course you don't, dear. There's nothing *to* say. Just don't pay any attention when he goes on like that. The dust'll settle pretty soon. Everything will work out. I'm sure of it."

Chapter Fifteen

I WISH / WERE that sure everything would work out, Allison wanted to say. She stood up and helped Isabel to clear the rest of the dishes from the table.

Isabel filled the sink with hot, soapy water. "I'll just rinse off these dishes, and then we can get going. I know you want to get there early."

"Yes." Allison watched Isabel scrub a crust of oatmeal from the rim of a bowl. "Were you really engaged to someone else when you met Abel?"

Isabel pursed her lips. "Oh, that. Well, sort of. You see, I knew Abel since we were kids. We both grew up on the island. But there were never any sparks between us then. After grade school everyone had to go to high school on the mainland. That's where I met Roy. He was a nice boy, kind of quiet and steady. You know, dependable. And I guess we talked a little about getting married after I finished school and all. It was nothing formal." She picked up the dishcloth and wiped a pool of water from the edge of the sink. "We dated on and off for quite a while. Then I got a job keeping house for some summer people here on the island. I was seventeen. Abel was supplying their lobsters. He had a little skiff and he used to go out hauling on weekends. That's when he started paying attention to me. He just swept me off my feet. I fell like a ton of bricks. He proposed on our first date and then just kept after me, until I thought I'd go crazy." She grinned over her shoulder at Allison. "The trouble was, I didn't want to hurt Roy. It took me quite a while to work it all out in my mind, until I realized it'd hurt Roy a lot more to marry him when I didn't love him than it would to break up with him." She rinsed a handful of spoons, stuck them into the drainer. "It worked out just fine, though. Roy got married only a couple of months after we did, to a real nice girl from down in Bangor. They've got grandchildren now, too. In fact, I heard the other day that Roy's granddaughter just made him a great-grandfather last week."

Allison smiled. The mental image of the young Isabel falling in love with the handsome, mischievous Abel was vivid and compelling. Something about the way Isabel told stories brought the people alive in a way she'd never experienced. Her own parents were quiet, sedate people, not given to storytelling.

"Well, enough about my life. We'd better get moving." Isabel dried her hands on a towel, plucked her sweater from the back of a chair. "Abel should be done with his pipe by now. And those kids will be arriving before we know it."

The sun had just risen over the long hill of pine trees as the truck rolled up to the schoolhouse. A tongue of sunlight touched the building, making the clean windows glow.

"A good omen," Isabel said as she climbed out of the truck behind Allison. She turned to Abel. "You can pick us up at noon. And don't go pestering Brent today. He has enough on his mind."

"He ought to," Abel growled.

Allison looked at the cloudless sky, the bright blue water stretching into infinity beyond the hill. She felt excited and eager to meet the children. It was going to be a wonderful day.

When the children began arriving shortly after eight, in little groups of two and three, Allison was ready for them. By half past nine there were twenty children playing tag on the schoolhouse lawn. Ricky Flory's bright red hair flashed in the sun. He was a strong child, Allison noted, both fast and fearless. Twice in the first hour she had to call him down off the roof. She understood what a handful he must be for his mother, but she admired his spirit. He was a cheerful boy, not sullen or sour. He made her think of a sunbeam more than anything else.

After lunch she gathered the children into a circle on the lawn and read to them. Then, while the youngest ones stretched out on blankets on the grass under Isabel's supervision, she led the older children in quiet games and some simple crafts. At two, when the last of the children headed off down the hill, Allison collapsed onto the porch steps.

"Tired?" Isabel sighed as she sat down beside her. "They can be a handful. Especially those Flory children. I don't know how their mother does it."

Allison grinned. "Actually, I really enjoy them. Especially Ricky. He's so full of life and enthusiasm. I hope I'll have a little boy like him someday. Always getting into mischief, but so happy all the time. It's like a breath of fresh air, just watching him."

"I know what you mean." Isabel smiled. "He reminds me of Brent—running all over the island, always up to something. But when he'd get in trouble, he always had this big grin that just melted your heart." She chuckled. "I never could scold that boy properly."

The whine of a truck engine broke the silence. "Ah, there's Abel." Isabel got to her feet, shading her eyes as the truck came up out of the trees. "Oh, it's not Abel. It's Brent."

A knot formed in the pit of Allison's stomach. She got hastily to her feet. "I think I'd like to walk home," she said to Isabel. "It's so nice out today."

Isabel gave her a quick glance. "Why, of course, dear. If you like."

The truck pulled up in front of the schoolhouse and Brent leaned out. He whistled softly. "Nothing I like better than seeing two pretty women on a summer day." He winked and grinned as Isabel marched toward the truck and aimed a swat at his arm.

"Behave yourself! Anyone would think you were brought up in a barnyard the way you act sometimes!" Her tone was playfully angry, and Brent withdrew into the truck with a look of mock injury. Isabel went around to the passenger door, pulled it open and climbed in.

"Aren't you coming?" Brent glanced expectantly at Allison.

"No." She shook her head and made herself smile. "I want to walk. It's such a beautiful day. I can't resist the temptation."

His smile widened. "I know exactly what you mean." For a moment his gaze was so intense that Allison instinctively lowered her eyelashes.

"Well, see you around." Brent waved and gunned the engine. A moment later the truck was roaring back down the road, kicking up a thin golden trail of dust in its wake.

Allison started down the hill toward the Cutler house, relishing the touch of the warm sun on her back, the cries of the gulls that swung above her head. Tired as she was, she was already looking forward to the next day. She was particularly excited about working with Ricky. He was a natural leader; with a little guidance and encouragement, he would be a credit to the island.

She felt so at home on Harper's Island; it was hard to believe she'd only arrived a couple of weeks ago. The thought of leaving at the end of the summer was depressing. She pushed it away; she was too tired to think of such things now. She'd have to take things one day at a time, the way the children did. As if to confirm her thought, she heard Isabel's reassuring voice in the back of her mind: Things will work out, dear. They always do.

The week flew by. Allison was up with the sun every morning, eager for the challenge of the day ahead. When she returned to Isabel's house early in the afternoon, she always found Martha in a good mood, waiting to hear the adventures of her day. She was grateful for her friend's listening ear, but it puzzled her that Martha wasn't doing more complaining about her confined state. It wasn't like her friend to endure such restrictions in silence.

On Friday morning Allison discovered the reason for her friend's contentment. The children had all left just after ten to go the mainland where a children's carnival was running for the weekend. Matt Flory and Newt Emory had offered their lobster boats for transportation, and four high school girls had volunteered to chaperone, along with several of the mothers. Although she had originally planned to go, Allison decided against it at the last moment, when she realized that there were almost as many chaperones as children, and a sudden wave of fatigue had reminded her that she needed rest more than more excitement. She left the school at eleven and walked back to the Cutlers'. When she came down the road and rounded the curve above the house, she saw Brent's truck parked in the driveway. She instantly understood why Martha had been so cheerful during her convalescence. Brent had been visiting her daily.

She hesitated at the end of the driveway. The fact that she hadn't seen Brent in four days had slowed the emotional roller coaster she'd been on since her arrival on Harper's Island. She didn't want to see him now. Maybe she could sneak in the back door and up the stairs without either Martha or Brent knowing she was in the house.

She moved quietly to the back door and opened it. As she'd expected, Brent's low voice came from the living room. She heard Martha's answering giggle and straightened her shoulders resolutely. She wasn't going to let him get to her this time. The truth was unmistakable: Brent was a man who made time with any pretty woman available. Just because he was handsome and charming, Allison thought, didn't mean she had to be one of them.

"You *are* wicked!" She heard Martha's laughing voice, imagined the two of them locked together on one end of the couch. Her heart pounding, she hurried across the kitchen to the stairs. On the first step she stumbled and, arms flailing, backed into the table and sent one of the chairs crashing to the floor.

"Damn!" She bent quickly to right the chair, then heard Brent's footsteps crossing the living room. Even though her back was to the door, she knew the instant he entered the kitchen. She gritted her teeth in rage and frustration. The last thing on earth she wanted was to face him.

"Allison." There was a trace of laughter in his voice. "Are you okay?"

She straightened and forced herself to look at him. "I'm fine. I'm sorry if I bothered you."

"No bother." He came across the room toward her. He was smiling. "I have good news. Or rather, Martha does."

"Good news?" Her heart shriveled. Were they about to announce their engagement?

His grin widened. "Cabot's here."

"Cabot? Here?"

"Well, not *here* exactly. He's settling into the guest house at the Hollingsworth place. I'll take you up there. Right now, if you want."

"Take me there?" She licked her suddenly parched lips. She felt dizzy, confused.

"Are you sure you're okay?" He frowned, extended a steadying hand toward her.

She swallowed. "I'm fine. Just a little tired."

"Well, I'll take you there after you've had a chance to rest, then. Whenever."

"I don't—" She stopped, blinked up at him. She had almost said she didn't want to go! What was happening to her lately? The only time she was happy was when she was with a bunch of little kids!

He was watching her intently. She had the uncanny sensation that his blue eyes were penetrating her brain. She turned and started up the stairs. Her back stiffened as she heard him follow her, felt his fingers brush her arm.

"You're scared, aren't you? You don't really want to face him." Was there the trace of a taunt in his voice, or was his tone a measure of concern?

"No, you're wrong!" She whirled on him. "I'd love a ride. I'm going to get freshened up right now. I'll be ready in five minutes."

She ran up the stairs before he could see the consternation in her eyes.

* * *

When Allison came into the kitchen fifteen minutes later, dressed in a sleeveless blue sweater and a soft, denim skirt, Brent was leaning against the door frame, talking with Martha. "I'm ready." Allison touched a lock of hair that had escaped the ministrations of her brush. Her hair was piled high on her head, knotted into a bun, the way Cabot liked it. He couldn't tolerate anything wild-looking or unkempt. Well, she'd done the best she could. Not bad for spur-of-the-moment elegance, especially when she was dog-tired.

Brent turned and gave her an appreciative grin. "Not bad. But your hair looks much better down."

"I didn't put it up for *you*."

"No, indeed. And I'm sure it's perfect for Cabot."

Martha appeared beside him, leaning on her crutches. "Have a great time, Allison. Give him a kiss for me."

"Sure." Allison gave her friend a weak smile.

Brent crossed the room to her and placed his hand lightly on her back. "We'd better get going." He steered her toward the back door. Her skin tingled under his hand.

"Are you coming back here, Brent?" Martha asked.

He nodded. "You bet. Isabel's got a big shindig planned for tonight to welcome Cabot to the island."

"What fun!" Martha grinned. "I can't wait!"

Allison groaned inwardly. She dreaded the thought of being in the same room with both Cabot and Brent.

Outside, Brent insisted on helping her into his truck. "Don't want to mess up those fancy duds." He grinned, climbed into the driver's seat and started the engine. A moment later his fingers touched her neck, stroking the sensitive curve of bare skin.

"Stop that!" She glared at him and jerked her head away.

"Sorry. I couldn't resist. I'm beginning to understand why Cabot likes your hair up."

Allison sighed. "Just take me to the guest house, please."

"Anything you say, love. How's the play group going?" He seemed lighthearted and congenial. Apparently his gesture hadn't meant anything; it was probably just the mischievous boy in him coming to the surface. She wondered if he was oblivious to the fact she was trembling.

"Fine," she said, trying to smile. "The kids are great."

"Could you use any help?"

She glanced at him warily. "I'm managing."

"That's not what I asked."

"If you mean, can you come and watch me sweat, the answer is no." She thought her words would silence him, but he seemed undaunted.

"I thought maybe I'd come around some afternoon, take them on a hike along the north cliff. It's a little tricky up there. You wouldn't want to do it alone."

"I had no intention of doing it at all."

"Prickly today, aren't we?"

"I've got a lot on my mind," she snapped, and turned away from him to look out at the pine trees flashing past the truck.

"I'll bet you do," he said softly. Suddenly he slowed the truck, turned onto a narrow dirt side road and pulled to a stop.

"What are you doing?" There was no house in sight. "Where are we?"

He had stopped smiling. He was watching her closely. "Look," he said quietly, "how much longer are we going to keep up this charade?" He slid across the seat to her, put his arms around her. Little shivers of joy ran down her spine. "Allison, you could resolve this thing right now. Get it over with today."

"Resolve what? Get what over with?" Her mind told her to open the truck door and get out, to put as much distance as possible between herself and Brent Connors. But her body seemed paralyzed, powerless.

He cupped her chin in his hand, turned her head gently to face him. "Give him back the ring, Allison. First thing."

She had to lower her eyes, retreat from his penetrating gaze, before she could speak. "You don't understand," she murmured. "You don't know Cabot."

"You're just making it harder on yourself. It doesn't have to be this difficult. We don't have to play these games, love."

She tried to turn her head away, but the pressure of his hand held her immobile. "Let me go," she said. "Please, Brent."

He closed his eyes for a minute. A huge sigh came from him. He released her and slid back behind the wheel. "Well, you can't say I didn't try." He backed up, turned the truck onto the larger road again. "I want you to know where I stand, Allison. But I'm not trying to make your life miserable."

"I know where you stand," she said tightly. "That's been pretty clear from the first day."

"Good," he said cheerfully. "One thing I like is being clear."

A few moments later they pulled up in front of a

small, gray Cape tucked behind two ancient pines on the hill below the Hollingsworth cottage.

"This is it." He opened the door and jumped down, but Allison managed to get out before he could come around to her side.

She forced herself to smile at him. "Thanks for the ride."

Brent leaned against the truck, watching, as Allison walked up the narrow brick path to the front door. She felt his eyes on her back, like two hot coals burning through her.

The door opened before she reached it, and there was Cabot, tall and handsome in a polo shirt and tweed blazer and casual, camel-colored slacks. He lifted his hand in a small wave to Brent, and opened his arms to Allison.

She ran into his embrace, aware with every step that Brent was still observing her. She smiled. This would prove to him that she really loved Cabot. A woman didn't run to greet a man she didn't love. Cabot gathered her into his arms, but when she raised her face to his, he didn't kiss her, simply smiled down at her fondly. His lips were cold and hard, unmoving. Allison felt an icy claw slice into her chest. He took her wrists and gently lowered her arms.

"How nice you look, darling." His smile looked etched onto his handsome face.

"I missed you, Cabot!" She pleaded with her eyes for him to kiss her, but he was wooden, unreachable. She stood with her arms hanging at her sides while Cabot crossed the lawn to the truck to shake Brent's hand.

"Thanks so much for bringing her here. I hope I can return the favor sometime."

She saw Brent's grin and cringed inwardly.

"I hope so, too." Brent nodded to Allison and climbed back into his truck. "I'll be back to pick you both up for dinner at six o'clock sharp. Isabel's orders."

The truck left with a roar, and Allison found herself following it with her eyes all the way down the hill.

Cabot walked slowly back to her. "How are you feeling, darling? When I received the news about your ankle, I was quite concerned." He took her hands. "It was difficult not being able to come immediately."

"My ankle's fine." She waited while he opened the door for her, despite her instinctive urge to yank it open and stalk into the house. "How did the merger go?"

"Fine, fine." He followed her inside. "It was actually more of a takeover. We had the other company right where we wanted them. They couldn't do a thing." He chuckled. "You should have seen them squirm."

She pushed away a little ripple of revulsion. "I'm glad things worked out so well for you." She smiled up at him. "And I'm even more glad you came."

He smiled and embraced her again. She leaned against him, tried to melt into his arms; her anger slowly ebbed away. He kissed her carefully, his lips dry against hers.

"There," he said, smiling down at her. "I've been waiting for two whole weeks to do that."

She had no heart to tell him that his kiss wasn't really a kiss at all. How could Cabot's embraces have satisfied her only a short time ago? She felt a flash of anger. It was Brent's fault. His kisses had spoiled her. Would she spend her whole married life with Cabot hungering for a passionate kiss?

No, other things would take the place of passion. She would find plenty to keep her busy and happy in Cabot Wilder's world of wealth and privilege.

"Come, darling." Cabot took her hand and led her into the small living room, pulled her down beside him into the deeply upholstered couch. "We have so much to talk about. Mother has a million plans for the wedding and she's unbelievably frustrated that you aren't in Boston this summer so she can fill you in. Worse yet, you're incommunicado on this godforsaken island! She made me promise to bring you back as soon as possible."

Allison frowned. "But I can't go back! I've started a play group for the children."

"Ah yes, Brent told me all about it when he drove me up here from the ferry. Apparently you're the talk of the island." He sandwiched her hand between his. "But surely someone else can run around after the little ones for the rest of the summer. You have more important things to do."

"There's nothing more important than taking care of children! I love children!"

He leaned his head against the back of the couch, chuckling softly. "Children will always be around, darling. You have only one wedding in your lifetime."

She stood up. "I'm really tired. Is there some place I can lie down for a little while?"

He frowned up at her. "It's not like you to run off in the middle of a conversation, Allison."

"I'm not running off. I'm just tired."

He sighed. "There's a bed upstairs, if you can call it that." He twisted his face into a grimace. "I can't believe the Hollingsworths would put their guests up in a place so *primitive*."

Allison shrugged. "I think it's very comfortable."

He smiled and settled deeper into the couch. "I can see you still have a great deal to learn, Allison. Luckily, my mother has decided to spend considerable time visiting us after we're married. She'll be able to teach you a great deal."

Allison turned and left the room, resenting his arrogance and disdain. What if she told him the real reason for wanting a rest? That she needed strength for the evening ahead, when she'd be seated at the same table with Brent Connors? She climbed the stairs and found the simple bedroom at the top. It reminded her of her room in Isabel's house; a narrow cot, a chair, a plain wooden bureau. She lowered herself onto the bed, kicked off her shoes, lay back and fell immediately asleep, exhausted by the emotional chaos of her day.

Chapter Sixteen

ALLISON WOKE from a troubling dream. In it, Isabel was scolding her for having forgotten some ingredient in a cake.

"Don't you understand?" she'd said. "If you leave out the lovage, there won't be a cake. Just a pile of dried-up batter."

Allison sat up and glanced at her watch. It was six-fifteen. Why hadn't Cabot woken her?

She put on her shoes, reached to smooth her rumpled hair. Several tendrils had come loose from the confining combs, but she had no time to fix it now. Brent had said he would pick them up at six o'clock.

She went to the window, peered out. Brent's truck was parked in the driveway, but there was no sign of either him or Cabot. The house was totally silent.

She ran down the stairs, ducked into the empty living room, caught a glimpse of herself in the hall mirror as she went through into the kitchen. She scowled in disgust. She might just as well wear her hair down. It would look better than this rumpled, frowsy mess on top of her head. She yanked the combs savagely out of her hair and stuck them into the pocket of her skirt.

She heard the sound of male voices outside, and

followed them quickly. She saw the two men before they saw her. Brent was leaning against a huge maple, smiling, while Cabot strutted around like a peacock, boasting about his latest polo game. She pressed her hands together at her waist.

"Hi!" she called, forcing her voice to register a cheeriness she didn't feel.

Brent and Cabot both turned toward her at the same moment. But it was Brent who crossed the lawn to her first.

"Well, Sleeping Beauty! I wish Cabot had let me come up and kiss you awake like the prince that I am." His right cheek dimpled. "It's his fault if Gran's got her dander up."

"What happened to your hair?" Cabot came toward her, frowning.

"I took it down. It was a mess."

"It *is* a mess. Take a few minutes and fix it, darling. Please."

Brent turned to look at him. Allison could see the flint in his eyes as he spoke.

"Her hair looks fine to me."

Cabot didn't return his glance. "Allison, we're going to *dinner*. You don't want to look like a hillbilly."

A month ago she would have done exactly as he wished; she had been brought up to please the man in her life. But the set of Brent's shoulders, his look of disgust, fired her own anger. She lifted her chin.

"I happen to like it this way, Cabot. I've been wearing it down most of the summer."

Cabot took her arm and pulled her around the corner of the house, away from Brent's penetrating gaze. He leaned down so that he could speak directly into her ear.

"You're embarrassing me, Allison. And making yourself appear to be some sort of hoyden."

"Hoyden?" She fought back a grin. The word was so old it creaked.

Brent appeared at the corner of the house.

"Sorry to break this up, guys, but we really have to get going. Isabel's going to be pulling out her hair. And everyone else's, too."

Allison jerked her arm from Cabot's grasp and marched over to the truck. She opened the passenger door and climbed in, sliding over so that she was sitting in the middle. Brent grinned as he climbed in beside her, and she had to look away from the impish twinkle in his eyes. When Cabot got in, he didn't look at her and she was careful not to touch him.

Brent did all the talking on the way to the Cutler house, chatting amiably about the weather and the price of lobsters. Allison sat, staring down at her hands, intensely aware of the nearness of Brent's thigh to hers. Once, when he was shifting, his hand casually brushed her knee, and she gave Cabot a startled glance, wondering if he'd noticed. But he was staring stonily out at the trees, apparently oblivious to her.

When they pulled into the Cutler driveway, Cabot got out immediately and stood waiting for Allison to join him. For a moment she was tempted to slide out on the driver's side, just to let him know that she was still angry with his arrogant, superior attitude, but one glance at the gleeful look on Brent's face changed her mind. The last thing Brent needed was any encouragement. He was undoubtedly already blowing their little lover's quarrel all out of proportion.

She climbed out the passenger door, closed it behind her, slipped her arm through Cabot's. "I'm sorry, darling," she said softly. "I'll go fix my hair as soon as we get inside."

He acknowledged her apology with a quick nod, and together they followed Brent into Isabel's bright kitchen.

"So *you're* Cabot Wilder!" Abel was seated in his usual chair at the table as he pointed his empty pipe accusingly at Cabot. "You got yourself quite a little prize there." He nodded at Allison. "Be sure you take real good care of her." He got to his feet and came toward them, his hand extended to shake Cabot's. "My wife'll be right down. She's busy getting herself all dolled up." His eyes twinkled. "She loves company, you know."

Allison ran quickly up the stairs to her bedroom and pulled a brush through her hair, coiled it quickly in a tight bun, and fastened it firmly to her head. When she descended to the kitchen, she found Isabel bending over a large pot on the stove. The men had gone into the living room; she could hear their low, resonant voices and Martha's crows of delight from beyond the doorway.

"It's so good of you to have us all to dinner," Allison said brightly. "What can I do to help?"

Isabel smiled and handed her the wooden spoon she was holding. "You stir this while I go meet your young man." She disappeared through the doorway, and Allison plunged her spoon into the pot and stirred the thick soup energetically.

She didn't realize that Brent had come into the kitchen until he was standing directly behind her.

"Allison." He took her left hand, held it up to the light.

A shudder ran the length of her arm.

"I see you still have the ring," he said.

She pulled her hand away. She wondered if he had detected the trembling in the tips of her fingers. "Of course I still have the ring. *I* never said anything about giving it back. That was *your* idea."

"I've never been so sure I was right in my life."

She felt his breath on her hair. Gentle, warm. For a giddy moment she wanted to lean back against him, feel his arms go around her. She straightened her back, set her teeth together.

"I'm glad you know so much about what's good for me, Brent, because *I* certainly don't most of the time."

He touched her neck lightly with his fingers, and a little thrill of pleasure danced down her back. His hands stroked her shoulders, and then he was rubbing her shoulder blades gently with his thumbs.

His voice was very soft. "I'd never do anything to hurt you, Allison. Ever. I know you don't want to hear what I'm saying. But, in time, you'll understand that I'm right about this. I just hope it won't be too late."

Tears started into her eyes as she responded to his voice, to the gentle caressing tone, the deep concern. Was Brent right? Would she be making a huge mistake if she went ahead and married Cabot? And what would her life be like if she broke the engagement? Suddenly all her dreams of financial security would vanish. Her family and friends would be shocked, stunned. She could just imagine the disappointment in her parents' eyes when she called to tell them she wasn't going to be marrying Cabot Wilder after all. Her mother would never forgive her for throwing such an opportunity away. She took a deep breath, put the spoon down on the stove and turned to face Brent.

"I thought you promised to leave me alone."

His face went suddenly pale, as if he was seeing something deeply disturbing. "You're right," he said quietly. His arms dangled at his sides. "I did promise to leave you alone. I'm just not sure I can keep my promise. It seems to be even harder than I expected."

"That's because you haven't even tried! Not once since I got here!" she said hoarsely. "You are the most difficult, upsetting man I've ever met in my life!" Her eyes were blinded with tears as she ran for the privacy of her room. Behind her she heard Isabel come into the kitchen and speak quietly to Brent.

Allison slammed the door behind her and threw herself down on the narrow bed to bury her face in the pillow. The soft foam muffled her sobs, but nothing could muffle the intense shame she felt. How could she have lost control that way? Her angry words had certainly been overheard by everyone in the living room. Including Cabot. What must he think of her now? His fears of her becoming a "hoyden," as he called it, must have all been confirmed. Perhaps he would no longer think she was refined enough to be his wife. She smiled grimly. How ironic it would be if he broke the engagement.

There was a light knock on her door. Allison sat up, wiping her wet face with the palms of her hands.

"Just a minute." She found a tissue in the clutter of things on her bedside table, blew her nose, and got up to open the door.

It was Isabel, holding a tray of steaming food and smiling fondly at her.

"I thought you might like to have your supper up here tonight." She bustled into the room, set the tray on top of the bureau. "It's nothing fancy—just chicken curry stew and biscuits—but it'll make you feel much better. You're welcome to join us, of course, but I thought you might not be up to facing everybody just now."

"Thanks." Allison sat back down on the bed, lowered her face into her hands. "I'm terribly sorry. I'm afraid I've spoiled all your plans."

"Nonsense! It'd take more than a few angry words to spoil an evening at the Cutler house." Isabel sat next to Allison and slid an arm around her sagging shoulders. "You've had a difficult day, dear. It's never easy for couples to be reunited. Don't be too hard on yourself."

Allison felt the tears well again, tried to shake them away.

"Maybe it would help if you talked a little bit, dear. I'm always willing to listen."

"Oh Isabel!" Allison couldn't hold back the tears any longer; she buried her face in the older woman's shoulder.

"There, there." Isabel patted her back with a gentle hand. "I understand. Brent can be a real trial at times. He's just like his grandfather—stubborn and opinionated."

"It's not that . . ." Sobs drowned Allison's words. She sniffed, swallowed. "It's . . . He wants me to break up with Cabot."

"Oh, my dear! No *wonder* you're so upset!" She stroked Allison's back. "I don't blame you for crying."

Gradually Allison felt her sobs subside. She straightened to wipe her face and look at Isabel. "It's been so hard! Brent's been after me to break the engagement ever since I came here. He claims I don't really love Cabot." She swallowed a hard knot, went on. "I know Cabot and I aren't a passionate couple. But things are different in Cabot's world. There are all these proprieties and important considerations that Brent just doesn't understand. . . ."

"Of course." Isabel smiled. "But maybe there's one important thing *you* don't understand, dear."

"What's that?"

"Brent isn't beleaguering you out of spite or arrogance. He's a boy who's always spoken what's on his mind, but he's not vicious." She smiled and tilted her head to one side. "To be perfectly honest, I think he's fallen head over heels in love with you."

Allison's breath caught in her throat. She shook her head slowly. "I don't think so, Isabel. He's never said anything like that."

"Oh, my dear, he wouldn't! It's a code of honor around here. I guess we're a little old-fashioned on Harper's, a *lot* old-fashioned, some would say. Brent isn't going to tell you he loves you while you're engaged to somebody else. But to me it's as clear as the sun in the sky. It's written all over his face every time he looks at you. I'm surprised you haven't noticed it yourself." She beamed happily. "I understand why you're not interested, under the circumstances. But you have to forgive a man for being a little insistent when he's so love-struck."

"But what about Tracy Lawton?"

Isabel's expression sobered. "If it were anybody else but Brent, I might think he was just on the rebound. But Brent's a man who's scrupulously honest with himself. If there was even a shred of possibility in his mind that he still loved Tracy, he would never even have looked at you. Believe me. The man is the most straightforward person on God's green earth. He's not the kind who can fall in love with more than one woman at a time."

"Well, he seems to be seeing a lot of Emily Potter."

"Emily? Oh, pooh! She hasn't got the brains she was born with. She's about as interesting to him as a stick. Brent's not going to get himself tied down with somebody like that. If he's paying attention to her, it's for your benefit."

"*My* benefit?"

Isabel nodded. "Maybe he's hoping to coax a little jealousy out of you. He's not used to women who keep him at arm's length. He's had more problems the other way—women throwing themselves at his feet. It's one of the hazards of being a handsome man."

"Some hazard. Most men would kill for it." Allison blinked away the last of her tears.

Isabel smiled and stood up. "Don't let it worry you, dear. Brent may be persistent and a little trying at times, but there's a line he won't step across." She reached down to pat Allison's hand. "And I'll have a little talk with him. I can't promise you anything, because he's as stubborn as they come, but if I explain how upsetting this is to you, maybe he'll leave you alone."

Allison took a short, sharp breath. "I appreciate it."

"Don't worry, dear. Things will work out. Enjoy your meal."

Isabel left before Allison could work out the confused emotions that tumbled through her. There was a part of her, she realized suddenly, that didn't want Brent to leave her alone. And there was another part that sought the peace that only his distance could bring her.

She went to the bureau and lifted the tray down, carried it to the little ladder-backed chair. As she spooned the thick, spicy stew into her mouth, she could hear Brent's laughter from the kitchen. Her stomach turned over. She fought the sudden desire to run down the stairs and throw herself into his arms.

* * *

For the next ten days Allison didn't see Brent at all. It was as if he had completely vanished from the island. She spent the weekend showing Cabot around the island and listening to him and Martha talk about the exciting social world of upper-crust Boston. She went back to the schoolhouse on Monday, while Cabot buried himself in his papers and stock sheets.

Her days quickly developed an enjoyable, predictable rhythm. She threw herself wholeheartedly into supervising the children. She grew increasingly fond of Ricky Flory. His mischievous intelligence drew her to him; she liked his spunk and creativity. She remembered what Isabel had told her about how much he resembled Brent as a small boy. As she watched him lead the other children through the complicated patterns of an old island chanting game, she was struck by the maternal feelings that rose in her. More than once she imagined herself as a mother on Harper's Island, sitting on the front porch of her little cottage, watching her children playing in the sunshine of a summer's afternoon. The bright green schoolhouse lawn that sloped down to the sea was an idyllic setting of great peace and beauty. She enjoyed the children's sweaty hugs as they left to go home at two, and she felt a kind of bereft sadness creep through her as she walked along the wooded path to the guest house to meet Cabot for a late lunch.

He always greeted her warmly at the door, pulling her into his arms and kissing her tenderly. While she prepared their meal in the tiny kitchen, he regaled her with the rigors of price wars and company mergers. She had no desire to study stock reports, and was relieved when he didn't offer them for her perusal. She savored the mild domesticity of the after-noons, eating in the dining room at the small wooden table by the window, looking out to sea and chatting casually with Cabot. On good days sail-boats regularly passed the island. Cabot pointed them out to her, elaborating on the design and sea-worthiness of particular boats. He was planning to buy her a fifty-foot yacht, he told her. On summer weekends they could cruise up the coast all the way to Prince Edward Island. She noted ironically that, in contrast to the pleasure boats, the fishing boats were out in all weather.

It rained on the last day of June. Sitting by the window in the guest house kitchen while Cabot paced up and down, complaining about the cramped quarters of the cottage, Allison saw the *Blue Lady* go by. She thought she could make out a figure in a yellow slicker standing in the shelter of the pilot-house. Something tightened in her throat and she couldn't swallow the crabmeat sandwich she'd been chewing. She hadn't seen Brent in almost two weeks. She took a sip of white wine. The comfortable famil-iarity of her pleasant afternoon with Cabot suddenly struck her as constricted and lifeless. She pushed the thought away, took another sip of wine, and gave Cabot her most brilliant smile.

Cabot smiled back. "You look so lovely today, dar-ling. But when *are* you going to have your hair cut?"

She reached to stroke a strand off her forehead. The length of her hair seemed to be the only point of contention between them. She wondered suddenly if her long hair was responsible for Cabot's lack of pas-sion. If she were to cut it, would he become sud-denly sensuous and masterful? The thought excited her. If she could only feel the same thrill in Cabot's arms that she had in Brent's, she would be the happiest woman alive.

She leaned toward him across the table. "I was keeping it as a surprise. But if you must know, I'm cutting it this afternoon."

She fought tears later, as she hacked off her long curls alone in the cottage's tiny upstairs bathroom. But she resisted the temptation to save even one long tendril. After she washed and dried her hair with Cabot's expensive blow-dryer, she decided that she didn't look so bad after all. Her hair hung to her shoulders, gently swaying as she moved. She sighed as she ran a brush through it one more time. It was merely something she had to do as a woman marrying into the Wilder fortune. The first of many things.

She went downstairs and found Cabot sitting in the living room, reading. He rose when she entered the room and came toward her, his arms open, a huge smile lighting his face. "That's so much better, darling! As soon as we get back to Boston, we'll have André trim it. You'll look gorgeous on our wedding day!"

For a moment she thought he was going to take her in his arms and kiss her passionately. Instead he grasped her hand and suggested they go out for an afternoon walk.

The wind in her short hair felt strange. She no longer had the sensation of flowing beauty all around her body. She struggled once again against the tears that threatened to overwhelm her, and grasped Cabot's arm tightly as they walked along the path to Lookout Point.

She thought suddenly of Brent, of the many times he'd complimented her on the length of her hair. What would he say when he saw she had cut it? She lifted her chin resolutely. It didn't make any difference what Brent said. She was going to be Cabot's wife. He was the man she had to please. She raised her hand to shield her eyes from the setting sun. Maybe it was a good thing she had cut it. Her short hair would send a clear message that Brent was wrong about her lack of love for Cabot. It would show him that his opinion didn't matter to her in the least.

Cabot was full of wedding plans the next day, excited about the lengthy guest list he'd received in the mail from his mother, pleased with the Regency Hotel accommodations for the reception. He'd already chartered a private yacht for their honeymoon trip to Greece, and he spent hours detailing the luxuries that would be at their disposal and the beautiful sights they would see on their trip. Allison smiled, trying to imagine what it would really be like to be catapulted into his world of elegance and power. Her hand went frequently to her hair, as if in search of a long strand, but she felt less bereft, more relaxed about its length, especially since both Isabel and Martha had complimented her on the new style.

That evening, she and Cabot ate dinner at the Cutler house and talked with Martha, who had recently had her cast removed. She was starting to hobble around without her crutches, and chattered excitedly about her plans.

"I'm definitely going to be ready by the fourth," she boasted happily. "Don't forget our double date!" She looked meaningfully at Allison.

Allison gave her a doubtful look. "The fourth is only three days away. Are you sure you'll be ready to *dance* by then?"

Cabot laughed. "You don't know Martha very well if you think anything can keep her from dancing."

"That's right!" Martha lurched toward the living room doorway and did a wobbly spin. "See, I've been practicing every day! The doctor said it was amazing that I'd recovered so fast!"

Allison couldn't help grinning back at her friend. She was looking forward to the July Fourth Social herself. The only cloud on the horizon was that Martha's determination to double date meant she would have to see Brent. She hoped that Isabel had had her little talk with him.

Isabel was filled with plans of her own, for the traditional Fourth of July Social was one of the most important events of the year on Harper's Island, and she was the president of the Ladies' Auxiliary, which supplied all the refreshments. She filled in Allison and Martha while they were doing the dishes, after supper.

"First, there's the parade. It's not much, but it's all we've got on Harper's Island. Then the auction. Joe Barnes is a great auctioneer; I really think he missed his calling digging clams for a living. Of course, in the evening there's the chicken pie supper. Everybody comes, even the littlest ones, and they all have a wonderful time. I can promise you the best food in the state of Maine will be eaten that night—maybe in the whole of New England. Then there's fireworks. After that's the best part—the dance out at John Bailey's barn. We've got a real live band coming from Bar Harbor this year. Everybody comes to the dance, too, and stays up until all hours."

"It sounds wonderful!" Martha crowed, doing a shaky waltz across the kitchen floor. "Look, I can really dance! So much for Brent's doubting my ability to get back on my feet! Now he *has* to escort me! I can hardly wait. I intend to dance with every eligible man there!"

Isabel laughed. "Well, I'm sure you will. Probably a number of the ineligible ones, too. It's a real community event." She turned to Allison. "You'll have to share Cabot, I'm afraid. It's not the kind of event where you just dance with one person all night, even if you *are* engaged to be married."

Martha gave her an enthusiastic glance. "That's right, Allison. And with Cabot's dancing ability, he's going to be very popular."

Allison smiled. "Okay, I'll share him. Just this once."

"You don't have a choice." Martha giggled. "He's already promised me a tango."

Chapter
Seventeen

THE FOURTH OF JULY DAWNED clear and warm; a gentle sea breeze lifted the long needles of the white pine tree outside Allison's window as she woke to the sound of Martha's knock.

"Come on, lazybones," Martha ordered, sailing into the room, her long arms dancing in the sunlit air. "We've got to get ready for tonight."

Allison rolled over and sat up in bed. "Get ready?"

"Of course! We have to figure out our outfits and hairstyles. This is the event of the summer. We have to look *gorgeous*!"

Allison smiled wryly. "I was thinking of wearing my denim skirt."

"Don't you dare, Allison Curtis! We're going to knock them off their feet when we go to that dance! I'm going to wear my blue paisley chamois, and you . . ." She cocked her head and squinted at Allison. "I think you should wear that pink thing, with the lace. You know, the one you wore to the engagement party."

"That's much too formal, I'm sure." Allison thought of the frothy pink dress that hung in her closet, and wondered why she'd brought it to the island in the first place. It certainly wasn't appropriate here. It was cut very low in front, accentuating her full breasts, and it sheathed her hips tightly under the double skirt of lace that spilled from her waist.

"Cabot loves it. He told me you look very sexy in it."

"Cabot said I looked *sexy*?"

Martha shrugged. "Well, maybe those weren't his exact words, but that was the general idea."

"I'll bet." He'd probably said something like, Doesn't Allison look becoming? and Martha had, as usual, exaggerated his meaning.

"Oh, please wear it, Allison!"

"You just want me to wear it so it will set off your blue."

Martha wrinkled her nose. "That's not the only reason."

"I'll think about it." Allison yawned. "But right now I want to get a few more minutes sleep. It's Saturday morning, and I've been working all week, remember? There's plenty of time to plan my outfit later."

"But there isn't, Allison! The parade begins in just two hours. You don't want to miss that, do you?"

"I don't have to dress up for that. Cabot's not meeting me until later this afternoon. I'm on my own for the parade and auction."

"You can come with Brent and me, then."

"Brent's taking you to the parade?"

Martha's eyes sparkled. "He's taking me to *everything*! I had to twist his arm a little. He said he was only obligated for the dance, but I insisted it was a package deal." She giggled. "He didn't fight too hard."

Allison's heart gave a hard thump. "I think I'll go

to the parade on my own. I don't want to cramp your style."

"Don't be silly. I *demand* that you come. I won't take no for an answer."

"You're going to have to, because I'm not going."

Martha pouted. "Then I'll get Brent to roust Cabot out of his den and we'll all go together. What does Cabot *do* with his time all day, anyway? I thought the merger was signed, sealed, and delivered."

Allison shrugged. "It's not something he ever finishes with. There's always new deals on the horizon. You ought to know that. Isn't your father the same way?"

Martha sighed, nodding. "It's deadly. You're going to have to make him take regular vacations, like my mother does. Go off to places like Kenya and Sri Lanka."

Allison laughed. "I'll certainly do my best." She slid back down on the pillow. "But I don't have to worry about that right now. And if I'm going to be up until all hours tonight, as Isabel says, then I want to get a little more sleep."

"Okay. But be ready by nine-thirty or I'll make Brent turn you over his knee."

Allison's stomach flip-flopped. "Spank me? That's not Brent's style."

Martha grinned, her eyes dancing. "You'd be surprised." She bounced out of the room, leaving Allison to stare up at the ceiling, wondering why she had suddenly lost the desire for more sleep.

At nine-thirty Allison came into the kitchen dressed in her denim skirt, a pale yellow chamois blouse, and open sandals. She had decided to risk Cabot's disapproval and wear her hair down for the morning; since she'd cut it, he really couldn't object. She'd put it up, the way he liked it, for the supper and dance. She found Martha in the kitchen, wearing a green cotton dress that set off her tan complexion and gray-green eyes. Her short, dark hair curled attractively around her face. She looked stunning.

A moment later Allison's throat tightened as she heard Brent's truck in the yard.

Martha went to the screen door. "We're all set, Brent!" she called cheerily.

Allison sank into a chair, unable to bring herself to look through the window and watch Brent's confident stride across the lawn.

"Where's Cabot?" Martha asked, opening the door for him.

"He's not coming." Brent slid past Martha and looked at Allison, who had to force herself to lift her head and meet his eyes with her own.

He stopped, his legs frozen in mid-stride. Two small frown creases appeared between his eyebrows. "What happened to your hair?" There was something cold in his voice.

Allison raised her chin. "I cut it."

"So I see."

"Doesn't it look wonderful?" Martha tugged on Brent's sleeve. "Cabot's been begging her to do it for months, and finally she gave in." She beamed up into Brent's face. "Ain't love grand?"

Brent didn't respond. He was still staring at Allison. She watched the muscles of his jaw tighten. She looked down at her hands.

"Brent, why isn't Cabot coming?" Martha leaned against his arm, trying without success to pull his gaze away from Allison.

"I don't know. Something about a new takeover bid. He said Allison would understand."

Allison shrugged and glanced at Martha. "I didn't

really expect him to come. It was your idea to get Brent to ask him, Martha."

"Does he always work on national holidays?" She saw the disgust on Brent's face and looked away.

"Let's try again. Maybe if *you* talk to him, Allison." Martha looked hopefully at her friend.

Allison shook her head. "I've already tried."

Brent turned suddenly to Martha. "I guess that leaves you as our last hope, Martha. Take my truck."

Martha blinked up at him in surprise. "You're offering me the keys to your precious truck?"

"Just take the curves under sixty, please. As a favor to me." He pressed the keys into her hand and steered her quickly to the door. Allison watched as he opened the door and escorted her outside. She stood up quickly and headed for the stairs. She'd wait for Martha's return in her room. The last thing she wanted was to face Brent alone.

"Wait." Brent's deep voice slashed through her.

Allison froze. "I have some things to do in my room." She couldn't look at him.

"Tell me why you cut your hair."

She turned slowly to face him. "Martha told you already. Cabot's been after me for months to cut it. He doesn't like it long."

Brent's jaw tightened. "And you *wanted* to cut it?"

She lifted her chin. "I did it to please Cabot."

"I see." His voice was very low. He gazed at her, nodding slowly.

Her eyes stung. "I don't need to justify myself to you. What I do with my hair is my own business."

"Yes, exactly. Not mine. Not Cabot's. What did he do, tell you it wasn't stylish enough for his circle of friends?"

Allison heard the derisive tone and her anger flared. "It really isn't your business, is it? There's nothing criminal in wearing my hair to please my fiancé. And he's very pleased."

Brent's mouth quirked upward in a sardonic grin. "I'm sure he is. Anything to tame the wildness of the beauty around him. The question is—are *you* pleased?"

She straightened and looked directly into his eyes. "Yes, Brent. I'm sorry to disappoint you, but I like my hair this way. It's much easier to take care of; it's not as hot, and, believe it or not, I don't object to being stylish. And"—she took a short, deep breath —"since you find my looks so distasteful, I certainly don't intend to impose them on you any longer." She whirled and started up the stairs, taking them rapidly, her legs pumping furiously.

His hand found her shoulder almost instantly. When he turned her, Allison found her lips only inches from his.

"No, Allison," he whispered. "I certainly don't find your looks distasteful. You could shave it all off and I'd still want to do this."

His mouth claimed hers before she could think to move away. He kissed her hard, more insistently than ever before. His strong tongue pressed her lips open and entered the warmth of her mouth. Allison thought momentarily of resisting him, but when she brought her hands up to push him away, her muscles turned to jelly. Her trembling hands found the column of his neck as he stroked her hair and spine.

When he pulled her closer, she lost her balance and fell against him. His arms gripped her tightly, lifting her. Lost in the sweetness of desire as his tongue probed the sensitive recesses of her mouth, Allison was only dimly aware that he was carrying her, until he laid her gently on her bed in the little guest room at the top of the stairs. She heard the door close softly and then felt him lie down beside her.

She gasped with delight as his hands found the buttons of her blouse and his fingers explored the tender skin of her breasts. She touched his back, ran her hands down the hard muscles and over the rippling biceps of his arms.

"Oh, Brent!" she moaned as he kissed her neck and the soft swell of her breasts.

The slam of the screen door in the kitchen below brought his head up instantly. Allison watched the glazed look clear from his eyes. She reached for him, then froze as she heard Martha's triumphant crow at the bottom of the stairs.

"Hey, I got him to come! Cabot's here!"

Allison gasped. What had she done? She was lying here on her bed with Brent, half undressed, while her fiancé waited for her downstairs!

Brent sat up. "Sounds like we've got company." He ran a hand through his thick hair.

Allison stared at him with wide eyes. "You said it wouldn't happen again," she whispered.

"I know." He closed his eyes, rubbed the bridge of his nose between his thumb and index finger. "It's a lot harder than I thought it would be, Allison. I'm not sure how much longer I'm going to be able to wait." He turned to her, his eyes tender and sad.

She buttoned her blouse quickly, concentrating on each button so she wouldn't have to meet his gaze. "Wait for what?" she said hoarsely.

"For you to break up with that insufferable snob you call your fiancé."

She took a sharp breath. "I've told you already, Brent, I'm not breaking the engagement. And he's *not* a snob! He's the most polite, most considerate man I've ever met."

He sighed. "And the richest." He stood up, took her hand and pulled her to her feet. "That's what it's really all about, isn't it, Allison? It's not love; it's money."

She went rigid with fury, but he only smiled down at her.

"Looks like I hit the nail right square on the head this time." He released her hand and stepped to the door. "It may be a little awkward to explain what we're both doing up here. Why don't you change your blouse, and I'll tell them I was up here checking a leaky faucet? Isabel's orders." He gave her a quick wink and left the room.

A moment later she heard Brent in the kitchen, his deep voice mingling with Martha's higher one.

She changed to a red and blue paisley blouse, and slowly descended the stairs. Cabot was standing with his back to her, watching Martha as she told Brent the details about how she had lured Cabot into coming. Allison went to Cabot and touched his elbow. He turned and gave her a distant smile before his eyes slid back to Martha.

Her friend was cavorting around the room like an eager puppy, frolicking from Cabot to Brent and back again. When she finally spotted Allison, she grinned. "Hey, let's get going! We want to get a good place to watch the parade!"

Brent laughed. "This isn't Boston, Martha. There's plenty of space and plenty of time." He sat down at the table. "How about a cup of coffee?" He looked directly at Allison.

"I'll get it." Allison forced a false lightness into her voice as she hurried to the stove, grateful for the excuse to turn her back on Brent. "Is instant okay?"

"You bet. I'm not a man who likes to wait too long.

For coffee or anything else." His tone turned her stomach to jelly.

"Ohhh," Martha groaned loudly. "I can't believe you're going to hold us up like this, Brent! The rest of us want to get going. Don't we, Cabot?" She waltzed over and tucked her arm through Cabot's.

Cabot smiled at her fondly. "I'm in no rush, Martha."

"Just what I need! Two party poopers! Maybe Allison and I should just go by ourselves." She jutted her narrow chin into the air and giggled.

"Fine with me," Brent said. "Cabot and I can sit here and have a man-to-man talk."

Allison stiffened. She knew that Brent was joking, but the thought of Cabot and Brent talking alone in the kitchen was profoundly unsettling. She tried to imagine Cabot outlining his takeover bids while Brent stifled a yawn. No, Brent wouldn't be that polite. If he wasn't interested in something, he'd come right out and say so. What if he started talking about her? Would he dare to mention what had just happened between them in her bedroom? Her mouth went dry.

She glanced at Brent and was startled to find his blue eyes looking straight at her, twinkling with mischief. Quickly she turned way. "Let's all have a cup of coffee, Martha. There's plenty of time before the parade."

"All right, but if we miss anything, I'm holding each of you personally responsible." Martha flung herself into a chair and Cabot sat beside her.

To Allison's relief, the teakettle started to boil, breaking the tension with its raucous shrill.

They watched the parade from Brent's front porch. Allison managed to position herself so that both Martha and Cabot were between her and Brent, and she found herself thoroughly enjoying the little procession of children and adults that marched up the road. They carried flags and balloons; some of the children had decorated their bicycles in red, white, and blue crepe paper. When she saw Ricky Flory flash by in a blur of patriotic color, she couldn't resist the urge to cheer.

There was no music; the participants seemed to carry their own rhythm inside their heads. The parade went up the road to the bend by the Cutlers' house, then turned and came back, bikes flashing, balloons bobbing. The procession disbanded at the general store, where the spectators and marchers mingled together over ice cream cones and sodas.

Martha insisted on joining the crowd, and before Allison knew it, she was in the middle of a group of familiar children, all wanting to know if she'd seen them, and wasn't it the best parade ever? She assured them that she had and it was and, in fact, she honestly believed that this little motley group had been more enchanting than the massive parades she'd witnessed when her parents took her to Boston as a child.

She looked up once, to find Brent gazing at her with a strange, vulnerable look on his face. Cabot had moved to the edge of the crowd and was busy wiping something from his slacks; his face was folded into a look of loathing. A hand tugged at her skirt, and she looked down to see one of the younger Flory children grinning up at her.

"Did you see me, Miss Curtis?" the tiny girl lisped.

"Oh, yes I did, Hannah!" Allison squatted to embrace the child. The smell of the sun in her hair made Allison want to bury her face in the soft curls.

A few moments later she heard Martha's excited giggle.

"Come on! We don't want to miss the auction!" Martha came up to her, urged Allison to her feet. "I told Cabot and Brent to save us some seats."

Martha pulled her away from the children, and Allison reluctantly followed her down a path behind the row of houses to a barnlike structure. It was filled with people who were milling around happily, chatting with each other in little groups and sitting in the folding chairs which were set up in jumbled rows. They found Brent and Cabot deep in conversation in the fifth row back.

When Martha called and waved cheerily, both men's heads went up.

"We saved you a place," Cabot called. He stood up, while Brent swiveled in his seat. Allison followed Martha past the people in the row and watched her drop into the empty chair between Brent and Cabot. The only other empty seat in the entire row was next to Brent. She slid into it, trying not to touch him, but the chairs were set very close together, and her arm settled unavoidably against his. She looked quickly away, wondering if he could hear the rapid pounding of her heart.

Joe Barnes, the auctioneer, was a large, heavyset man who opened the proceedings with a series of Maine stories, all told in the lilting, down-east accent that Allison was beginning to love. When he began auctioning off the array of "attic treasures," as he called them, his transformation was striking. He was no longer the lazy, slow fisherman, but a fast-talking, clever manipulator of the crowd.

Allison enjoyed herself, in spite of the distraction of Brent's closeness. Her only moment of disquiet came when Martha bounced up to the front of the pavilion, dragging Cabot with her, to examine one of the articles she wanted to bid on. They stayed there, chatting with townspeople for several minutes, while Allison sat in uncomfortable silence beside Brent, deliberately looking away from him, but intensely aware of the warmth of his body next to hers.

When he placed his hand on the back of her chair and spoke, every fiber in her body tensed.

"You could look at me, you know," his soft voice challenged her. "Isn't it considered impolite to ignore the person you're sitting next to?"

She turned her head, made herself smile at him. "I'm sorry. I'm just having a wonderful time looking around. It's so picturesque here."

He looked at her, hard. "It doesn't suit you, Allison."

"What?" Her cheeks reddened.

"That pseudosophisticated tone. Cabot may be fooled, but I'm not."

"I don't know what you're talking about." She crossed her arms quickly over her breasts.

"Yes, you do." He leaned toward her and his hand slid under her hair, rested on the back of her neck. She almost gasped with the thrill that went through her. "It's not going to work, you know," he whispered, his fingers burning against her skin. "I can only keep my distance for so long on an island this size. I've stayed clear of you for two weeks. But I'm afraid I've reached the limit of my own willingness to go on with this charade."

"Then maybe I should go back to Boston." There was a bitter taste on the back of her tongue.

"No. Wrong solution to the problem."

"Well, what are you suggesting I do, Brent?"

"You know the answer to that, love."

"No!" she whispered. "I'm *not* going to break up with Cabot!"

"Well," he smiled, "at least you're not still claiming that you love him."

Allison bent her head to hide the sudden tears in her eyes, and was relieved to feel his hand slide away from her neck. A moment later Martha and Cabot reappeared. She looked up at them with a grin of such false brightness that even Cabot looked puzzled. He reached out and squeezed her hand as he moved past her to his seat, but when his fingers slipped away, her own hand dropped heavily into her lap.

Beside her Brent slid his arm casually over the back of Martha's chair, and Martha leaned against him. Allison lifted her chin and forced herself to concentrate on the rippling melody of the auctioneer's words.

By the time the auction was over, Allison had managed to gain control of her tumultuous emotions. She was able to join in the superficial chatter as the four of them returned to the Cutler house, weighted down with the collection of worthless items that Martha hadn't been able to resist.

"You have to stay for lunch," Martha commanded the two men. "Isabel fixed it this morning—it's already in the fridge."

Brent shook his head. "I've got other plans for this afternoon."

Martha pouted playfully. "The deal was, you have to spend the day with me."

He pointed an admonishing finger at her. "The deal was, I'd take you to the dance. Nothing more. You know I don't like being tied down. If I want to be somewhere, I'll be there."

Martha sighed with an exaggerated shrug of her

shoulders. "Okay, but you have to pick us up at five so we can all go to the supper together."

"Right." He glanced at Cabot. "Want a lift?"

"Thanks. I'm sure Allison needs some time to get ready for the dance. She looks a bit disheveled at the moment."

Brent gave him a quizzical look and then studied Allison thoughtfully. She felt his eyes travel the length of her body.

He grinned. "She looks pretty good to me the way she is." He turned and was gone before it registered to Allison that he'd just winked at her over the top of Martha's head.

Chapter Eighteen

ALLISON AGONIZED over her clothes all afternoon. She took the pink lace dress out of her closet a dozen times and kept putting it back again. She knew the color emphasized the rosy fairness of her skin, but the cut and style of the dress seemed too bold, too sexual, for Harper's Island. She considered and rejected the denim skirt. Comfortable as it was, it was too casual for the dance. That left her with only two choices: a cream-colored knit dress that hugged her breasts and fell in soft folds from her waist, and draped her arms in wide bell sleeves; and a pale blue linen shirtwaist, with a high lace collar and pleated bodice. She didn't dare ask Martha for her advice, knowing that her friend would argue for the pink lace because it set off the dress she was planning to wear.

She finally decided on the knit dress. It was simple and summery, and the contrast with her hair was stunning. She looked thoughtfully at her reflection in the mirror. She hadn't really given much thought about how to wear her hair. She hadn't had much time to experiment since she cut it, but there was still probably enough length to put it up in a small twist on the top of her head. Cabot would certainly like it that way. For a rebellious moment she yearned for her long curls. How lovely they used to look against the creamy dress! She sighed and gazed into the mirror, fingering a short tendril. She imagined herself twirling around the dance floor in Cabot's arms with her hair spinning out behind her in glorious, auburn profusion.

She sighed and shook her head. There was no use crying over spilt milk. Her long curls were gone forever. Quickly, she piled her hair on top of her head and secured it tightly with combs, telling herself firmly that, since she was going to the dance with Cabot, he was the man she wanted to please.

At five o'clock she was wearing the knit dress, a white silk flower in her hair, watching the sun sink toward the water from Isabel's living room window. It was strange how her heart was hammering away, as if she were about to go out on her first date. She put her hands to her cheeks, felt the heat and frowned. This was absurd! She forced herself to concentrate on Martha's happy chatter. But when she heard Brent's truck in the driveway, her chest tightened and she nervously fingered the white, hand-crocheted sweater Isabel had told her to bring along against the night air.

"They're here!" Martha cried, rushing to the window.

Allison got to her feet and slowly followed her friend into the kitchen to greet the men.

Cabot came through the door first, wearing light blue slacks and a matching blazer; a white silk scarf circled his neck. She saw a flicker of approval cross his face, and knew she'd passed the test of his good-taste critique. She went to him immediately and was just slipping her arm through his when Brent entered the room.

"Everybody ready?" He was dressed more casually than Cabot, in an open-necked lime shirt and brown corduroy jeans. He looked at Martha and then at Allison. She was aware of his eyes traveling the whole length of her body and back again. She forced herself to smile brightly up into Cabot's face.

"You both look ravishing." Brent's voice was hearty. "Let's go eat." He put his arm across Martha's shoulder and steered her through the door.

They walked along the road, Allison's arm tucked into Cabot's, Brent's big hand clasping Martha's. The sun was low in the sky; it threw long shadows across the bright green lawns as they walked up the hill past the houses. There were other people on the road, couples mostly, some with children trailing after them. Everyone looked freshly scrubbed and cheerful. They called out greetings to each other, and Brent was kept busy for most of the walk responding to the cheery shouts and giving them back in kind.

The Bailey barn was a large wooden structure set into a dip in the hillside behind a tall bank of spruce trees. It was recently built, and Allison could see immediately that it had never been used as a real barn. The wide doors and windows were flung open, revealing long tables where people sat, conversing happily.

They managed to locate four seats together along one side of a table, on the far wall opposite the kitchen. Allison sat between Cabot and Brent. After a few brief moments of consternation at Brent's proximity, she found herself relaxing. To her great relief, Brent paid no attention to her, nor to Martha, either, who was seated on his far side, happily engaged in conversation with Dr. Johnson. Brent was in an exuberant mood, talking with the couple across the table, asking them about each of their four children. After a while Allison began to feel strangely isolated. Brent hadn't said a word to her since the auction, and Cabot was discussing the stock market with the elderly woman next to him. She sat in silence, grateful that at least the food was delicious. When Isabel, who was waiting on table, came up behind her and gave her shoulder an affectionate squeeze, Allison beamed up at her out of sheer relief.

"How's it going?" Isabel asked. "Would you like some more coffee?"

"No thanks. Everything's delicious, though."

"Good." Isabel bent down so that her mouth was close to Allison's ear. "Could you give me a hand in the kitchen for a few minutes, or is that asking too much?"

"No! I'd love to!" Allison followed Isabel eagerly, glad for the opportunity to share a few minutes of conversation with someone.

In the kitchen Isabel put her to work spooning mashed potatoes from a huge pot into serving bowls. Several other women worked busily at the far end, washing pots and pans.

"It was probably awful of me, getting you out here and putting you to work," Isabel apologized. "But Natalie had to go feed her baby, and I wanted to tell you something."

"What?" Allison put down her spoon. Isabel was wiping her hands on her apron, a worried line etched between her eyebrows. "Something's wrong, isn't it?"

Isabel shook her head. "No, it's just . . ." She sighed. "Actually, I don't really know why I'm talking to you. *Brent's* the one I should be telling."

"What is it?" Allison leaned toward the older woman. "What's happened?"

Isabel licked her lower lip. "I just learned that Tracy Lawton's on the island."

"Tracy Lawton?" Something contracted inside Allison's chest.

Isabel nodded. "Brent hasn't seen her since she left last winter. I'm afraid . . ." She paused, rubbed her hands on her apron. "I'm afraid it might upset him to see her. But I don't know how he can avoid it. She's on her way over here right now."

Allison stared. Her brain didn't seem to be working; it was as if it had been submerged in cold water. "Well," she said slowly, "maybe Martha and I can get him out of here before she comes."

Isabel shook her head and reached to touch Allison's arm. "I'm sorry. I probably shouldn't have said anything to you. It's just . . . I thought *some-one* should know."

"No, you're right. I appreciate your mentioning it."

Isabel gave her a small smile. "Well, if he leaves suddenly, you'll understand. You can explain to Martha."

Allison nodded. "I guess I'd better get back to my table. Thanks."

She walked out of the kitchen and crossed the wide floorboards to the table, her eyes scanning the barn for anyone who matched the description of Tracy Lawton. When she sat back down, Cabot leaned toward her, smiling.

"I missed you, darling," he murmured into her right ear.

She smiled back at him, but there was something cold in the center of her back. She was startled by the sudden realization that she didn't believe him.

She looked down the line of tables toward the

door, glanced sideways at Brent. He was talking with Martha, tilting his tall body toward her. His blond hair looked soft under the light.

The door opened a few minutes later, revealing a small group of young well-dressed men and women. Allison instantly knew which one was Tracy; the long hair and the startlingly dark eyes were dead giveaways. The woman was slender and graceful, and she walked with a pronounced sway of her hips. She wore a form-fitting black sheath that made her deeply tanned skin glow. She had her arm linked around the elbow of a tall, dark-haired man who looked like a male fashion model.

Allison glanced at Brent. He had straightened in his seat and was staring at the group, who still stood in the doorway, laughing and talking among themselves. She had an impulse to put a solicitous hand on his arm, but she didn't move. He rose slowly to his feet.

Martha looked up at him. "What is it, Brent?"

"There's someone I have to see." He was smiling; a thin, strained smile.

Martha followed his glance. "Who are *they*? I don't recognize any of them."

But Brent didn't answer; he merely slipped out of his seat and strode down the row of tables toward the door. Allison watched as he made his way to the group. She saw the black-haired woman turn toward him, smiling, as he came up to her. A moment later he had taken her by the arm and led her outside. The rest of the group stood for a moment in surprised immobility before they were escorted to a table by a gray-haired woman in a flowered apron.

"Who is that woman?" Martha said. Her voice was indignant. She scowled at Allison, who gave her a sympathetic smile.

"Her name is Tracy Lawton. She's somebody he met last winter."

"How do you know all this?" Martha asked. She slid into Brent's chair so that she could be next to Allison.

Allison shrugged. "Isabel told me." She knew that Cabot was looking at her. She turned and smiled at him. "I think I know stories about practically everyone on the island, after living with the Cutlers for three weeks."

Cabot frowned. "I'm not surprised. These people don't have much entertainment except for country music and local gossip."

Martha laughed knowingly.

Allison felt herself bristle. "I think these people are wonderful!" she said hotly. "And what's wrong with country music?"

"Nothing, if you're living in the boondocks." He glanced at Martha, who laughed again. "It's just not the sort of thing I care to listen to. Nor does anyone else I know."

"Well, it may come as a shock to you, Cabot, but I happen to *like* country music!" Allison knew her face had reddened dramatically and that her voice was much too loud. She pushed her chair away from the table. "If you'll excuse me, I think I'll go see if I can help out in the kitchen." She stood up quickly, bumping her hip on the table. Cabot's glass of water sloshed dangerously close to spilling.

"Allison!" His voice was a hiss. "Sit down!"

She ignored him, whirling away from the table and heading for the kitchen. Her heart was slamming against her ribs; there were drops of perspiration along her hairline.

Isabel met her at the door. "You look like you just

lost your best friend!" She pulled Allison into the kitchen, tucked an arm around her shoulder.

"I think maybe I did." Allison gave her a stricken look. "Brent left to see Tracy, and then Cabot made a nasty comment—" She blinked against the stinging sensation in her eyes and looked at Isabel. "I came to see if I could help before I head back to the house and go to bed."

"But my dear! You can't go home now! The evening's just beginning!"

A tear welled up and escaped Allison's left eye. She shook her head. "I can't cope anymore . . . everything's falling apart." She glanced at the women workers, who were busily washing dishes and storing leftover food in large containers. They were studiously ignoring her, but she sensed they were hearing every word she said.

Isabel saw her glance, and steered Allison into a little side pantry. "It can't be as bad as all that. Now tell me something: how did Brent look when he saw Tracy?"

"I don't know—upset, pale."

"Was he smiling?"

"Sort of. But he didn't look very happy."

Isabel let out a long sigh. "Well, that tells me that I still know my grandson pretty well. Unless I miss my guess, he'll be back here inside of five minutes. He's on the cleanup crew, you know, and the supper's almost over."

Allison gratefully accepted the tissue that Isabel handed her and wiped her eyes. "I guess I'd better go apologize to Cabot. I left in kind of a huff."

Isabel patted her hand. "That's a good idea, dear. Lovers should always make up as quickly as possible after they quarrel." Allison opened the door from the kitchen to the main hall, and was startled to see that only a few people were left sitting at the tables. There was no sign of either Cabot or Martha. "Oh dear," she sighed, giving Isabel a gloomy look, "he's already gone. I was so angry, I just left. I didn't think he'd leave, too."

Isabel sent her a compassionate smile. "Don't worry; he'll come back. Give him a chance to cool off." She handed Allison an apron. "In the meantime, you can help me by drying those dishes." She pointed to a large drainer filled with coffee cups and saucers.

Allison was grateful for the work, for something to do with her hands to take her mind off things. But she couldn't help thinking of Cabot and Martha walking outside somewhere in the warm evening. It was her own fault, she knew, for getting angry. And it wasn't like her to lose her temper, especially not with Cabot. Maybe Isabel was right, maybe it was just as well that he had taken a walk with Martha. Allison had to admit, Martha had a way of handling Cabot that she envied.

She was standing on her tiptoes, stacking saucers in a high cupboard, when Brent came into the kitchen. She sensed his presence even before Isabel's cheery greeting alerted her.

"Well, where have *you* been hiding?" Isabel said. "The men are already taking down the tables."

"I had some business to take care of, Gran." His voice was low.

Allison slid the last of the saucers onto its pile and closed the cupboard door. She had to make herself smile as she turned; she wiped her clammy hands on her apron. Brent was looking at her over the top of Isabel's head, his eyes darker than usual. She flushed and went to the drainer for a load of cups.

"So you saw Tracy," Isabel said.

Brent nodded.

"And?"

"And nothing. No sparks, no fireworks, nothing. It's over, Gran. I told you that three months ago." He gestured toward the door to the main room. "Where's Martha?"

"Apparently she and Cabot went for a walk."

He frowned. "Without Allison?"

Allison heard the disgust in his voice and winced. She finished stacking the cups and turned to look at him, forcing a bright smile. "I didn't mind. I wanted to help Isabel in the kitchen."

He gazed at her for a moment, then something moved across his face, a look of comprehension that sent shivers down her spine. She picked up a stack of cups, carried them quickly to the cupboard.

"Let me help." He was across the room instantly, opening the cupboard door, taking the cups out of her hand, placing them carefully on the shelf. His arm brushed hers, and then his hand touched her back.

She glanced up at him, started to speak, but for some reason, words wouldn't come to her lips. Instead she felt her eyes prickle with tears.

"Well," Isabel said brightly, "that about does it for now, girls." She beamed across the kitchen at her workers. "We'll clean up the rest after the dance." She untied her apron and turned to Brent. "Why don't you take Allison out for a bit, Brent? Find a good spot to see the fireworks."

Brent raised a quizzical eyebrow: "Didn't you just get through lecturing me for not helping take down tables?"

"Oh, pooh! Don't give me a hard time, young man! You know they've got more help than they know what to do with." She bustled across the room to

Allison and reached out for her apron. "Go on, get out of here, you two. Shoo!" She pushed them to a side door and out into the evening.

The door swung shut behind them, and Allison shivered a little in the slight breeze that came toward them over the water. The sun was setting, spilling pink and gold light across the cove.

Brent laughed. "Well, I guess we got told." He took her hand and she felt his touch on her fingers as a burning heat. She couldn't have removed her hand from his if she'd tried. She realized, with some surprise, that she didn't want to.

"I have an idea," he said softly. He was looking at the boats resting on the wind-rippled water.

She looked up at him. His eyes were dancing with excitement.

"We'll take the *Blue Lady* off Lookout Point. It'll give us an awesome view of the fireworks."

She took a deep breath. The thought of being out on the water in the darkness with Brent made her feel almost dizzy.

"What do you say? Are you game, love?"

She shook her head. "I can't go, Brent. Cabot might get worried."

He grinned down at her. "That might not hurt him, if you catch my drift."

He was right. She was suddenly aware that she'd been seething ever since Cabot had left with Martha. Any man with a shred of sensitivity wouldn't have gone. This wasn't about being with Brent; it was about teaching Cabot a lesson.

"All right. I'll go."

"Great!" He tucked her hand tighter into his own, and a moment later she was running beside him down the hill toward the wharf, out of breath and laughing like a child.

The sky was turning deep indigo as Brent helped her into the stern of the painter and sat facing her while he settled the two small oars into their locks. Over his shoulder she could see the evening star shining above the distant hills on the mainland. Her heart was beating rapidly; her face was flushed with excitement. A tendril of hair had come loose in their wild run and hung near her cheek. She started to put it back when Brent reached out and circled her wrist with his fingers.

"Take it down," he said softly. "Let it go free."

She didn't know what made her obey him. Was it something in his inflection? Or was it because his words gave voice to her own desire? She pulled the combs out and let her hair spill around her shoulders.

"That's better." He caught a strand in his fingers. "A bit short, but it'll grow." He winked at her, grinning.

The painter nudged the *Blue Lady* before Allison could think of an adequate reply. Brent tied it quickly to the mooring and leaped aboard. He turned and leaned over the gunwale, lifting Allison easily into the boat.

He kept his arms around her, cradling her body against his. She knew that he was going to kiss her, and she had no will to resist. The truth that she had tried to avoid for so long was staring her in the face in the warm darkness of the summer night: she was deeply in love with Brent Connors.

He took her face in his hands and kissed her gently, his right hand moving to the back of her head and caressing her neck before pressing her face against his shoulder. A long sigh came out of him as he released her.

Allison blinked up at him. "What's wrong?" She was startled to see tears in his eyes.

He turned away from her quickly. "Let's go." His voice was hoarse. He stepped into the pilothouse, started the *Blue Lady*'s engine and headed out of the cove. Allison stared at his back, the cool night air blowing against her face, her hair streaming out behind her. Her lips ached and there were tears in her own eyes. She wanted to go to him, embrace him, dissolve in his arms, but she didn't move.

Chapter
Nineteen

THEY ROUNDED the island slowly, Brent carefully avoiding the scattered moorings and lobster buoys. Behind them the boat trailed a long, silver wake.

The first rocket exploded as they came out under the cliff head by Lookout Point. It lit the water around them with hundreds of blue and gold darts.

Allison gave a little cry of delight. "Oh, it's so beautiful!"

"What'd I tell you?" Brent was leaning against the cuddy wall, smiling across the deck at her.

Another rocket exploded, showering the sky with green and silver. Then there was no sound but the idling of the *Blue Lady*'s engine and the soft lap of waves against her hull. Allison's desire to feel Brent's arms around her again was intense.

"I wonder where Martha and Cabot are," she said quickly, to break the heady spell.

"Probably up at the schoolhouse with everybody else." Brent crossed the deck to her. "That's the best viewing spot on dry land."

"I hope they're seeing this." She was intensely aware of the nearness of his body.

"I'm sure they're having a wonderful time." His

voice was tight. "Besides, they went off on their own, remember?"

"We should have looked for them. It's so gorgeous out here, with the reflection on the water and everything!"

He put his hand on her shoulder. "Have you been blind to what's been going on between them?"

"Going on?" She frowned up at him. His face was a silhouette in the darkness. "What do you mean?"

"Martha and Cabot. They've been seeing an awful lot of each other while you've been running the play group."

She licked her lips. "I didn't know that. But they're old friends. I'm sure it doesn't mean anything."

He was silent for a moment, as if weighing his words with great care. "I think it's more than simple friendship."

She stared at him. He was lying to her. He had to be.

"Cabot happens to love me. He's not the kind of man who takes relationships lightly. He's not interested in other women, Brent."

A breeze rippled her hair, throwing a lock of it across her face. She pushed it away, crossed her arms over her breasts.

"I know this isn't easy for you to hear, Allison." His voice was gentle. "I'm sorry I had to be the one to spill the beans. But it's been going on ever since he came to the island. He's been spending every morning with Martha."

"And how do *you* know all this? I thought you went out hauling in the mornings."

"Gran told me. She's really upset about it."

"If that's true, then why didn't she tell *me*?"

"Why do you think? She didn't want to hurt you. Besides, she's a great believer in things working out for the best. Everyone lives happily ever after. Gran's a romantic."

There was a hard knob at the base of Allison's throat. It took considerable effort to speak. "I can't believe Martha would do this to me. She's my friend."

He looked away from her, out over the water. Lookout Point loomed above them, a black mass against the dark blue sky.

Her tears came slowly and silently. She knew that Brent was right. She had seen it all along, and had deliberately ignored the signs: the animated way in which Cabot always spoke about Martha; the excitement with which her friend had greeted Cabot's arrival on the island; Martha's insistence that they double date; her ability to coax Cabot into doing what she wanted. Allison realized she had tried to make herself believe that Martha was still carrying a torch for Brent. But it hadn't had anything to do with Brent; it had all been designed so she could be near Cabot.

A rocket flared, red and gold; Allison bent her head into her hands.

When Brent's arms went around her, she pressed herself gratefully against his chest.

"I didn't want to be the one to tell you," he whispered. He lifted her head and wiped her face gently with a handkerchief. "I'm sorry."

She forced herself to pull away from him. "I want to go back," she said huskily. "It must be almost time for the dance."

He stared at her for a long moment before he spoke. "This doesn't change anything for you, then?"

She stiffened slowly, her spine like a hard cord of metal in her back. "So that's what this is all about!

You're trying to make me doubt that Cabot really loves me!" Her voice thickened. "You're saying all this just so I'll break the engagement!"

He shook his head. Another rocket lit the sky, briefly revealing his troubled eyes. "No, Allison, you're wrong."

"You'll stoop to *anything* to get your way, won't you?" Her voice rose, harsh and angry over the silent water. "What is it with you? Pride? Ego? Why is it so important to you that I live my life *your* way?"

His arms dangled at his sides. "I know you're upset, and you have a right to be," he said quietly. "But not with me. Cabot's the one you need to have it out with."

"It's always Cabot, isn't it? Why do you hate him so much?" The words shot out of her mouth like vicious, barbed hooks. She couldn't stop them. "Is it his money? His social standing? Are you jealous? Why do you despise him when you hardly even know him?" She was shaking with anger.

"I don't hate him, Allison." His voice was so low she could barely make out his words. "But, yes, I suppose I am jealous. I wish *I* was the one who inspired that blind devotion in you."

"Don't say that!" she cried. She put her hands over her ears, bent her head away from him. "Please take me back to the dance!"

He made a small, helpless gesture with his hands. "All right, I'll take you back."

They rode back to the cove in silence. The final rockets burst above them, but Allison didn't look up. The beauty of the night had been destroyed for her, by the cruel import of Brent's words.

She climbed into the painter by herself, deliberately ignoring Brent's helping hand. As soon as the boat bumped the dock, she scrambled ashore and marched back up the ramp alone. She would have nothing more to do with Brent Connors. He was a liar and an egotist, the most despicable man alive.

The barn was radiant with warm, yellow light. The band, which was set up on a small platform at the far end, was playing a tango as Allison entered. Only a few people were dancing, so it was easy to spot Cabot and Martha in the center of the dance floor. They were locked together in the tense passion of the dance, performing flawlessly. Allison felt her stomach clench. She ran her hands over her hair, trying to smooth down the wild strands. When the dance ended, she marched across the floor to Cabot and placed her hand possessively on his arm.

"Ah, Allison!" He turned to her with a little smile. "All over your pique, are you? Where have you been? Martha and I have been looking all over for you."

"Did you miss the fireworks?" Martha beamed at her.

"No, I saw them." She looked directly into Cabot's eyes. "We have to talk."

"Talk? Now?" He patted her hand. "Darling, this is a dance. We can talk later."

The band started a waltz; Martha and Cabot exchanged quick glances.

"I'm afraid I've already promised this dance to Martha." Cabot smiled his thin smile and squeezed Allison's hand. "I had no idea where you were. But I promise you the next one."

Allison lifted her chin. "Of course, Cabot. Don't let me stop you."

She retreated to the row of folding chairs lined up against the wall and sank into one.

So it was true. Every word Brent had spoken was

absolutely factual. She watched Cabot swing Martha gracefully onto the floor. Their hips were pressed close, their eyes locked together, their bodies swaying easily in three-quarter time. They were both wonderful dancers, but it was more than that. It was so obvious that even a child could see it: they were in love.

She forced herself to look at the other dancers. There was Natalie and Matt Flory, Dr. Johnson and his wife, a number of young couples she didn't recognize. She saw Emily Potter swing onto the floor in the arms of a tall, gray-haired partner.

Out of the corner of her eye she saw Brent enter the barn. For a moment he stood in the doorway, his eyes sweeping the dance floor. Then his face hardened and he started toward the refreshment table, next to the entrance to the kitchen. There were several people milling around the table. Allison spotted Tracy Lawton among them and her heart contracted.

She seemed paler than when Allison first saw her; her face looked strained, almost old, but she was smiling. Allison watched Tracy place her hand on Brent's arm, saw Brent smile down at her. They would dance, Allison knew. No man could resist a body like Tracy's. And Brent wasn't just any man; he had recently been in love with her.

The waltz ended and the band swung into a samba. Allison waited for Cabot to find her as he had promised. Couples were leaving the dance floor; apparently not many knew how to do this Latin dance. For a minute her view of the far side of the room was obscured, then the crowd parted and she saw that Martha was still in Cabot's arms, gazing up at him with a look of delight as he led her through the complicated, sensuous steps of the samba. There was only one other couple on the floor, a young man and woman Allison didn't recognize.

Then Brent and Tracy emerged from the crowd at the table. He put his arms around her and swept her into the rhythm of the dance. Allison was astonished at how graceful he was. As he glided around the floor with Tracy, she realized that he was an even better dancer than Cabot. His eyes met hers once, in a sad, questioning glance, then flicked rapidly across the room to Cabot and Martha. Allison flushed; if he was trying to tell her something, she had already grasped the message. She was surprised that he wasn't looking at Tracy while he danced. She glanced back at Cabot and Martha. They were still gazing at each other. She knew it was part of the dance, but the intensity of their look was beyond form; it was pure passion.

Allison bent her head. She felt sick. When the samba ended and another waltz began, she didn't even wait to see if Cabot would dance with her. As the couples moved back onto the floor, she got to her feet and stumbled to the door through a hot blur of tears.

Allison ran through the warm night. She didn't know where she was going, but she had to get away, to put as much distance as possible between herself and the barn. She knew she would never recover from this moment of pure pain.

She blindly followed the narrow trail up the hill to the schoolhouse. It was a path she had walked so often, she didn't have to think about it; her feet instinctively avoided the roots and stones. By the time she reached the top of the hill, her anger was gone and she felt only a deep, heavy shame. She collapsed on the schoolhouse steps and buried her face in her hands. The tears came slowly at first, then with a profound intensity. She wept for a long time, and when she finally raised her head and looked around her, she was surprised to see that the full moon had risen, casting a silver glaze over everything.

She stood up, dazed by the light on the water. No matter how long she lived, she would never forget the incredible beauty of moonlight on the ocean. She started down the hill toward the sea. The sand beach stretched in a white crescent before her. She ran down the rest of the hill, slipped off her shoes, dropped them onto the grass.

The sand was cool under her feet. Allison walked toward the water. The tide was low, the water black and still. What would it be like to walk through the mud flats into the water, her bare feet sinking into the cold, slippery muck? What would it be like to keep on moving into that cold blackness? Tears stung her eyes again and she collapsed onto the sand, let the tiny grains spill through her fingers.

There was a soft, animal sound behind her. She gasped, lifting her hand to her throat.

"Allison?" Brent's voice lay like a warm tongue against her ear. He walked toward her, the shush of the sand under his feet strangely loud in the darkness. He put his hand on her shoulder. "Are you all right?"

She swallowed. "I'm fine."

"No you're not." His hand didn't leave her shoulder. "I'm sorry."

She bit her lip. "I told you, they're old friends."

He was silent.

She shivered. "I suppose you're going to tell me that she looks more in love with him than I do."

"The thought occurred to me."

"So you came down here to rub it in."

"No, Allison." He sat down beside her on the sand

and slid his hand under her hair to stroke the curve of her neck. "I came here to ask you to dance."

"I can't go back there," she whispered.

"Yes, you can, love. In fact, you have to. It's the only way to get past the pain." His fingers caressed her neck, stroked down the small bones of her spine to the top of her dress.

Allison trembled and closed her eyes. "I can't believe I've been so blind. I feel like such a fool!"

"You're not a fool, Allison. It can happen to anyone. It has happened to most of us, at one time or another."

She looked at him. She could see his eyes shine in the moonlight.

"The day I watched Tracy push that little girl away, I thought I'd never forgive myself for loving her. I felt that I'd wasted four months of my life. I didn't believe I'd ever have the courage to love anybody again." He picked up her hand, cradling it in his large palm.

She stared at him. "But you danced with her tonight."

He nodded again. "For the same reason you have to go back to the barn and face Martha and Cabot. To prove that no one has the power to destroy who you are."

"I can't," she whispered.

"Yes, you can." He gave her hand a gentle squeeze. "I'll be right there with you."

She had to smile then. "Are you saying that all my problems will be solved if I dance with you?"

"Not exactly, but it's a beginning."

"All right," she said, lifting her chin. "I'll dance. As long as you promise not to abandon me for Tracy or Emily."

He laughed gently. "You have nothing to worry

about, love. Once I get my arms around you, your only problem will be getting away from me."

He stood up and pulled her to her feet. Her heart was hammering rapidly, her face flushed with excitement. He led her up the hill, her hand captured tightly in his. It wasn't until they reached the schoolhouse that she remembered her shoes.

"I dropped them in the grass by the beach." She waved her free hand in the direction of the water.

"I hope this isn't just a delaying tactic." He gave her a playful nudge. "I ought to let you go in your bare feet. Or better yet, make you dance with me right here."

He swept her into his arms and spun her around so quickly that she gave a little shriek and clung to him dizzily.

"Stop!" she gasped. "Let me go!"

But he was laughing out loud, spinning and dancing her across the wide lawn, making a huge circle around the school. If he heard her, he paid no attention, and she was forced to follow his lead to avoid collapsing against him. He was incredibly supple; his feet flew over the lawn and she found herself following him with a willowy ease that felt like the result of months of practice.

When he finally slowed to a stop, she was breathless and light-headed. He slipped both arms around her waist and pulled her firmly against him. His smile widened in the moonlight.

She had to force herself away from him.

"Relax," he said, his arms tightening, pulling her closer.

"Please let me go," she whispered. "We shouldn't do this." But her body had become strangely languid.

Brent's hands stroked her back. "You're right," he

murmured. "Maybe if you weren't so incredibly beautiful in the moonlight, I'd be able to control myself."

His mouth descended tenderly on hers, and the thrill of desire that went through her took her breath away. She moaned softly as he kissed her, pressing her even more tightly against him with insistent, loving hands. She felt herself melt against him, her brain swimming dizzily in the dark fire of passion.

When he pulled her down onto the grass, she pressed herself eagerly against him, running her hands up and down the long column of his spine. She felt his hard, muscular body through the soft fabric of her dress. His hand slid over her hips, down the curve of her leg, then back up to gently cup her breast.

She moaned again as his hand slipped under her skirt and caressed the sensitive skin of her thigh. She no longer had any will of her own; the only thing she wanted was to feel his body against hers, to surrender herself completely to the man who held her in his arms. When his fingers touched the zipper of her dress and inched it downward to her waist, she felt a shock of joy go through her. The cool night air touched her back, and Brent deftly undid the clasp on her bra. His sensitive fingers stroked her naked skin, drew the dress down from her shoulders, exposing her breasts. He caressed them with expert hands and bent to kiss them.

She arched her neck and breathed his name as if her whole body was one word.

He kissed her mouth again, a long, probing kiss, full of yearning passion. His fingers traveled the length of her arm and stroked her hand.

Suddenly he pulled away from her and sat up.

She gaped up at his hard jaw, his bent head. She saw him shudder all over, then get to his feet.

"I'll go find your shoes." His voice was gruff.

"Brent? What's wrong? Wait!"

But he had disappeared around the side of the schoolhouse, and she was alone in the darkness.

For a moment she lay dazed and shivering on the grass. The sky above her was spangled with stars; a cool breeze ruffled the grass around her. Yet she had never felt more dejected and bewildered in her life. She wondered dully if Brent had been trifling with her all along. Perhaps all he had ever wanted was to prove that he could overwhelm her with passion. Perhaps he played with women like toys and she was just one in a long line of conquests. She shook her head and wiped the tears from her eyes. That wasn't possible. The man who had held her in his arms only moments ago wasn't a manipulator; he was the most principled man alive; she knew that in her heart.

She sat up slowly and slipped her dress back over her shoulders. As she reached back to zip the dress, her engagement ring made a scraping sound against the metal zipper. Her heart froze. Brent had touched her ring. That was why he'd pulled away from her. She remembered Isabel's comments about Brent's strange, old-fashioned code of honor. Touching her ring had reminded him of her engagement. He wasn't going to let himself love her as long as she belonged to another man.

Angrily, she yanked the ring off her finger. All the wealth and prestige in the world didn't matter if she wasn't really in love with the man she married.

"Brent!" She got to her feet and started after him, racing as fast as she could through the cool grass. What if he'd gone home? Or back to the barn to dance with Tracy again? What if he would never see her again because of her blindness and stupidity? She tore around the side of the school and almost whooped with delight. Brent was climbing the hill toward her, her shoes in his hand.

She raced toward him, the ring clutched tightly in her hand. She would give it to him, tell him that he was right, that she didn't love Cabot; she never had. She understood what she hadn't before, that Brent was the only man she'd ever loved. He'd changed the meaning of love for her forever.

Chapter Twenty

ALLISON WAS CLOSE ENOUGH to see the hardness of Brent's jaw when she heard a shout from the road at the top of the hill. She watched Brent turn.

The shout came again, urgent and forceful. "Brent? Is that you?" It was Abel's voice, sharp with alarm.

He emerged from the shadow of the trees beyond the schoolhouse and came down the hill toward them, his stride tense and rapid.

"What is it?" Brent dropped Allison's shoes at her feet and started running up the hill to meet his grandfather.

"There's trouble, son. Bad trouble."

Allison's heart moved into her throat. She slipped into her shoes and hurried after Brent.

". . . he's been missing for a least two hours," Abel was saying. "Which means he could be anywhere on the island. All we know is where he *isn't*."

Allison twisted her hands together to keep them from trembling. "Who is it? Is someone lost?"

"I'm afraid so." Abel gave her a troubled frown. "Young Rick Flory."

She gasped. "Ricky?"

Abel nodded. "Seems he's gone off on one of his

wild adventures. Not the first time it's happened. But he's never picked nighttime before. It's going to make it wicked hard to find him."

"Well, at least there's a full moon and everyone on the island is searching for him," Brent said.

"Yep. Most everybody, anyway."

Brent's eyes narrowed. "Someone's not joining the search?"

Abel shrugged, glancing sideways at Allison. "No offense, miss, but that fiancé of yours has a lot to learn about priorities."

Allison felt the blood drain from her face. "What do you mean? He was at the dance with the others. Didn't somebody ask him?"

"Sure did. But he wouldn't help. Said he's not trained in rescue operations and he had stock reports to go over." Abel shook his head. "Afraid his thinking is beyond me."

"Come on," Brent said quickly. "We'd better get moving. Who's heading up the search—Pete?"

"Yep. Glad I found you. Pete says the *Blue Lady*'s the only boat with the lights to check out the shoreline."

"Okay. Tell him I'll start right away. As soon as I find a copilot to keep a lookout."

Abel nodded and started jogging back to the road.

Allison put her hand on Brent's arm. "Let me be your copilot."

He frowned down at her. "You're not familiar with the shoreline. Besides, we don't know what we'll find —or when. We could be out there all night and then some."

"Please, Brent! This is important to me. Ricky— he's a special kid. I couldn't stand it if something happened and he . . . he . . ." Her throat clenched against the thought.

He searched her face with his eyes. "You're really serious, aren't you?"

She nodded. "I may not know the shoreline, but my eyes are as good as anyone else's. Please let me go with you!"

He gave her a quick grin. "This is the first time I've ever heard you begging to be with me. Maybe things are looking up." He grabbed her hand. "Okay, you're hired. Let's get going. We don't have any time to waste." He started running down the hill, pulling her along with him. It was all Allison could do to keep up with him. This was no romantic chase; it was a matter of life and death.

As soon as they were on board the *Blue Lady*, Brent started the engine, and its deep, powerful roar filled the night. He turned a switch, and a brilliant searchlight flooded the cove.

"Look," he said, taking her hand and placing it on a cold metal lever. "This controls the direction of the spotlight. Aim it at the shore, and keep your eyes peeled."

She shivered in Isabel's lightweight sweater as the boat started its slow grind around the island. They were towing the painter this time; Brent had said they might need it; it followed the *Blue Lady* like a dark shadow. She could see people scattered along the shore, many of them carrying lanterns. She thought of Cabot going back to the cottage in the middle of this crisis, to work on his stock reports. Why would refuse to help in the rescue effort? A little boy was lost, and even Cabot knew the island could be a place of danger and death, despite its beauty.

She aimed the searchlight carefully, keeping it focused on the curve of shoreline just beyond the water's edge.

"Tide's coming in." Brent came over to her, touched her back lightly. "You're shivering."

"I'm all right."

He moved briefly to the pilothouse wall, returned. She felt something cover her shoulders and realized he had placed his jacket around her.

"Thanks." She didn't dare take her eyes off the circle of light.

"I don't imagine he's on this side of the island or they'd have found him by now." Brent stared out over the water. "Still, I don't dare skip anything."

They rounded the curve of land by the schoolhouse beach. Allison's eyes hurt with the strain of staring. Her mouth was dry, and her back ached because of the tension in her shoulders. It was hard to believe that only a short time ago she'd been sitting with Brent on the sand that was now flooded with brilliant light.

She felt his hand on her arm. "Warm now?"

She nodded. His hand moved up her arm to her shoulder, massaged it gently. "Relax. We'll find him." He turned back to the wheel, guiding the boat carefully through the dark water.

She stared out at the shore, praying that he was right. He had to be right. Nothing could happen to Ricky, not on this night, not when she'd finally made the decision to give Cabot back his ring.

The ring! She felt a balloon of fear rise inside her. It was gone! She'd been holding it in her hand, but it wasn't there any longer. She must have dropped it somewhere. She groaned out loud.

"What is it? Did you see him?" Brent was instantly alert.

"No. It's not that." She bit her lip. "It's the ring. I lost it."

"Cabot's ring?"

"Yes. I took it off. I must have dropped it."

"You took it *off*?"

She nodded, but didn't turn to him, didn't dare take her eyes off the circle of light. Just as she opened her mouth to explain, his sudden shout cut her off.

"Look! There he is!"

Allison peered at the ragged jumble of rocks where he was pointing. All she could see were gray and black shadows and the white spray of the surf.

"Ricky?" Her breath tightened. "Where?"

"Look! There by the thunder hole. See—on that ledge there." He placed his hand on the side of her face and turned her head slightly to the left.

She focused on the deep cut in the rocks that was the thunder hole. She remembered Isabel explaining how the sea carved out caverns in the rock. When the tide rose, powerful waves created a booming sound as the water hit the back wall of the cave. Her eyes traveled over the dark rock face, and finally she saw him: a tiny figure crouched on the narrow ledge directly over the surging channel of water that led into the cave.

"Oh my God!" She raised her hand to her mouth. She was trembling all over. "He's going to fall, isn't he?"

"We'll get him out of there. Though, God knows, it won't be easy."

He jumped to the control panel and yanked the CB receiver out of its cradle. Allison kept the searchlight trained on Ricky while Brent barked orders into the CB. A moment later he had slowed the *Blue Lady*'s engines and was easing the boat closer to the shore.

"What are you going to do?" Allison's voice was plaintive with worry.

"Go in there and get him. I'm taking the *Lady* as close as I dare, then I'll row over in the painter. It'll be a little while before the others can get there, and the tide's coming in fast. If we don't get him off that ledge in the next few minutes, then . . ." He didn't finish his sentence.

As the boat drew closer to shore, Allison could make out Ricky's form more clearly. He was hunched on a narrow lip of rock, clinging desperately to the wet granite face. With every surge of the surf below, a soaking spray covered him.

"He must be scared to death," she murmured.

Brent cut the boat's engines and, with a grunt, threw the heavy cement anchor overboard. He ran to the stern, reached over the gunwale to pull the painter against the side of the *Blue Lady*.

"What can I do?" Allison was shaking like a leaf. "I can't just stay here and do nothing."

"You won't be doing nothing. I'm going to need the spot trained on Ricky the whole time."

"Isn't it dangerous, going in so close to the rocks in that little boat?" She frowned doubtfully at the painter.

He shrugged. "We don't have a choice." He jumped into the painter, untied its mooring rope, and picked up the oars. He was half standing as he rowed quickly away from the *Blue Lady*. Allison stared after him, dazed, until he called to her.

"The light, Allison!"

The boat was swinging slightly to the west, and the circle of light had moved away from Ricky. She ran to the searchlight and adjusted it so that it was focused once more on the thunder hole.

"That's great!" Brent's voice was reassuringly strong over the roar of the surf.

Allison shivered violently as she watched the little

boat move closer and closer to the thunder hole. How could the painter survive the crashing waves? It would be dashed to pieces against the rocks!

She heard a high-pitched scream and looked at Ricky. His right foot had slipped off the rock ledge and he was dangling precariously over the foaming spray.

"Hold on!" she yelled, hoping that her voice carried over the sound of the water. "Don't let go, Ricky!"

The boy struggled upward and finally managed to regain his foothold on the rock.

She saw Brent turn the painter toward a ridge of low rocks near the shore. A moment later he had scrambled out of the skiff and was climbing a granite outcropping. The painter lay on the swells until a huge wave came and lifted it high into the air. Allison watched in horror as it fell against the jagged rocks and splintered into a thousand pieces.

"He's almost there, Ricky!" She kept calling to Ricky, praying that whatever words came into her head might encourage him to hang on. Her throat hurt and her voice grew hoarse. With shaking hands she kept the searchlight focused on the boy, and soon Brent's tall figure was standing on the bluff above Ricky.

An angry crash sent spray high into the air. For a terrible moment Allison thought Ricky had been washed off the ledge. But when the mist cleared, she saw that he was still there. Above him, Brent was easing his way down the rock face to the ledge.

"Be careful, Brent!" she cried.

Another wave crashed into the thunder hole; the echoing boom sounded like a death knell. Allison trained the light on the two figures, her body aching with cold and tension.

Brent continued to maneuver his way down until he was just a few feet above Ricky. Clinging to the rock with one hand, he reached toward the boy with the other. Ricky clutched it eagerly, and Brent pulled him slowly upward. It seemed an agonizingly long time before Ricky was finally anchored to Brent's side. For a moment the two figures gripped each other without moving. To Allison, it looked like the stopped frame of a film, the two dark bodies clinging motionless to the darker rocks. The only thing that told her time hadn't halted was the continuing crash of the surf below. Then, very slowly, and very carefully, Brent lifted the boy onto his shoulders.

With a cry of joy Ricky scrambled up to the safety of the bluff. Allison took a long breath and let it out. Her palms were damp and her hands shook on the light control.

Suddenly she froze. Something was wrong. Brent was slipping bit by bit down the rock face to the narrow ledge where Ricky had been standing.

"No! Brent!" Allison screamed. "Oh my God!" And then she was silenced by the horror in front of her eyes as Brent fell through the air into the turbulent water of the thunder hole.

Her scream seemed to last forever, ringing out over the raging water. She saw the group of men appear on the bluff over the thunder hole, but her brain didn't register their significance. Mechanically, she kept the light trained on the place where she last saw Brent. Every few seconds a cloud of spray leaped into the air. There was no sign of him.

Gradually she realized what the men were doing. Someone was being lowered in a rope sling, dangling over the thundering water, lower and lower. A bud of hope opened inside her. Was it possible that they could save Brent? Could he still be alive?

Fear coated her tongue. The rescue rope dropped lower; the man in the sling disappeared briefly in a burst of spray. She heard the shouts of the men on the cliff but couldn't make out their words. She held her breath, her eyes riveted to the rope.

Then, slowly, the rope was being pulled back up. She strained to make out the figure on the end of the line. He was holding something over his shoulder. Her heart slammed against her chest wall as she recognized what it was. He had Brent's body.

When the rope was finally hauled all the way back to the bluff, she watched the men lay the body on a stretcher, and then they disappeared from the ridge. Her hands continued to cling to the light control, although she was dimly aware that there was no longer any need for the searchlight.

She'd never felt more alone or helpless in her life. Brent had been killed before her eyes, taken from her, just at the moment when she was going to tell him she'd decided to break the engagement. Tears filled her eyes and overflowed, running down her cheeks. If only she'd listened to him! He'd been right all along; she had never truly loved Cabot. Now it was too late. She would never again feel his strong arms around her, taste the sensuous warmth of his lips. Now she would never be able to tell him that he was the man she loved, had loved from her very first day on the island.

It seemed an eternity that she stood there, weeping and leaning against the gunwale. She had no anxiety about what might happen to her, about how she would get back to shore. All she was aware of was a deadness inside, a huge, black hole of pain. When she started trembling, it seemed as if she would never stop. Weakness flooded her, and her shaking became so violent that she sank to her knees.

Something dug into her right knee, something hard and jagged. She looked down. Her knee was bleeding; a deep gash had been cut into her flesh. She groped along the deck until she found the cause of her wound. When her fingers closed over it, she recognized it instantly. Cabot's ring.

Rage surged through her, white-hot and blinding. So much misery in the past four weeks had been caused by the ring! She pulled herself against the gunwale and lifted the ring to fling it into the water, but something stopped her. It was as if Brent was standing in the darkness behind her, speaking. He had told her so many times to give Cabot back the ring. To do anything less now would be a betrayal.

She got to her feet, bumping the spotlight. The circle of light swung across the water. It was then that she saw the rowboat coming toward her, a small oblong carrying two figures. A moment later she heard a familiar voice.

"Allison? Is that you?" It was Isabel, her tone high and clear in the darkness. It sounded like an angel's.

"Yes!" Allison ran to the stern. The next moment Isabel and Abel were climbing aboard and she was sandwiched between them in a tight, three-way hug.

"You poor thing!" Isabel murmured. "You must be scared to death! Out here all alone!"

"Thank God you were," Abel said. "We couldn't have located Brent without the searchlight."

"Brent—is he . . . ?" Allison's throat knotted with tears and she closed her eyes against her thought.

Isabel patted her shoulder. "He's alive, dear. They've taken him to the hospital."

"Alive?" Allison blinked at her. Something warm opened deep in her chest. She brushed at her wet face. "He's really alive?"

"He's pretty beat up, but he'll make it," Abel said. "He's as strong as he is stubborn." He went into the pilothouse. "Now let's get you back home where you belong."

"No, please. I want to see Brent. I have something I have to tell him."

Isabel put her arm around Allison's shoulder. "We'll go first thing in the morning, dear. All three of us, and half the town besides. But there's nothing we can do for Brent now. They wouldn't let us see him tonight."

Allison was too exhausted to argue. But she knew she wouldn't be able to sleep until she'd seen with her own eyes that Brent was alive.

Abel flicked off the searchlight, started the *Blue Lady* and swung her around. A few moments later they were heading into the cove.

Allison sagged against the wall of the pilothouse. "How's Ricky?"

Isabel laughed. "Oh, he's just fine. Full of vim and vinegar five minutes after he was rescued. But I do think he'll be a bit more careful from now on. Some kids just have to learn their respect for the ocean the hard way."

Abel grunted. "As I recall, Brent was one of those kids."

Isabel nodded. "And you, too, Abel Cutler, if I remember correctly."

He gave her a sheepish grin, and despite herself, Allison laughed.

At the house, Allison took a hot shower, then washed and bandaged her cut knee. It was a deep gash, but it would heal. In her room she changed into jeans and a sweater and examined her dress. It was dirty and grass-stained; a hole had been torn in the skirt. She'd never be able to wear it again, and yet she hung it carefully in her closet, remembering vividly how it had felt to be in Brent's arms. Her tears came again, and she collapsed weakly on the bed.

When Isabel came quietly into the room, Allison was still sobbing loudly.

"You poor dear!" The older woman sat beside her on the bed and gently rubbed Allison's back. "You've been through so much! Why don't you come downstairs and have some hot chocolate before you go to bed?"

Allison sat up and made a halfhearted attempt to dry her eyes. She sniffed loudly. "I'd love to, but I have something I have to do first."

"Nonsense! What you have to do is get some sleep so you'll be fresh in the morning."

"No, really. I have to see Cabot."

A frown creased Isabel's face. "He went home hours ago. I'm afraid, dear, that people aren't saying very nice things about him."

"I know. And they have good reason. Isabel, I'm going to give him back his ring."

"Oh, my dear! Surely it's not necessary to break your engagement because he didn't join the search." The older woman continued to frown, but her voice lacked its usual conviction.

"Yes, it is. And it doesn't really have anything to do with tonight. The fact is, I don't love him."

Isabel cleared her throat. "Well, I won't deny that I've had my doubts about this marriage, dear. You didn't exactly seem head over heels for the man."

"I don't think I even knew the meaning of love before I came to Harper's Island," Allison whispered.

The older woman looked at her thoughtfully, then her face folded into a wide smile. Though she didn't say anything, Allison had the feeling that Isabel knew exactly what she meant.

Chapter
Twenty-one

T HE MOON WAS SETTING over Lookout Point as Allison
approached the guest cottage. The little house
was dark. She marched up to the front door and
turned the knob. It didn't open. She frowned, tried it
again. Nothing.

She knocked loudly. "Cabot?" Her voice was startlingly resonant in the darkness. There was a thump
from deep inside the house, and then the sound of
footsteps. The door opened.

"Allison!" Cabot smiled at her, but his eyes were
cold. He was wearing a gray velour bathrobe. His
bare legs and feet looked curiously vulnerable.
"What are you doing here? I was sleeping."

"May I come in, Cabot? This will only take a minute."

He cleared his throat. "It's not a very good time,
darling. Can't this wait until morning?"

"No."

She heard the sound of a toilet flushing from inside the cottage. He reached behind him to close the
door. She felt a finger of ice at the base of her throat.
"Is Martha here?"

His smile stiffened.

She knew instantly that she'd guessed correctly.

"Never mind," she said quickly. "I'll say what I came to say out here. I'm breaking our engagement."

He frowned. "I don't understand."

She pushed the ring into his hand. "Give it to Martha. She's much better suited to wear it."

"But Allison, I love you—" He reached toward her, but she stepped quickly away.

"No you don't, Cabot. You never did. I'm not your type at all."

He swallowed. "I didn't intend that you should find out. Martha and I have been very discreet."

"I'm sure you have," she said bitterly. "That's the trouble with how you see things, Cabot. There's so much concentration in your world on discretion and appearance, there isn't any room for trust. Love is just an incidental detail, something that has to be fitted in with all the corporate business deals and the charity balls."

"My world, as you call it, is something you wanted very much to be a part of, Allison. You can't deny that."

"You're right. That was my first mistake. My second was loving you."

"There's no reason we can't work this out, Allison."

"Yes there is. Because I don't want to work it out."

He gave her a startled look. "Mother is going to be very upset."

She looked at him. "That's what it's really been about all along, isn't it? Pleasing Sarah. *You* weren't the one who chose me for your wife. It was your mother."

"I never intended to hurt you, Allison."

"No, you just assumed that I would look the other way while you had your affairs. That's the way it works in your world, isn't it?"

He was silent.

She sighed. "It doesn't really matter. I couldn't have gone on much longer pretending I really loved you. It was only a question of time before I listened to my heart." She felt hot tears well into her throat, swallowed hard. "The thing that's unforgivable is that you didn't join in the search for Ricky Flory. There was a little boy in terrible danger on this island tonight, Cabot. They needed every available man to help search for him. You refused to help."

"I had my work to do," he muttered. "You don't understand the pressure I'm under."

"It wasn't your work. You saw an opportunity to go off alone with Martha—a time when no one would be wondering about where the two of you were—and you took it. Your lust took priority over a child's life!"

"Now, just a minute! You're not being fair!" He reached for her arm, but she jerked away.

"I think I am. You've just slept with my best friend. You've made a travesty of our engagement. You ignored a little boy's desperate plight. I think I'm being more than fair, under the circumstances."

"Don't think that you can speak to me this way and get your ring back in the morning, Allison!"

"I thought I made it clear. I don't *want* your ring back! I'm breaking the engagement. You're a coward and a hypocrite. I'm only sorry that I wasn't smart enough to see that months ago and save us both a lot of misery."

She turned on her heel and marched away. She heard the door close firmly behind her and she felt a sudden, welling joy. She raised her left hand and looked at her bare fingers. She was free! She started down the hill, jogging and skipping, as if she wasn't tired at all, but had just awakened from a bad dream.

* * *

At the Cutler house Isabel was waiting up for her. A steaming pan on the stove filled the kitchen with the aroma of hot chocolate.

Isabel gave her a warm, sympathetic hug before she took a mug from the counter, poured it full of hot cocoa, and handed it to Allison. Allison sat down at the table, clutching the mug tightly between her hands. "How did things go with Cabot?" Isabel's blue eyes were full of concern.

Allison smiled. "Very well, considering. I just wish I'd done it a long time ago."

"Still, it's not easy when two people break up, even if it is for the best. I remember when I told Roy that I was in love with Abel. It was the hardest thing I'd ever had to do."

Allison gazed down into the creamy brown liquid. "I don't think I was ever really in love with Cabot. I was attracted to what he represented, and he's really quite handsome, but that's not love, is it?" She glanced up at Isabel, who shook her head sadly. "Actually, I think our relationship was a matter of social convenience for Cabot. And I was brought up believing I should marry somebody with a lot of money, if I was really going to be a successful woman."

"Well, if that's true, then you're well rid of him. No marriage can survive that sort of beginning. A good marriage has to be based on love. It's the only thing in life you can really count on."

"Yes. I can see that now." Allison took a sip of cocoa. The chocolate slid down her throat, soothing it warmly. "Anyway, I think he's always been in love with Martha."

Isabel nodded. "I wondered why he spent so much time over here while you were with the play group."

"He was sleeping with her tonight, Isabel. She was at the cottage when I got there."

Isabel gave her a pained look. "Oh, my dear! That must have hurt terribly!"

Allison smiled. "Actually, I was so angry when I went up there, so eager to tell him off, I wouldn't have cared if he'd had a dozen women in his bed."

"But Martha's your best friend."

"I know. That's the worst part." Allison tried to blink away the stinging tears, but they spilled out of her eyes and ran down her cheeks. She watched a tear drop into the mug of cocoa.

Isabel handed her a tissue and patted her shoulder gently. "Well, to be honest with you, dear, I never thought Cabot was the right man for you. He always struck me as rather stiff and cold." She tucked a stray wisp of white hair behind her ear. "Maybe this is for the best in the long run."

Allison nodded up at her. "I know she's always been half in love with Cabot. I just never thought she'd betray me like this." Tears choked her once again.

"If they're so attracted to each other, why isn't he engaged to *her*?"

Allison wiped her face with the tissue. "Because of Sarah, Cabot's mother. She doesn't like Martha, even though she's from Cabot's social class and went to all the right schools. His mother thinks she's too flighty for Cabot."

Isabel brushed her hand across the table. "Seems to me Cabot ought to make that decision for himself. Maybe the flighty type's exactly what he needs. Might loosen him up."

"You're right. I never thought of it that way."

"Well, if Cabot's going to grow up, he's going to have to make his own choices, and act on them."

Isabel went to the sink and rinsed out the empty saucepan.

Allison looked down at her bare left hand. She felt relaxed and sleepy; the cocoa had done its work. "Now that the wedding's off, I've got a lot of choices to make myself. I'll have to go back home and explain everything to my parents. That won't be easy. They were absolutely thrilled about my marrying Cabot."

"I'm sure they'll understand, dear. Sometimes parents get temporarily caught up in a dream for their children, but what they really want is their children's happiness."

Allison nodded. "They'll approve when I explain it to them. I wonder if I'll be able to get my old job back next fall."

Isabel came up behind her, put her hands on Allison's shoulders. "Don't make any hasty decisions, dear. You'll always have a home here with Abel and me. And those kids still need a play group for the rest of the summer."

"Oh, I wouldn't desert them!" Allison twisted in her chair to look up at the older woman.

"Good." Isabel beamed. "I hoped you'd say that. Now finish up that cocoa and get to bed. We'll be heading over to the hospital in less than six hours."

Allison smiled back at her and placed her hand over Isabel's. "Thanks. For everything."

"You're more than welcome, dear." Isabel gave her a warm hug and headed up the stairs to her bedroom. Allison felt the house settle into silence around her. How good it was to be sitting in this warm, cozy kitchen, drinking Isabel's hot cocoa, knowing that Brent was alive, that she would see him in the morning.

She had finished her cocoa and was getting to her

feet to carry her mug to the sink when the back door opened and Martha stepped into the kitchen.

"Allison," she said, her mouth open in a small O of surprise. "I didn't think you'd still be awake. Is everything okay?"

"No. Everything isn't okay." Allison felt heat flood her cheeks as anger rose through her body like fire.

Martha ran a hand through her short curls. There was something wistful and sad in her eyes, something that reminded Allison of a child. "I heard about the boy. What an awful thing!"

Allison's hands curled into fists. "I know where you were, Martha."

Martha gave her a weak smile. "I took a walk after the fireworks. The moonlight was so lovely I just lost track of time."

"You're lying! You've just come back from the guest house. You slept with Cabot." Allison stepped toward Martha, her voice rising toward a harsh sob. "How could you, Martha? How could you do this to me? He was my *fiancé*!"

Martha's face crumpled. She gave a little moan and collapsed into a chair, covering her face with her hands. "Oh, Allison, I didn't mean to hurt you. I didn't . . . I didn't know what I was doing."

"How could you not know what you were doing?" Allison wanted to shake her, dig her nails into the soft flesh of Martha's shoulder. Her voice slid to a hiss. "Do you realize *I* never even slept with him?"

Martha gulped, nodded, raised a tearstained face. "I know. I'm really, really sorry. Honestly. I just couldn't help myself." A tear broke loose from her right eye, ran down her cheek and dropped onto her dress. She sniffed loudly. "I've always loved Cabot, from the first day I saw him, way back when I was twelve years old." She swallowed, held out her hands to Allison. "He was so sophisticated, so brilliant, so handsome. I used to fantasize about marrying him. I had everything all planned out, my dress, the seating arrangements, the reception . . ." Her voice trailed off and she bit her lower lip. More tears welled out of her eyes. "I couldn't believe it when he proposed to you. I just couldn't believe it. I've been so jealous—" She gulped and licked her lower lip. "Tonight, when he asked if I'd walk back to the guest house with him, I couldn't refuse. I know it was wrong; I should have said no, but one thing led to another and—" A huge sob cut her off; she buried her face in her hands again.

Allison felt a deep stab of pity as she watched Martha's shoulders convulse. Martha had been such a good friend for so long, had supported her through the tough, early years of college, had generously introduced her to so many remarkable people. Had invited her to Harper's Island. She placed her hand on Martha's shoulder.

Martha raised her head slowly. Her eyes were red and puffy from crying; her face looked like it had been slapped. "I'm so sorry, Allison. Can you ever forgive me?"

Allison sighed. "I just wish you'd told me before. If I'd known how you and Cabot felt about each other, I never would have accepted his proposal."

Martha closed her eyes, wiped her face with the back of her hands. "I know, I should have. I don't think I really knew how much he meant to me until after you were engaged. I kept hoping something might happen, that the two of you would break up." She gulped and cleared her throat. "I think that's the real reason I wanted you to come to Maine with me. To put distance between you and Cabot."

"Well," Allison said quietly, "I guess it worked.

Only it wasn't the distance between us that made the difference. It was Harper's Island itself."

Martha gave her a puzzled frown. "What do you mean?"

"I mean that I learned something really important here. Something that changed my life."

"What?"

Suddenly Allison was smiling. "That love is the only thing that really matters. That no amount of money or social status or luxury can make things all right if love isn't there."

Martha gaped at her. "Are you saying you don't love Cabot?"

Allison nodded. "I don't think I ever did." She sat in the chair next to Martha, leaned over and pulled her friend into her arms. "So I guess that explains why it's really not so hard for me to forgive you. And anyway, I have you to thank for the best summer of my life. If you hadn't talked me into coming to Harper's Island, I'd never have met all these wonderful people, Isabel and Abel and the Florys . . ." Her voice trailed away.

"And Brent," Martha added, hugging her friend tightly.

Allison smiled. "And Brent," she murmured, her inflection as tender as a prayer.

The trip to the mainland hours later was a tourist's dream. The sky was high and clear. Gulls wheeled above Abel's lobster boat, *Belle II*, and a breeze fanned Allison's face gently. They arrived at the hospital just before nine and took the elevator to the third floor.

A stocky, pleasant-faced nurse greeted them, smiling. "You must be Allison."

Allison gave a startled nod.

"He's been asking for you."

"He has?"

She nodded. "All night long. I'm glad you finally came. It'll make my job a lot easier." She laughed and turned to Isabel and Abel. "Are you the grandparents? I'm afraid there's only one visitor allowed at a time. He's still pretty weak."

"We'll wait, dear." Isabel patted Allison's shoulder. "You're the one he wants to see."

Allison followed the nurse down the long hall to a wide door.

"It's a private room," the nurse said, her eyes twinkling merrily for a moment before she disappeared. Allison took a deep breath, smoothed her blouse and denim skirt, pushed open the door slowly and slipped inside.

Brent was lying in a high, white hospital bed, staring out the window. His face was bruised and swollen; there was a deep gash across his right cheekbone. But he was smiling as he turned to Allison.

"You came." His voice hadn't changed. It was the same deeply resonant voice that sent shivers down her back.

"Are you in a lot of pain?" She took a step toward him.

"Nothing that time and TLC won't heal." He moved his right arm from under the sheet and reached for her. She saw that it was bandaged from the wrist to the elbow. He frowned. "What happened to your knee?"

Allison glanced down at her bandaged knee, smiling as she remembered the cause of the cut. "It's just a little scrape." She crossed the room to the bed. His warm, masculine smell filled her nostrils.

He gazed deep into her eyes, and a tremor of heat

ran up her spine. "God, you're beautiful," he said softly.

She tried a grin. "I'm afraid I can't say the same for you."

He reached for her left hand, which was closest to his bandaged arm, lifted it to his lips, kissed the tips of her fingers. Her chin trembled.

She saw his sudden, bright look of astonishment as his glance slid over her bare fingers. He looked up at her.

"The ring."

She grinned. "You weren't the only one who did something dramatic last night. I had a little adventure myself after you saved Ricky's life."

He gave her a baffled look.

"I gave it back to Cabot. The engagement's off."

He took a deep breath, blew it out slowly, released her hand. He sagged back against the pillow and put his arm over his face.

"What's wrong?" She leaned over him anxiously. "Should I ring for the nurse?"

He shook his head and lowered his arm. She was stunned to see tears in his eyes.

"I didn't think you'd do it," he said hoarsely. "It was killing me to watch you throw your life away. Nothing I said seemed to make any difference."

"But it did! I was all torn up inside. Terribly confused. It just took me a long time to sort things out. I guess I've got a stubborn streak of my own."

He reached for her. "Come here." With a surprisingly vigorous thrust of his arm he captured her wrist and pulled her down beside him on the bed. He wrapped his arms around her so tightly she could barely move.

"Kiss me," he commanded, his blue eyes shining.

She obeyed, brushing her lips very gently against

his. His arms tightened around her, his lips moving against hers as she opened her mouth to his tongue. Then he kissed her eyes, her cheeks, her neck, and the swell of her breasts at the opening of her blouse. She dissolved against him, pressing her body closer and closer into his as wave after wave of desire pulsed through her. When he finally released her, she felt weak and dizzy.

He took her face in his hands. "I've wanted to say this since that first day when I watched you get out of Martha's car. So listen carefully." He smiled deep into her eyes. "I love you, Allison Curtis."

"Oh, Brent!" She was flooded with incredible joy, unlike any she had ever known. When he pulled her into the circle of his arms again, she knew that she never wanted to leave.

Time dissolved in bliss, and when Brent took a deep breath and pushed her gently away, Allison felt a sense of loss so palpable she could taste it on her tongue.

He grinned. "I think you'd better leave, or something will happen that isn't appropriate to a hospital setting."

She got up reluctantly, tucked her blouse into her skirt, smoothed her hair with her hands. She was still trembling.

"How long will you have to be here?"

He shrugged. "A few more days. Enough time for you to make the arrangements."

"Arrangements?"

"For the wedding."

"What wedding?"

His eyes flashed. "*Our* wedding, love. You *are* going to marry me, aren't you?"

Her breath caught in her throat. It took her a moment to find her voice. "Are you proposing to me?"

"I certainly am."

She tried to swallow the grin that pushed against her mouth. "I'll have to consider it. I'm not a woman who makes snap decisions."

"Fine. I've waited four weeks already. I can wait a little longer." He glanced at the watch on his left wrist. "I'll give you thirty seconds." He grinned up at her.

"All right, all right!" She laughed. "I accept."

He captured her hand, drew her back down toward him. "I don't have a ring yet, and when I do, it won't be anywhere near the size of Cabot's. But I'll put one on your finger the day I get out of the hospital. In the meantime, consider yourself taken."

He pulled her face down to his. Their lips met hungrily, sending shudder after shudder of delight through Allison.

A soft knock on the door startled Allison; she straightened quickly, putting her hands to her blazing cheeks.

Brent smiled. "Don't worry, love. You've never looked more beautiful." He looked at the door. "Come in."

Isabel poked her head in. "Sorry to disturb you, but we thought we'd break the rules and pop in for a minute, since morning visiting hours are almost over."

Brent grinned at her. "Come on in, Gran. Abel, too, if he's there. We have something to tell you."

Isabel entered the room, followed by Abel.

"Well, out with it, boy," Abel said, giving Brent an exaggerated wink.

Brent took Allison's hand firmly in his own. "We're going to get married as soon as I'm out of the hospital."

"Wonderful!" Isabel turned to her husband. "There, what did I tell you?"

Abel grunted. "Took you two long enough. I was beginning to think I'd have to take you both out on the water, dump you overboard, wash some sense into your heads."

Isabel embraced Allison. "Don't listen to him, dear. He's all bark and no bite. You look absolutely radiant!" She turned to Brent. "I must say, you two both had a bad case of love at first sight. Seemed pretty clear to everybody but you."

Brent's eyes twinkled. "It was wicked clear to me, Gran. It was Allison who had a hard time figuring out what was going on."

Allison blushed and nodded. "Brent's right. I didn't want to admit the truth."

Isabel patted her hand. "Well, that boy's loved you from the minute he first laid eyes on you."

Abel nodded. "Plain as the nose on my face. Which is wicked obvious, as you can see."

"I knew once you broke the engagement it wouldn't take two minutes for Brent to pop the question." Isabel beamed. "The only doubt in my mind was how long it would take you to say yes."

"About four seconds, Gran." Brent's eyes danced. "She had to decide if she was willing to trade big city excitement for the simple pleasures of a fisherman's wife. I had to convince her that, in the pleasure department, I'd make it well worth her while."

"Brent!" Allison swiped at him playfully.

Isabel laughed. "We'd best go find some lunch before that nurse comes storming in here."

"Yep." Abel grinned. "Think this calls for a celebration, don't you? How about dinner at the Blue Lobster?"

"That's a wonderful idea!" Isabel cried. "You

haven't taken me out to dinner in months." She gave him an affectionate kiss on the cheek.

Abel grinned roguishly at Brent. "Sorry you can't make it this time, boy. Next time you rescue somebody, hold onto the rock a little tighter, okay?"

Brent laughed. "It's a deal." He caught Allison's hand once again and gave it a warm squeeze. "Remember what I said about being taken, love. No flirting with the waiters."

She grinned down at him. "I promise."

"And don't ever forget, even for a minute, that I love you." He pulled her down to kiss her good-bye.

When he released her a moment later, Allison was flushed with joy.

At the door Isabel linked her arm through Allison's and gave her a triumphant smile. "Didn't I tell you, dear? Things always do work out for the best."